TO
THE
WHITE
SEA

....

TO THE WHITE SEA

James Dickey

A Marc Jaffe Book

Houghton Mifflin Company

BOSTON • NEW YORK

1993

For information about permission to reproduce
selections from this book, write to Permissions,
Houghton Mifflin Company, 215 Park Avenue South,
New York, New York 10003.

Library of Congress Cataloging-in-Publication Data
Dickey, James
To the white sea / James Dickey
p.   cm.
"A Marc Jaffe Book"
ISBN 0-395-47565-1
I. Title.
PS3554.I32T6   1993   93-1247
813'.54 — dc20   CIP

Printed in the United States of America

Book design by Robert Overholtzer

MP 10 9 8 7 6 5 4 3 2 1

The author is grateful for permission to quote
from *The Way Things Are: The "De Rerum Natura"
of Titus Lucretius Carus*, translated by Rolfe
Humphries, published by Midland Books,
Indiana University Press; and from *Les Barricades
Mystérieuses* by Olivier Larronde.
Copyright 1948 by Editions Gallimard.

Portions of this book previously appeared in *Playboy*,
Partisan Review, and *South Carolina Review*.

To my wife and children

This fire was made by nature, and refined
More than all other fires, with particles
Diminutive, quick, and irresistible,
For lightning bolts go through the walls of houses
As voices do, or noise; they go through rocks,
Through bronze, they can fuse bronze and gold together
In a split second; wine evaporates
Under their force from bowls or jars which show
Never a crack; and this occurs because
The heat is so intense it opens up
All of the pores, and, boiling through, it melts
The motes of wine, dissolving them in ways
The sun could not accomplish in a lifetime,
So burning is this force, this flash, this fire . . .

— LUCRETIUS

Si je suis . . . d'une autre étoffe,
La trame n'en est pas de vos oiseaux de mer
Mais de leur froides proies ourdie.

— OLIVIER LARRONDE

TO THE WHITE SEA

Tinian Island, March 8, 1945

"We are going to bring it to him," the Colonel said with satisfaction. A lot, more than usual.

"Fire. This is what you've got to look forward to. This is what *he's* got to look forward to."

He leaned into it, from the heels, you could say. I sat and waited, looking straight ahead.

"We're going to bring it to him." He looked down the rows of us, but I didn't watch him do it; all this was like before. "To the enemy, you know. Up yonder, friends. Up yonder to the north." He pointed at the ceiling, not north. "North and fire."

"Fire," he said again. "We're going to put him *in* it. That's saying, friends, that we're going to put fire around him, *all* around him. We're going to put it over him and underneath him. We're going to bring it down on him and on *to* him. We're going to put it in his eyes and up his asshole, in his wife's twat, and in his baby's diaper. We're going to put it in his pockets, where he can't get rid of it. White phosphorus, that'll hold on. We're going to put it in his dreams. Whatever heaven he's hoping for, we're fixing to make a hell out of it. Soon, good buddies. We just got the good word this morning. White phosphorus and napalm. That's our good stuff for the little yellow man and his folks. We're going to make him a present of it, in his main city. Bestow it. Give it away. With both hands. With three hundred airplanes. Tokyo is going to remember us. Within a week, I clue you. That's all I can tell you right now. But we're going all the way with incendiaries. All bombs. No ammunition. No gunners. All payload, all fire."

I sat up a little. Some of the other gunners were grinning at each other. This was a raid they could sit out, another day and a night they would live. I didn't feel that way, though. I couldn't see any point in the pilots and the other crew going up amongst the fighters without any protection, and I didn't really want to sit out any raids playing Ping-Pong and watching Andy Hardy movies. No ammunition, no gunners. I wondered who had thought that up.

"But we're not there yet," the Colonel said. "The firebomb strike is going to be gravy. It's going to be history. But tonight is just regular, gunners and all. We rendezvous at angels nine, at sixteen three seven. Your course is three-five-six degrees true. The target is Tokyo."

I sat back. The mission would be like the others, and my part of it would be the same. I was glad the Colonel had quit talking about fire. That had nothing to do with me.

❖　❖　❖

We had a couple of hours, and most of us went back to the Quonset hut to check over personal equipment and do whatever we wanted. We had worked on the plane all morning, the crew and the armorers mainly, and it was ready, just as ready as it had been the other eight times. The armorers were good. They knew what they were doing, and I finished servicing my place in the tail before any of the others got through. I field-stripped the twin fifties, but there was really no need to do it. The parts were all nearly brand new, and the springs to the belt-holding pawl and the belt-feed lever were as strong as if they had just come out of the machine at the factory. I made sure that the belts were straight in the boxes and wouldn't twist when they fed. That was all I needed to do, as far as regulations went. With that done, I was not in any danger from my own equipment, unless I got excited or panicked and fired the guns too long, so that a shell cooked off in the chamber. That had happened in two or three of the other planes, and one gunner, a new guy, was killed. But I never felt like there was ever any possibility of that in my plane, at least not at my station back in the tail. When I was through with the guns, I checked the intercom jacks and the electrical outlet, and as far as the Air Force was concerned, I was ready to go.

But I had one or two more things to do that were not regulation. When they brought the chest chutes in and stacked them, I waited until the riggers left and took some tire tape and taped one chute by the harness snap to the bulkhead — I don't like anything of mine to be loose. Then I soaped the inside of my plexiglass and cleaned it down good with a rag I took out of the latrine. We were set to take off at sixteen hundred, which is what the Air Force calls four o'clock in the afternoon, and I wanted to be able to see as much as I could. It would be night when we got up over Japan, and even though at night you fired most of the time at the flashes you saw the Nip fighters giving out with, there might be something I would be able to see, somewhere along in there, and if that was so, I wanted to see it good. I was finished with everything, then, and sat looking through the plexiglass at the runway until the others got ready to go back.

The hut was all right, at least for what it was, though they kept it too hot in there. The crews went over their stuff, the things they carried with them and on them, and talked about it, and I got ready to go over mine. The armorers and mechanics and riggers and the other enlisted men who were not air crew were around and about, and they all tried to be friendly and do what they could, but there was so much difference of feeling between them and us that any talk you heard or got into was so hard to be honest about, so hard to keep going, that it didn't seem to me like it was worth it. Some of the crews played cards with the others, and there was a lot of letter writing. If it had been me, I wouldn't have done it, because if you've got your mind on somebody who's not in the air with you, you're giving something away, and you might not could get it back. I didn't know anybody back in the States or the territories, since my father died just before I went into the Air Force, and even if I knew people to write to, I would have kept them clear of what I was doing. I was sorry for the married fellows, and even sorrier for the ones who thought they wanted to get married. There couldn't be anything sadder than writing from where we were to a person who was out of it, and who wanted you out of it. I laid my personal equipment, or most of it, on the cot and started going over it, not because I had to or thought I should, but because I like to: liked the equipment, and the reasons I had got it together the way it was. They were all good reasons.

An open-bay barracks bothers some people, who will tell you

all about their privacy, and what it means to them, and all that, but you can be just as private as you want to anywhere you take a notion. The other crews let me alone, pretty much; they knew how I was. Every now and then one of them would ask me something, and I'd tell him what I thought. But they'd been on the same missions; they had their own ways of doing things. The new guys, though, the replacements, always wanted to talk, and I looked up and there were two guys standing over my bunk. Recruits were always coming around, these or others like them. Some I knew and some I didn't. I had never seen either one of these before. One was a pale, redheaded fellow who I judged hadn't been out from the States very long. The other was taller, as rough looking as a placer miner. He had a snake tattooed on one forearm, with the sleeve pushed up on that one and not the other, and a hardscrabble beard, probably two or three days old.

"You fixing to fly this mission?" I asked him.

"Yeah," he said. "What's that to you?"

"You better shave, then," I told him, "while you got time."

"I've already said it, and I'll say it again. What's that to you?"

"You been up before?"

"No," said the redhead. "We both just got in and been assigned. This one is the first one."

"You're going to be up there seven or eight hours, and at least part of the time you'll be on the mask. It'll fit better if you shave. If you don't, your face will drive you crazy. The main thing is that if you're on mask discipline, you can't get at your face and it can give you a bad time."

"I'll do it or not do it, little man," the tall one said.

"Have it your way," I said, and went back to going over my stuff. But they wouldn't leave.

"Take off, will you?" I said. "I've still got to count up and check off."

"You say you're gonna jack off?" And when I didn't look up, he went on. "If I've got time to shave, you can do that. You're giving me free advice. Take some of mine."

They stayed, shifting from one leg to the other. I packed the fishhooks and twine into my emergency kit.

"You the big Nip knocker around here?"

"My name is Muldrow. You don't need to know any more than that."

"Four kills. That right?"

"Seven."

"The board says four."

"Go read the board, then."

"Does it bother you to kill people?"

"No," I said. "That's what I'm here for." Then, "What business is that of yours?"

"Don't fool with him, Arlen," the redhead said, looking back and forth between us. "Don't fool with him. The other guys told us that just as soon as we got in. Don't fool with this one."

"This little prick?" the tall one said. "He don't have his guns now. I could bust his back with one chop."

I pulled both feet up on the bunk. "He's right," I said. "You better listen to him. Don't give me any trouble. You might lose that snake, and that would be too bad. Your mama might want it."

He leaned over, and I organized, bunching.

"Do you like money?" I asked him.

He wasn't sure. He didn't know where I was taking him.

"Yeah," he said finally. "Yeah. I like money."

"You got any?"

He felt around. "Some," he said.

"Twenty?"

"Yeah. I got twenty."

"I'll bet you fifty against twenty that I'm stronger than you are."

"How're you gonna tell?"

"I can tell right quick. It's just something we take on, you and me. We both try to do it, but you can't do it and I can. That's all."

"I could bust your ass in half, you little shit."

"Maybe, but I wouldn't try that either. You're missing the point, mama's boy. Let's see if you've got any guts. Let's see if that snake can give you what you ain't got."

"Try me," he said.

"You see that brace right over your head? That long two-by-four?"

He looked up. "I see it."

"Jump up and grab it. Chin on it."

"I can do twenty."

"One is enough."

He got off the floor, and I must say that he looked good doing it; he might have been a basketball player. He chinned on the brace, and came down. "How's that, asshole?"

"Average," I said. "Now jump up and catch it like this." I showed him: four fingers together, thumb opposite — a pinch grip.

"I ain't ever tried it," he said, glancing at his hands.

"Try it."

He jumped and caught the brace, but couldn't hold. He tried hard but he fell, purple in the face. "No grip," I said. "No grip, no guts. That's what they say." He went an even deeper color, with veins and frustration. "Stand clear," I said, and launched up from the bunk to the brace. I caught it pretty well with one hand and then adjusted.

"You see where I am," I said, keeping my voice down, down and level. I had quit swinging by this time. "Now watch."

I went up slow to the bar, holding the pinch with everything I had. Everything was in my fingers, thumbs, forearms, and wrists. My body had almost no weight, only strength, main strength. I went up a second time, a little faster, and then once more, slow again. I dropped off and the two of them jumped back, like a snake or a lynx had hit the floor between them.

"Now," I said, turning square into the tall one. "You want to shake hands?"

"You mean . . . How do you mean?"

"Friendly or unfriendly."

"You think you can mash my hand?"

"Put it out there."

"No," he said, "I don't think I'll try. You got me convinced." He made a kind of smile, but I didn't answer. "With the grip you got, might not be too much left."

"Maybe a few bone splinters," I told him. "I might could use those. You can sew with them, you know." I waited a second. "I was raised up north. Some of my best friends are Eskimos. I could use a few needles out of your hand. I'll put 'em in my emergency kit. Might be just the thing, later on."

He smiled again, with not much strength. "I think I'll hold on to them," he said. "I need them to fire the fifties."

"OK, then," I said. "Pay me."

He had trouble getting out the twenty, but he gave it to me.

I handed it back. "This is for using your head," I said, "and for not making any more trouble. And for shaving before we take off. Go on, now, do what I tell you."

He left. The other boy, the redhead, stayed. "Can I ask you one thing, Sergeant Muldrow? Just one?"

"I guess," I said. "What is it?"

"I've been assigned to your crew. Have you got anything special you can . . . clue me in on?"

"No," I said. I looked at him finally. "Don't waste your ammunition. Never fire at anything out of panic. Make it count. That's all."

"How about the crew?"

"Major Sorbo is a good pilot. He's cool enough. He knows what to do. You're lucky to be on with him."

"If you don't mind me saying so, I'm lucky to be on with you, too. I never have to ask anybody but once who the best gunner in the squadron is. The guys — the Major and the rest of them — you don't fly with them, they fly with you. It's a damned honor. I'm fucked if it's not."

"Well," I said, "there's not any reason to go on and on. I don't do anything special. I just wait for what I want and then I center in and cut loose. So take your time. Be fast, but take your time. Know what I mean?"

"Not exactly," he said. "But I'll work on it."

"You do that," I said. "I'll see you later on, out on the truck."

"Just one more thing. How did you learn to do this? How can you be all that sure?"

"I learned just like you did. Buckingham Field, Fort Myers, Florida. That where you went to gunnery? Or Harlingen, maybe?"

"No. I was in Florida, too. At Tyndall. I just barely graduated. I come from Florida, too."

"Well, you got through, anyway. You're here. Just do what they taught you in gunnery school."

"You mean you never shot a gun before you went to gunnery school?"

"I didn't say that," I said, facing him a little more and looking at him, but not for long, because I don't spend time on anything I can't use. "I was raised in Alaska, on the north face of the Brooks Range, which is away from everything, facing away from the States, and I could shoot as soon as I could hold a gun." That was not quite true, though, and I set it straight. "No, I could do it before that. My father would prop the rifle up on a stump, and I'd get down behind it and cut loose."

I would like to get back to that, I told myself before I could think about it. I was impatient, I guess. It couldn't be too soon for me, to get down behind the twin fifties, like behind a rock, and cut loose when the time came, when it was time for it. I looked up from the Florida boy into the rest of the hut. The trouble with the whole damn place was that the people — the gunners and the rest of the enlisted personnel — were trying to make it look like somebody's house, a home of some kind of person, when it could never really be like that, be anything like it. There were posters of different places in the States — a lake, a field full of flowers, the buildings of some city or other — and all over the hut were pictures of people, mainly women and children, little children, and mostly ugly, and even a Christmas card every now and then, over this guy's bunk, up from me, and another one farther along. All that was strange, and wrong. The hut was nobody's house. The people who were in it ought to have taken it like it was, and for what it was. There was no reason for Betty Grable to be up on the wall in a white bathing suit, with her fat ass in your face, looking over her shoulder. Not a one of those gunners, not a one, had any idea what the real feeling of a home is like, like it used to be when I came in off the snowshoes, when maybe I hadn't brought anything back with me, hadn't found anything to shoot, and found the trap lines empty, too, and would just come in off the snow and look right straight into that red wall, the wall my father had painted, just for the color. There's not much color on the Brooks Range, and you're glad for a little while when you come back to your place, and before you go out into the snow again, where you belong.

"They said you didn't talk much," the Florida boy said.

"Who told you that? I don't mind talking, I'll tell you anything I know."

After a while he said, "All this don't bother you?"

"No. And it ought not to bother you, either. You've got a good pilot and a good crew. The airplane's been checked out every which way. You got every chance in the world. Just get up there and do what you know. Get them Nip fighters on the pursuit curve, like they showed you in gunnery school, showed you in the mockup. Let 'em slide on down the string, lead 'em just like it feels is right, and cut loose on 'em. They'll back off, or go down. If they don't do neither one, keep on shooting. Keep the Nips off you with that fifty caliber and the Major will get you on back here. He'll do it. And that's a fact."

That seemed to be not too bad a thing to tell him, because he got friendly, or tried to get friendly, and sat down on the foot side of my bunk, running his eyes back and forth over what was there. I picked up my knife and the sharp-stone I used with it, and put a touch or two to the blade, whether it needed me to or not.

"What kind of knife is that?" he asked after a while, like I knew he would. "Is it issue?"

"No, it's not issue," I said. I let him hold that.

"What kind is it, then?" he asked.

"It's a bread knife," I told him. "The only difference is that I brought the point on down real fine. The edge is good, too. Kitchen steel is good steel. As good as you can get."

He seemed not to understand, so I spelled it out for him. "Look," I said, bending the knife almost double. The light from the roof bulb curved, wires and all, into the light of the blade. "That means it won't break off. It's not like one of these stiff issue blades, like a bayonet or a commando knife, that ain't got any give to it. This one will bend, it'll go around."

"Go around what?"

"Go around something, say, like a rib. It'll go around and come back. It'll straighten out on the other side and keep on going."

"Where do you keep it on the mission? Do you stick it in your flying suit?"

I looked at him. I looked at him and stood up. "No," I said finally. "I put it in the case and strap it, or tape it, to my left hipbone, with the blade going down my leg."

"And you're left-handed?"

"No," I said again. "I'm not left-handed. I pull the blade out across me. Cross-handed, you could call it."

He was not going to understand, so I went on. "That way, the handle is in your hand so that you can hold it lower than the blade and come up." I showed him. "Come *up* with it. The other way, where you pull it out with your right hand, from your right side, the blade ends up higher than your hand, or level with it, and you have to come down when you use it. You can't do nearly as much with it that way. With a knife, you need to come up." I showed him. "So I pull the knife in just two moves, to do what I want. Once across, and then up." I waited and watched. "Up, and up hard. If it hits anything going in, the blade will just flex and go on around." I put the knife back in the case. "And that's what you want."

I wasn't going to give him a chance to ask me what he wanted to; I wouldn't have told him anyway. It was just something I had learned in Alaska. I sat back down and tried to get him interested in the other equipment. It wasn't hard to do. I had a mixture of the same emergency stuff he had, along with some other things he didn't have.

"What are these for?" he asked, pointing. "Some kind of lucky stones? From up in Alaska?"

"No, but they might be lucky on down the road." I picked them up. "They're flints. To make fire."

"Don't you have matches in your emergency kit?"

"Sure, and I take 'em along, just like you. But there're just so many of them. When they're gone, you got no more fire. With the flints, you got all you want."

"Can I try? Can I try them?" he asked, like a little boy.

"Sure," I said. "You can try all you want."

He did, and nothing sparked.

"How do you hit them together? Is there a trick to it?"

"In a way," I said. "It takes practice. A lot of years. Everybody in this barracks could knock these rocks together all night and there wouldn't be a single spark. If you needed fire, you wouldn't get it. You'd all freeze to death."

"Show me."

I did, and blew out the spark on the blanket. "There's plenty of fire in the rocks," I said. "All you want. It stays there. The rocks have kept it for a long time, just waiting for this blanket, in this barracks building. But I won't burn you up," I said. "I promise."

"We got to go burn the Japs up," he said, coming back to where we were, "in a couple of days."

"That's right," I told him. "Napalm and white phosphorus. That's going to be our big play. Just like the Colonel said." I grinned, myself. "But not tonight. Tonight is just routine. Tokyo one more time, with the frags and the two-thousand-pound GPs. Guns and gunners and all, right up there amongst the fighters. It'll give you a chance to knock on 'em."

"Yeah," he said, and turned away.

But he came back. I couldn't get rid of him. "Is this emergency equipment OK?" he asked.

"Sure," I said. "If you know how to use it." I took apart my kit. "You've got a little knife. It's not hardly more than a toy, but there are things you can do with it. You've got fishhooks and some twine. You've got matches in a packet that's supposed to be waterproof. And you've got a little, a real little, compass. Didn't you get briefed on all this?"

"I did, but I don't remember much about it, to tell you the truth."

I held up the compass. "This is not a bad little compass," I said. "You can hide it easy. You can even stick it up your asshole if, like, the situation comes up."

"I can't figure out what the situation might be," he said, and was relaxing, which was a relief.

"You can't ever tell," I said. "You just can't ever tell."

"Do you put the kit in your leg pocket?"

"No, I tape it right square onto me." I hit my chest with my fingers. "I like to keep everything together."

"You sure use a lot of tape."

"I do," I said. "I don't like to have anything loose, where it might get away from me, or I might have to hunt for it. Hunt for it on the way down, like."

When I said down, he lost his relaxation, and even might have changed color a little; that'd be hard to tell under those kind of lights, though.

"What would you do if you went down?"

"I don't know. I'd have to see when I got there."

"I do remember one thing from the briefing, the first briefing I got when I came in." He breathed a lot, and then did it again. "You can't expect any mercy from the Japs when you go down."

"No, you can't. But why should you get any? This here's a war, and we're up there knocking their cities around. Ain't no need to talk about mercy. They don't have any. Especially for air crew. They cut off your head. Balls, too. Them first, most of the time. So don't go down if you can help it." When he didn't say anything, I changed gears. "Remember this: if you go down, it ain't going to be your GI emergency kit that'll save you."

"What will, then?"

I touched my head. "Whatever you can come up with that's already in there." I looked at him and propped up on my elbows. "There's plenty in there that you ain't using. If you go down, that's what you need."

"I don't know if I've got anything . . . anything like what you're talking about."

"Sure you do. You ain't got what I've got, and I ain't got what you've got." I picked up the flints and juggled them in one hand. "But we've all got something. It comes out of where we've already been. Stuff that's happened. Stuff that's stayed with us."

"You want to tell me?" Then, "*Will* you tell me?"

"Tell you what?"

"What you've got. What you remember."

"Well," I said, thinking, "all the time I was growing up, I was hardly ever off snowshoes, except in the summer, which is mighty short up on the Range. I hunted all the time, and trapped. My father had a bunch of lines, and I walked 'em over and over, years at a time. I got to know what lived up there in the snow, and how they lived. Some of the animals, and birds, live by being able to hide, and the others live by being able to find 'em. But being hard to see, to make out, is part of it on both sides. The rabbit don't want the lynx or the weasel to find him, and the lynx and the fox and the weasel don't want the rabbit to know they're around till it's too late." He kept waiting, and I said, "I could take you up on the slope right now, or on out into the muskeg, and you wouldn't be able to see a single animal that was there. And they'd be all around you. Stillness is a big thing with rabbits and marmots. The meat hunters will get after anything that moves. But the rabbits can fool 'em a lot of the time. In that snow, all you can see are the eyes, and you have to be close to 'em to do it. Without the eyes there's nothing there. Or there might as well not be."

He was not sure, but it didn't make any difference to me. "You ever see a human do anything like that?"

"Well, no," I said. "A human's not a rabbit or a lynx. But you can do something like it. Don't think you can't. You don't have the fur, but you got more sense than them."

"I've never seen snow," he said, changing the subject, because he saw I didn't want to say anything else about that one. "I like the ocean, myself."

"I do, too," I told him. "But for me the ocean ain't the ocean unless it's got ice in it. It's just what you're used to, I guess."

❖   ❖   ❖

A little after fifteen hundred the trucks came for us, and I climbed in with the rest of the crews. As it turned out, only nine planes were making the strike, which meant there was likely to be more fighter concentration. I told the Florida boy, who was riding with me, that we'd have more to shoot at, but it didn't seem to make him feel any better. As for me, I was pretty well rested, and ready for whatever might be up there. The mission would take around fourteen hours, which is a lot of time to sit and think, with nothing going on most of the time. When we got to the ship I stretched and loosened up, and felt over myself for my gear. I had a .45 and two clips, my emergency kit and a can of C rations, and my knife, down there where it should be. I stretched some more and said hello to Major Sorbo.

"Ready for 'em, Ace?" the Major asked me.

"Not an ace yet," I said. "Maybe tonight."

Along with the others I got in, then went back to my station to see if everything was exactly like I had left it. It was, except that somebody had put a tarp cover over the pile of chutes, and I couldn't think of any reason I might need to take it off, though I would've liked to check the one chute that was taped down. I was more or less sure it was all right, and I got in behind my guns, hooked my suit up to the electrical system, and plugged my headset into the jack. After a while Major Sorbo started the engines, and we wheeled out to take off.

The back end of an airplane is not one of the worst places in it. There were at least a couple of yards between me and anybody else, and it was like I had all that section of the plane to myself. When I called in on the preflight check, Major Sorbo might have been back in the States, he seemed so far away, off in another part of things.

We took off, and I settled in against the side of the plane until we got up past the Jap picket boats, and the night fighters scrambled and got after us.

That new gunner, the Florida boy, had got me thinking with his questions, and there was not any reason I couldn't just go along on the same track, just to have something to do. I had left off when I was telling him about the icebergs, and I started in now, thinking about them like I remembered. I looked out through my plexiglass, and it came to me that clouds and icebergs were a lot alike, because they were beautiful just like they were, and there was no use to them at all. There was no reason for them to be like they were, and have the shapes that they did, except that that was the way they happened to be, for nothing.

Where my father and I had lived was on the lower side of the north slope of the Brooks Range, in a kind of a draw that kept off most of the wind. It was easy to follow the draw on down to the flat country at the bottom of the mountains, and it was also easy, more or less, to stay on the slope where you could see more, down under you. We had most of the traps along the slope, in different places from the flat up until it got too steep. We had our best luck where there was some slant, but not too much. My mother died before I ever knew anything about her, and my old man, who was originally from Virginia, got hold of the land up there for almost nothing, learned to make out with weather and the traps, and as soon as he could he brought me

over from Barrow, where I was born, to the cabin. I never did go
to school, at least not when I was young. My father taught me to
read and write and what he'd been able to learn about staying
alive up in that country. He had his own reasons for being there,
which he never did get around to telling me, or that I ever really
understood. It may have been he got into some kind of trouble,
back in Virginia or somewhere in the States, though I don't
think it had anything to do with the law. But something had
happened to him that made him want to be by himself; or
maybe he was just that way all the time. Like I say, he never did
give me the straight of it. But he liked it up there in that place,
where you hardly ever heard anything but the wind, and where
anybody who didn't know how things were could get lost as
quick as he could take five steps.

But I was brought up in the snow. Until the time I was fifteen,
I used snowshoes more than I used my natural feet; my feet felt
wrong when I took off the shoes. My father used to tell me I was
half snow goose and half wolverine, and before I was more than
ten or eleven I was showing him stuff that I'd picked up by
myself, rambling around all over, as much as I could, from
Teshekpuk Point to the Colville River and back. In all that time
I never saw but one wolverine, and my father never did see one;
he's just heard the stories about them, like the other trappers.
But I was proud of mine, which I saw on the gut pile of a down
caribou, because I knew then that the wildest animal in the
world, the one with the most stories about him, the most bad
and strong magic of any of them, had looked at me — looked
right at me, for a good half a minute, through the feather snow.
That was enough. I'm glad my old man thought of me like that.

It bothered me that I had told the Florida boy anything. He
had probably already forgotten everything I'd said, in the time-

wasting time before the mission. But what I knew, I knew. Wherever it's cold enough, I can get along. Snow and wind are right for me. Dark weather is right. Nearly everything about the cold is good. The cold-weather birds are the best to eat and the prettiest by far; there's not a bird in any jungle that can compare with them. The cold-water fish are better, and stronger, and taste like fish ought to taste; the cold water makes the meat good and firm. And I love fur, and the animals that grow it. I like to sleep in a fur parka with ice all around me. Eskimos, the Nanamuit in our range, at a town there, Anak-tuvuk, showed me how to cut the slabs of snow and ice, fit them, and seal them, so that you've got yourself a real quick strong house. When you get in there, you don't need anything but your parka. It's all good; you're OK.

I nodded back against the airplane, took off my glove, and felt the aluminum. But it was the wrong cold. The cold of high air is not real, it's not honest. Cold should be connected to the ground, even if it's at the top of a mountain.

I eased back again and started to move with the caribou from the tundra through the tree line into their winter range.

I looked at my watch. It had moved some, more than I would have thought. We were probably past the picket ships by now. I got into position behind the guns, and as soon as I did, the Major called and told us we were over the Kanto Plain, and that we could expect fighters. We all knew the Kanto area could scramble a lot of them.

I charged both guns and fired off a few rounds, and then leaned forward and watched and waited. I had a way of doing things that was about half the Air Force's and half mine. When I came into gunnery school, it took me time to adjust to the way you set up the lead when you're in an airplane and the target is another airplane. I had shot with a lead all my life: birds, caribou, rabbits, you name it. But I had never shot at anything that was moving when I was in something moving myself, and for a while it threw me, threw me off. But there's really not all that much to it. If you're in the tail of a plane, you've got real good visibility.

In the daytime you can see anything that's close enough to shoot at you. At night it's a little different, because the other aircraft has to shoot first, before you can tell where he is by his guns. That bothers some people, but there's no need for it to. Usually the fighter will open up before he really gets into the range where his guns will do him any good, and when he does that you've got him, because when you see those gun glitters, you put together a couple of things and set him up. According to which side of you he's on, he's got to put his inside wing down and the other wing up to get his guns on you. If he's on the right side of your plane, the starboard side, he's got to put his right wing down; if he's on the port side, it'd be his left wing. When that happens you've got the situation you want, because the line that maneuver puts him on is all in your favor. It's like the fighter was sliding down a string, and he is; he can't shoot at you unless he is on it. All you have to do is put your sight in front of him, according to where he is on the curve, track with him, and let him have it. My favorite shot is two widths of the sight ring — two rads — down to one. I let him have a three-second burst, right in there. But zero rads is not bad, either, when he's dead behind you, and usually under you, before he breaks off and down. When he's at zero rads, you go right at him, right into his teeth with the fifties, and you can make him live hard.

So I waited for that. We were close to the bomb line, I was

sure. The bombardier didn't have the plane yet, and the bomb bay doors were not open, but there was that tension you always feel all over the ship when the time comes close to drop. There should have been fighters, and there weren't any. The part before the bomb run felt all right, but the rest of the situation didn't.

Then something hit us from underneath. Or, more like it, something hit *at* us, like it blew up the air right below us. "Hold on," Major Sorbo said, real loud; I believe I could have heard him without the intercom. "We got to leave this altitude. Hold on."

The 90 millimeter had never been on us this early before, not with the first crack of ground fire; it usually took them a lot longer to get us bracketed. We began to lose altitude, and I sucked on my tongue to clear my ears. We leveled out, and even before the half G of pull left me, I saw the sparkle of a fighter. Like always, he was too far off. He had showed on the port side of us, and I kept that in mind, and swung the guns. Then he was close to us, much closer than I would have thought, and firing. I fired back, but wasn't on him. I didn't think he hit us, though — at least not bad.

Another fighter showed on the same side, and this time I was ready for any rate of closure he might have. He fired again, and was in range, and hit us a little somewhere up the fuselage, as near as I could tell. He fired again, and this time he was on his curve. I led what I figured was two rads and cut loose. Nothing happened. I waited a second, until I judged he was point-blank line astern and below, and cut loose again, all three seconds.

The whole sky lit up. I must have hit his tanks, because the explosion was all over the place, and he was gone. I asked the

Major if he had seen the plane blow, and he said yes, everybody did, and get off the horn. I went back to watching for guns, but I was not really satisfied with myself, because I had been wrong on one or two points, and I never had before. The two fighters I had credit for had been knocked down in daylight, but the other three, which I know damn well I got, were at night. I know, because I do aerial gunnery in a certain way. I don't shoot at the plane, I shoot at the pilot. Or I shoot where I think he is, according to my feeling about it, which is like guessing, but not quite. You know that the pilot is halfway between his guns on most fighters, and right behind them on the others, and you just estimate that. When he fires at you from his pursuit curve, his guns have a relation to each other, a tilt, an angle, so that you can more or less tell how fast he's coming down the string. You feel, you guess, and then you fire. If he fires a little before you, you try to nail him between his guns, but when he's in close range, I try not to let him do that. I shoot before he does, by guess and by God. But all the time I'm going for the pilot, not the plane. The thing inside that I shoot by — guess or God or whatever you might want to call it — tells me when I'm on. The four confirmed kills that I had were hit that way; there was no blowing of the tanks, no fire. They were confirmed because they were going down out of control, and the people on my crew could see them, and some of the crews on the other ships could, too. I nailed the other three at night the same way, but the planes didn't explode, nobody saw them go down, and I didn't get credit. But they went, same as the others. I led them in; they came to me, came right down my throat. I fired on that split second, and they were gone. Long gone, I'm telling you. I know what I'm talking about.

At the new altitude we went into the bomb run. The bombardier, Lieutenant Madison, took over the plane, and we steadied on through the run, getting off the two-thousand-pounders and the payload of incendiaries we had, maybe as a warmup for the big raid the Colonel had been talking about. It's always a relief when you get the bombs off the racks and out of the plane. Major Sorbo circled us without drawing flak or any more fighters, and I could see two fires, one a lot bigger than the other, where we had hit the city, or the other planes had. It was an easy enough run so far. We were supposed to have dropped some two-thousand-pounders, some incendiaries, and some frag bombs on the Kiba area of Tokyo, the waterfront, and we had, and now we could pick up the home heading and get out of there.

The next thing was not fire, though later I realized that it had to do with fire, had fire in it, but it did not seem like fire that was separate from us, or that could have been to one side of us, or above or below us. No, it was like the inside of the plane had exploded and we, each one of us, had exploded. It was like we were *inside* an explosion, or maybe we had exploded from inside ourselves. That's as close as I can come to saying it. Major Sorbo was just coming out of the turn for home when it happened.

When I could think, I saw that I was over the butts of my guns. The wind was knocked out of me, but I could move all right, and I held on to the strap of my seat harness and turned around.

The plane leaned up on one wing like it was going into a turn, but it kept leaning. Nobody could have been controlling it and making it go any such way. Then the nose went down, and I knew we were completely gone; everybody on the flight deck was probably dead. One of the waist gunners, I think it might have been the Florida boy, was stretched out right in the middle of the air, his arms and legs going wild trying to fetch up against something solid, to get hold of a chest chute. Then he was gone — on the floor, on the wall, the ceiling, I couldn't tell. Equipment was flying all over the inside of the plane. You couldn't tell what anything was, except that I saw a chest chute bounce off one wall and a hand reach out for it and miss, and the chute was not there, or the hand. We were nose-down now, spinning, the wings going around the airplane.

"Man, I am here," I heard myself say, and it didn't surprise me too much. I unbuckled from the seat, and just as soon as I did I banged against a wall. But I was holding on to the seat-strap web, and I kept holding on to it, and worked my feet forward into the plane. I got banged around a lot, swinging like a clapper in a bell, but I caught on to another web strap — it must have been one of the ones for storage — and pulled on toward where the chutes had been, and the hatch was.

The chute I had taped was still taped, the only one there, and I pulled it loose, and, one hand after the other, holding to the strap with one hand and buckling with the other, I snapped the chute to my chest, over the emergency kit, everything going round and round, faster and faster.

The hatch was only a few feet farther on, and I scrambled and twisted along to it, and pulled the pins. The hatch stayed. And then the only lucky thing of the night happened. The ship yawed like it had been hit again, and swung me on the strap away from the hatch, so that I could get my feet around. When the plane swung back the other way, it swung me, too, and I hit the hatch with both feet, with everything I had.

It was gone. I could see the sky whirling outside the hole in the plane. The air would knock your teeth loose, but it was outside air. I had my door to the open, and went out through it, and had the whole thing, the whole sky.

The first thing was the cold, but like I said, not the right cold. I was tumbling — sometimes I saw stars and sometimes I didn't see anything, anything but black — and the wind seemed to whip the air out of my nose sideways. But I could see enough to tell that I had some altitude, enough to open the chute, and I waited a little to figure the best way to do it. You're supposed to be facing the ground, with your head a little lower than your feet, when you pull the chute, so that when the lines pay out and the chute opens, the risers will swing you under, and you won't get that terrific grab up through the crotch, that might be bad in a lot of ways. I spread out my arms to try to stabilize, and it was as easy as something in a dream. It crossed my mind how out of control the plane had been, there at the last, and how easy it was to control the way I was falling, and for a second it seemed to me that a man ought to be able to fly without an airplane.

But that was dangerous: I could have held on to the notion too long. I felt for the handle, and took hold of it with my right hand, though I hated to pull my arms back in; I was half believing they were wings. Dangerous, like I say. Then I put my left forearm across my face, because with a chest pack the risers whip right across your face when they come out, and pulled.

Something stuck. I pulled again, and it still stuck. I pulled again, hard as I could, and the handle came away. It felt like I had thrown loose my whole arm, thrown my arm away, but I was still falling, turning over from the position they'd taught me. What the hell, I thought; that's all I can do.

I was shot, through the armpits and between both legs.

There'd been a loud pop, a crack like a rifle, and I was sure I had been hit. My face had taken a lick, too; I felt of it, and it was wet on one side.

But the chute was open. I looked up at it, and started to make my thinking include it, and the reason for the cracking sound, and the new hurt under my arms and between my legs. The chute. It was the chute. I was in a very big, quiet place in the middle of the air, and not shot. Not shot. I couldn't get rid of the idea that I had been.

I looked around from my float, from my big wide calm place in the middle of things. Swaying back and forth, I concentrated on the situation. It was the first time I had ever tried to concentrate and sway at the same time, and it was not a bad feeling, though I wouldn't want to do it every day.

Right under me was dark, but to my left was a lot of silver, very beautiful, too. Water, sure enough. It went way out, out into the moonlight as far as I could see. I was not far from all that silver, and I started to wonder about where I would hit. Breaking a leg was not part of my plan, but you can always do that in the dark, and I couldn't see anything right under me at all. I felt for the risers, because I knew I could control where I hit, or control it to a certain extent. But I didn't have anything to sight on except the water. I think I could have slipped the chute enough to land in the water, just barely, but what would have been the good of that? I didn't need to be wet, I needed to be on the ground with no broken bones, dry and figuring.

Even though I couldn't see where I was going to come down, I was not near enough to the ground so that I couldn't spill part of the chute and make a move, a little move, in any direction I wanted, but it was the dark or the water, no matter what, and the more I thought about it, the more I wanted the land.

How close to the water, though? How close to the docks, or whatever was there? I didn't want to land on top of a building that I couldn't get down from, or on somebody's roof, if I could help it.

I was getting closer. I could hear a siren, a lot like the ones the Air Force has. I looked inland toward the fires. The smoke came past me, and there was cordite in it from some of our bombs. About a half mile from me there was a lot of stuff burning, and I hoped that would keep people away from where I was going to hit.

I was still high enough to get a fairly good view. I could see the docks now, and the ocean spreading out in another way from the first way. Between me and the water there were some big shadows, tall, thin, and bent, and I could see through them, see the ocean, like silver cloth that's been slung out and ruffled and sewed together with black thread: all that, on the side toward the moon.

Quicker than I would have thought it could be done to me, there was a terrific clutch up between my legs. Under my shoulders, too. My shoulders stopped where they were, and so did I, jigging up and down in the harness, wondering what the hell. I must have still been fifty feet off the ground, and I was hanging. Not hurting, but hanging, and could have swung myself if I'd had a mind.

I looked up at the risers. The chute was collapsed and hung up on something, one of the things that made the long shadows, maybe, or were the long shadows themselves. Though there were not any lights, I could make out the space between the buildings and the water, and I couldn't see anything that looked like a man. If I could get down without anybody seeing me, I could go on to whatever might be next, on my own.

But I couldn't just hang there in the smoke, which was colored with red and seemed to have some kind of wind that came with it, shifting back and forth, turning one way, then back the other. I felt down in it with my feet, felt around on all sides, twisting in the harness, trying to make contact, but there was not anything there for me. I pulled on the risers to see how my strength was, and I had some. I started up the lines, arming it out, hand over hand. When I reached the bottom of the nylon, like a sheet half off a bed, I went past it to where the chute was caught, and felt for what it was caught on.

It was a gantry, a loading crane, I was on, and at least fifty feet from the ground. Holding to the metal, I unsnapped the chute and was a lot freer, just in a second. I worked up the crane and out the arm to where the chute was caught, and cut it loose. A backswirl of the crazy smoke-wind caught it, and it disappeared, collapsing, toward the buildings back from the docks. I housed the knife, crawled head-first back along the arm, and started down the main body of the crane, not hurrying, but little by little, watching and listening all-out. The crosspieces of the thing hurt my feet pretty bad when I put both of them in the same place, and on one section I just had to slide down one of the main beams — shinny, kind of — but I did it. Getting to the ground was something I could tell I was going to be able to do, by now. When I got to the top of the cab, I turned loose all the beams and struts and looked around, and there still wasn't anybody there.

I saw a ladder on the cab, and I used it. The ground was level cement, and full of power. I leaned against the wheel of the cab, in the shadow away from the moon. The smoke was still blowing, though maybe not so much, and somewhere in it, down the dock from where I was, I heard voices, and they were coming. I

hit a stillness, a new stillness like a marmot's, and two little men
came by, shorter than me even, almost transparent with smoke,
talking right into each other's face. I hadn't had time to find the
chute, and I hoped they wouldn't notice it, wherever it was. I
had my hand on my knife but didn't even crack the blade to
light, to any sort of light. I didn't want to give light a chance at
it, even though I was in the shadow of the crane. They went past
till I couldn't hear them.

Using every bit of cover on the dock, I went looking for the
chute, and finally found it spread and crumpled over some
barrels and boxes, like it was making a display. I bundled it up
and shoved it under the boxes, piled some other boxes and
crates on it, then walked back a ways toward the crane — it was
friendly —and tried to size up the situation, decide what to do.
I really didn't have any notion just then; just a feeling something like the one I got when the guns of the fighter sparkled
and I knew he was on the pursuit curve; a feeling that was a kind
of guess but not completely; a guess with another thing added
to it, something I didn't have a name for. I didn't want a name.
It was not words.

What did I need? Where the bombs had hit had been concentrated in one place, I had seen from the chute, but the smoke
was fading off now and I couldn't hear any more sirens. In other
words, I couldn't bank on people having to deal with the fire.
And the bomb drop was only in a small part of Tokyo. Since I
hadn't seen any night watchmen on the ocean side of the docks,
I thought I might have a look down the streets between the
dock buildings and try to find out what they went into. I edged
out past the corner of the warehouse nearest to the crane,
looked as far as I could toward the city, and then started down

that way, in the fullest and longest shadows I could find. If I saw a single person, I would turn back and try something else.

I got almost to the end of the building, and could see a little way into the blacked-out blocks, when I heard voices — not one or two but a lot. A whole crowd went by the end of my truck alley, talking fast. There was no light but moonlight, but I could make them out against the cement of the street and the light-colored buildings on the other side. I couldn't have dealt with them. I had no odds going for me.

Using the same shadows, I went back to the dock and to the crane. What had bored me before, the words of the Colonel at the briefing, all his talk about fire, came up in my head, and all over me. Fire was what I needed, fire from my own side. I needed a whole city in panic, a lot of confusion, as much as there could be, and things would be different. I didn't know when the raid would come, but I knew that it would be soon. Soon. Maybe a day, another night. I would find a way to wait it out.

In the first shadows again, working from one crane to the other, I made it to the end of the dock and just stood paying attention, all the attention I had, to what was there, to what was only a step or two away, or might have been in a few more. Where the docks and the warehouses gave out there were more docks, more warehouses. But I was interested in the field be-tween, and what happened when it came together with the water.

There was no ladder down. I couldn't tell exactly, but I judged it was not far to the ground, though. I hung by my hands off the edge of the concrete, and dropped.

I hit almost right away. The field, whatever kind of ground it was, was slanted toward the water, and I didn't count on that, and hit wrong and fell. I rolled and had my knife out and ready to come up, but there was nobody around. Since it was out, I took the satisfaction of watching the blade flash off the moon. I looked around and did it again, and the satisfaction was as much as anybody could have wanted.

I could see a lot better, too, and I won't say that it wasn't because of the knife flash. Steel that good, and the ocean, that big silver light full of thread — well, you can't tell what might happen. Like I tell you, I believe in things like that. It don't matter why.

The field was set against the water by a kind of wall, cement — a breakwater, I think somebody called it. I inched along the top of it on my belly, like a lizard, running my hand, trying to feel if there might be some kind of hole in it, some place I might be able to wedge into. It took a long time to do it, and I really hadn't come all that ways from the docks when I felt into something, something not concrete, but hard and wet. I smelt of my fingers and knew where they'd been. Using one of my matches, letting it burn nearly all the way down to my fingers, I got a good notion of what was there: a sewer pipe that fell off into the ocean, big enough to hold a man; not running too much, but some. I let myself down and put my feet in.

The smell put my eyes out. I mean, it hit my eyeballs like the worst light, and one that would never quit. My eyes, you know, and that was not meant to be. But it was a hole, and I could go on into it if I wanted to. I took out another match and lit it, though I knew that sewers could blow up. That would be something else, I said to myself, to get out of a B-29 on fire and blow yourself up with shit gas. But nothing blew, and I went on up amongst the squishing shit and other stuff, to where there was a turn, where I was damn sure nobody would come. To do it, they'd have to come the same way I had, and I couldn't think of anybody who'd do that, not even the Japs, no matter what. For one day, maybe for a day and a night, I had shit and safety. What else, I asked myself, what else have you got a right to ask for in the enemy's own damn country, his main city? What else?

I broke back out, and the big air was good, I tell you. The moon was higher, and the stars were so strong they seemed to be blasting light at me, like studs or screw heads that had that kind of power. I broke off a stalk of something from the field and marked the sewer, and started back along the breakwater, this time standing up. So far, things were working. The whole thing was working, right where I stood, where I walked along the silver ocean of the Japs and looked out over the big sewed-together bay.

When I got back to the crane I had a sudden thought: how quick could I get to the pipe? I looked at my watch and took off, running light as I could along the front of the warehouses, my moon shadow in front of me. When I hit the end of the dock I took off, right into the air over the field, like I was trying to jump from the cement loading slabs of my dock toward that other one off as far as I could see, and I hung up there over the field-dark for the longest time, almost like being in the chute again, except that this time it was just me instead of a lot of harness and nylon, and when I hit this time I didn't fall. I found the stalk of stuff I'd left at the edge and let myself down into the hole and swung in, my eyes stinging.

I came out again and went back to the crane, listening for night watchmen but not all that much. It was two-thirty in the morning. I didn't have any notion of sleeping in the shit pipe, so

I climbed into the cab. It cut off the wind and had a big seat, big enough for two people. I took the control handles, set them off from the seat, and stretched out. I didn't know when they went to work on the docks in Tokyo, but I figured I could get at least a couple of hours of fresh-air sleep before anybody came. Before that, I would hit for the pipe.

I wanted to sleep in control, and not just like some desperate guy with no chance. There were certain things I had, and I knelt down on the floor of the cab and went over them, holding the matches down below the windows.

My knife I knew about, and left it alone this time. I laid out my .45 and two clips. There was no telling where I might use them, but it would have to be either in a place where nobody could hear or in a situation with so much noise and confusion that nobody'd care, or even notice. I thought about the Colonel's fire, and decided that I would wait a day or two in the whole concentrated stink of Tokyo, crammed into a little pipe, for them to bring the fire: for them to bring the fire, and make a situation where I could operate.

I needed to get outfitted, and that meant I needed some clothes different from a wired-up combat rig, a flight suit underneath it, and GI brogans. I couldn't last long in Tokyo, either in daylight or at night, in what I had on. If the fire came — *when* the fire came — I would go out with the .45 and get what I needed.

I broke open my emergency kit and spread the stuff on the seat, wondering what situations might come up where I'd use it — use this thing and then that thing. There was a little knife that I could use for little doings, like cutting string or scaling fish. There was a packet of fishhooks and some twine. There was a silk map of part of Japan, like a handkerchief printed with a topo layout of Japan up to the strait between Honshu and Hokkaido, and another piece of silk that had an American flag on it, and writing in five or six different languages; the intelligence officers told us that Japanese was one of them. I couldn't read them, but all the crews had had to memorize what they said: *I am an American aviator. My aircraft is destroyed. I am an enemy of the Japanese. Please take me to the nearest American authorities. The government of my country will pay you.* Like I say, I couldn't read any of this stuff, but I looked at all that writing, in Annamese, Burmese, Thai (it said), French, and Japanese, and I struck a blank wall on whether I should keep it. I looked by the match light, before the match went out, and tried to make a decision. But it was funny, anyway, and I think I laughed right there in the cab, and real loud, too.

It was quiet there. I sat on the floor of the cab with my things on the seat: gun, bullets, fishhooks, map, blood chit with all the languages, and leaned back against the metal of the wall. Nothing, nobody, could be more out of luck.

Except that there could be. Both times it was myself, and I knew that when I got down into the pipe — when the sun came up I had to get down into it — I would be even worse off, and if the fire didn't come down on Tokyo, it was only a question of time before somebody would find me, if I didn't drown in the flood of Tokyo shit, and no matter how hard I fought or however many I might be able to kill, I would lose. I would have my balls cut off, I would have my head cut off, and that would be it.

But not yet. I took out the C rations and wound the key around the can. It was not so bad: a kind of cold hash, and I ate it all, and stretched out on the seat when I'd put my stuff back the way it was. There was really nothing to worry about. I had

35

the next day planned, and the Colonel's B-29s would come, or they wouldn't. That was not up to me.

❖   ❖   ❖

There was a long dream in which a buffalo, something I had never seen except in pictures, ran across in front of me, and for some reason I couldn't move my eyes or my head, but had to stare front and center while he went by. He was big, and for some reason I felt like I could even ride on his back, but I couldn't reach him, or give him any notion of how I felt. He went by me on some kind of a raised platform that was like a breakwater. It was the breakwater that made the buffalo be there like he was. There was no doubt about it in the dream, or when I woke up, either.

It was all good, I mean it. All the problems were for the next day. Nobody was going to check the cab of a loading crane between three and five in the morning, no matter what the city was, no matter what the war was. I woke up, more or less, saw that it was still black dark, saw one star, and went back, waiting for the buffalo to come across again, on a line just above the ocean. That was something beautiful.

❖   ❖   ❖

Light, and I was dead. I knew it, and kept watching. Sometimes I looked, actually, and at other times I looked in my sleep and it was the same; through my eyelids it was the same; I could see the sun, and water. But when I heard feet, and voices amongst them, I knew I couldn't give away any more. I raised up, and twenty or thirty guys were going by, right by me, on their way somewhere. As much as I could, just at eye level over the bottom of the window, I watched where they went. The light was gray. It was first dawn, and if I was going to get into my hole, I had better do it before much longer. Little by little I let myself out of the cab and dropped down between the rails. Most of the men had gone into the warehouses, and as far as I could tell the few others would go in when they got around to it. I looked at my watch. It had taken me nineteen seconds to get to my hole before. Could I do it now? Could I time it so that nobody saw? Out on the Range, the Brooks Range, I had got where I was scared of the human voice; you didn't expect there to be one. I knew now that, when I made my move, if anybody sang out, I was dead. I crouched down between the rails and put my head up one more time. All but two or three of the men had gone into the warehouses. They were opening them up with big sick clangs and scrapes of galvanized iron. I stared at one guy especially, who kept hesitating and looking back out at the ocean. I made him the one that things turned on, and when he took a step or two toward the buildings, I broke.

I was on the wall in a second, not hunching but putting my head down and digging, but digging light, and there was not a sound but me. When I got to the piece of reed I had stuck up, I hit the top of the breakwater side-on and slid over, my feet going into the hole. I even broke off the stalk with my hand as I went down.

There I was. All the time I was growing up, I was on the side of the hunters, the foxes and weasels and lynxes, on the side of the wolverines, because we were doing the same thing: we were hunting the others. But when I got my feet into the sewer pipe, and was sure I was *in* that hole in the side of the sea wall, that I had found it and had come back to hide in it, I knew a little

37

about things from the other side that I hadn't thought about, or thought about enough. I knew how the marmot feels when he makes it to his hole, how the badger feels, how the snowshoe hare feels when he understands that the color that's been given him is right, that it works — or works right now, anyway — that nothing can get him because nothing can find him. Any animal would have had a better hole than I had, but it was all the same thing: we were in our place, me and the rest of them.

But my God, it was awful. I wasted another match, and risked blowing up on shit gas, to get back to the curve, and went on up beyond it and sat down in the shit and other slow-moving stuff. I waited, but I couldn't stay there long, and edged on out toward the ocean until I could see it, and smell it, through the shit and God knows what else was in there.

All day I was in it. All day, counting on the night and the fire. I had put it into my head that I shouldn't show anything around the curve of the pipe, because if anybody found the chute, there would be an all-out search. Somebody might even have a look into the pipe, or at least shine a flashlight up it. But I would be sure to hear them before they saw me, and could duck back. So, as it turned out I spent most of the day at the curve, looking out at the sky, which was a little blue circle at the end of everything, and that filled up with whatever I wanted to be there.

The caribou had been good to me, in my mind, especially since we took the first hit in the 29; before that I hadn't known how good. Them coming out of the woods was a beautiful thing to think. In such huge space they were, in snow that was more like ice, a little cautious, a little slow, but all of them coming, and then all in the open, in the overcast light that makes the snow more merciless than it is any other time, in the long afternoon that never ends. And then they are gone off into the winter range, and there's nothing left but the snow. Let there be a little more fall-down, I said, more snow. The caribou are good, the tracks are beautiful and good, but let the snow drift them down, let it drift them under.

It happened. The eye of the pipe I was in went away so far that there was not any more of it; everything there was snow. The snow of the Brooks Range, or some other snow. But snow. Snow, not a track on it. I knew, then, what I needed to do. The little compass would point north, no matter what I did, whether it was outside my body or in it. North was north, and it would stay that way. And there was the pull of something else to go with it: that other thing that was not called north but was at the same place, the thing nobody could say.

By feel I pulled out the compass again, though I didn't want to take too much of the adhesive off my body tape. It would be better, though, if I knew whether the compass was luminous or not. It was, and that was good; night was going to be my time, at least until I got to the heavy snow. "An asshole compass," I said out loud, my voice coming back from the sides of the pipe and maybe having some kind of roundness to it, from the shape of the galvanized tin or iron, or whatever I was in, looking off at the little circle of nearly black blue that was the bay, the ocean, the rest of the world. "Some compass," I said to the echo. "Right here I've already got a pretty close connection to half the assholes in Tokyo." The pipe walls told me it was so, and the slow-moving stuff I was sitting in. I wondered how I would smell when I got out among people. Something would have to be done about it, first thing. "Come on, boys," I said to Tinian Island, out through the round walls and the little ocean at the end of them. "Come on with all that fire. Let me out of this place. Come on, night. Come on, fire."

I thought of the snow, and one long kayak trip I took with an Eskimo buddy, Tornarssuk, east toward Kaktovik, hunting for seals. At one place we went by a big glacial berg that calved off about half a mile from us with a sound like a woman who had been reamed up through the gut. When the ice slid off the near side of it, the brightest blue I ever saw in my life came right at us, it seemed like, so deep and pale it could have been some new kind of scientific thing, a new kind of light that nobody had ever seen before. The ice just slid down off it, and it was there, a thing, a new color just invented, but one that had also been waiting in the ice for a long time, a real long time, just for two guys in a kayak to see it. We were the only ones who did.

We sat there for a while. Tornarssuk took his paddle out of the water, and so did I. We just stared off at that pale blue that came to us out of the big white, that came to us and went right through us, and I didn't ask Tornarssuk what he was doing or why he was doing it for so long, because I knew all that. There is not much color in an Eskimo's life, not more than three or four colors that are strong and simple: white most of the time, for almost everything that's on the ground; the blue of the sky when it's clear; the gray-green of the ocean when the floes break up; and red, which is blood, the brightest blood in the world, wherever you see it up there. So I let Tornarssuk stare on, let the split glacier come into him as it must have been doing into me — that pale, concentrated, pure, huge-sided light. And I used it now, in the shit tunnel, as part of the plan I was making. In the pipe I sat like I had in the kayak with Tornarssuk, with the iceberg coming through me. Every now and then I brought in the red of the far wall of my father's cabin, as I would see it coming in off the Range, as red as any blood in the snow, but always I came back, without trying, to the calm ocean and the berg, with the pack ice around the base of it, sending that light, just-invented blue color at me, keeping my paddle out of the water. That was the afternoon.

The blue-black at the end of the pipe left me, little by little, and even the circle of the pipe, at least as far as my being able to see it was concerned. I would give it another hour by my watch, and then poke my head out and see if I could pick up Polaris.

I didn't make it to the end of the pipe, or at least not right then. The whole thing squeezed together all at once, from all sides but especially the top, and drove my eardrums back into my head, pushed toward each other by some big quick clamp, like earphones coming together a hundred times harder than they were supposed to. There was a sound when this happened, but my head hurt so much from the in-driving on my drums that I didn't remember it until later. It was a big thump, though, one that was in the air, most likely. It was made out of air but had body to it, a lot of body, just for a second. The pipe shook with it; the water going past me sloshed. It happened again. I sucked on my tongue and started to crawl. It was not Polaris I was looking for now: those were explosions. "Come on," I said, crawling hard. "Come on. Let them have it. More. All you got." And then, "Let *me* have it." There in the shit pipe, heading for the outside to stay out, I called that fire down. I did all I could from where I was.

I got out and stood up, and looked back inland. There was a low red glow, very wide, with some white in it. I hadn't even straightened up when four or five more bombs hit, all in a line and spaced more or less even with each other. The line must have covered at least a mile, and right away the fire went wider, and a lot higher. There was already smoke, though the docks, at least my part of them, hadn't been hit.

But there were people on them, and I wasn't used to that at night. They were running back and forth amongst the cranes, and in between the bombs I could hear them screaming and gabbling. That was the way I wanted it, sure enough, and I took off across the field toward the fire, running easy.

❖   ❖   ❖

The field was tough and springy; my feet went down, went forward, and came back under me. I was not afraid of holes. I felt very light and a little better than usual, even. When I was a boy, in the summer, and the snow melted off the lower part of the Range below our cabin, I used to go down to where there was a field — a field that was like a road, though nobody had made it or used it — and run, the first day I got the snowshoes off my feet. I was so used to them that it was hard to believe I wasn't still lifting them step by step, and slowed way down from even normal walking. But after the thaw I'd go down and run with just my feet, and the whole land — the flat and the mountains to one side, and everything I could see — speeded up, and I really took off. I felt like I was the fastest thing in the world, the fastest-moving, the fastest thinking, the most free human there was. And freer than that: freer than any lynx, any mallard, any salmon or tern or bufflehead. I wouldn't be able to tell you that I couldn't fly; that would be next. Going over ground so fast and so free that it was wrong, except that I liked it so much, was so different from moving over snow that I wished every year for a few minutes that it would never snow again, or that we could move off the Brooks Range and live somewhere else. But when the snow came back I was ready, and happy to get back on the shoes where I belonged. There's too much easiness in just running on your feet. It's dangerous. The snow-shoes are solid, solid-down: they give you a balance you ought to have.

But now I was running just in my GI boots, and over the field I had the summer feeling. I had the freedom and the drunk power, and I knew I had better watch myself, and slow down before I went much farther. The smoke was beginning to sting my eyes bad; I was going right into it. As near as I could tell, two streets came together at the edge of the field, and every time the smoke shifted I could tell that there were plenty of people there, not going back and forth but all moving one way. They kept crowding past, to my right. I could hear them: a long moaning sound they all made together, and a sharp scream like a bird, or more like a trapped rabbit, rising out of it. I slowed down until I was almost walking, and then saw that wouldn't do because all of them were running, or trying to run, even if the whole movement of the crowd was slow, even slower than they would have been going on snowshoes. I picked up to a jog, because I wanted to get in amongst them at about the same speed, the same pace, and blend in.

I wasn't there yet, though. I was maybe seventy-five yards from the people in the crowd nearest me, but I couldn't say it was exactly that far. The wind would shift back and forth, and clear the view for a few seconds, and then the smoke would thicken up and I had to guess. The smoke didn't act like any smoke I had ever seen, and I listened more the nearer I got to the streets. In amongst the long moaning of the people there were low heavy crumps, like a rifle firing with a blanket around the barrel. This was the three-hundred-plane raid, all right. This was it. The more I listened, the more I could hear the incendiaries hitting behind the crowds in the street. Then all at once I felt my back warm up, a heavy slash of heat, and I turned around toward the docks. Up and down where I had been was on fire, with the deep orange of napalm and also the blue-white of white phosphorus, which is not so much like any fire you'd know, but was more like the end of a blowtorch, all spread out and shooting up curlicues and wriggles of itself like tracers that had gone crazy, and were meant to.

Even in the situation I was in, I couldn't get over the smoke, the way the smoke acted. In a low red light that was over everything before I even realized it was there, the smoke would all of a sudden stir itself, whirl around, and cut one way or the other. It would jog and slant, and settle, then jump and swirl again and go the other way, or come right at me. The incendiaries were hitting everywhere, in front of me and on both sides, but nothing else behind me; there was no more heat on my back. Now, though, as I got closer to the streets, whenever the smoke would blast one way or the other with the bombs — it was hard to believe those quick jumps and jogs were not something the smoke was doing to itself — I could see fire, low fire, buildings and not just white phosphorus twisting in the air, down the street I would be on if I kept running and came off the field and didn't turn.

Through the blasts of smoke I got into the crowd, making the turn to be in their direction and slowing down to their pace, which was a kind of fast shuffle. I couldn't tell much about the people, even the ones who were right next to me, except that they were women, a couple of them with babies. There was one old man bent over like a squirrel. I just caught a glimpse of him, and then he went down under all of us, and we went on over him, on past him.

The smoke in front of us stopped, stopped dead, and then

came back and hit us square, face-on. Then I was on top of somebody on the ground, and there was another one on me, or maybe two. I rolled a woman — I'm sure — to one side and got my feet under me. The others were getting up, and it bothered me that I might have stood up too quick and would show my difference, even in all the confusion. The new fire was right in front of us, on both sides of the street, and all of a sudden I looked down, because something was wrong. The zipper of my flight suit caught the light, and caught it strong just for a second, and without any pain I had the notion that I had been gutted, ripped right down the middle by fire, by lightning maybe, and that I was dead from it; that I had come out on the other side alive with another kind of life, still holding the print. I bent down again, and got up slow with the others. Nobody had noticed a thing. We started, and turned off into another street, the smoke jumping and slanting with the bombs. The sound of the crowd around me was made up of high yells, all you could put up with, but around them all was the low sound, which must have been coming from the whole city. How all those high screams could have added up to that one low tone, like a glacier when it first begins to calve off, was not something I could explain. It must have had something to do with the buildings — echoes — all those voices beating back and forth off the walls. Maybe, but I don't know.

On the second street the smoke was bad, even worse than on the other one, and for the first time I noticed how terrific the heat was, and steady, not just near the fires we could see. I kept as close as I could to the woman in front of me — for a while it was the same one — so that my zipper wouldn't show in the flames, but I knew I had better do something about my clothes while I could. I looked around as much as I was able, and I

45

started to figure, in there shuffling with the rest of them, sweating like a thaw, and adding up what I had with me.

I was sure glad I was a great believer in tape. My bread knife was riding down my leg, almost a part of me, just as much in place as it had been in the Quonset hut back at Tinian, and the emergency kit was square in the middle of my chest, breathing with me, and ready to do all the things it could do, from cutting wire to stripping down vines and cleaning fish. I had my .45 and one extra clip, and that was something I could use in what I needed to do; wanted to do, you might even say. It was one of those kind of times. And there was a war on, too, as the Colonel and everybody else used to tell us. That was all right with me.

In the building we were going by there were plenty of doors, some that shut on the street and some that went back a ways. I was interested in the deep ones, and I looked along the left for what I wanted. There was hardly any sidewalk, and I could be in one of the doorways in two pushes and one big step, or two at the most. There were a couple of men in the crowd now, on the side I was edging toward. They were ahead of me, but one of them was about my size, and I figured that there would be more than one to come along later, when I was ready. And I had noticed something else. A lot of people, even the babies, had things, some kind of bandages, over their noses and mouths, like doctors in hospitals; like some of the ones at the base hospital at Buckingham Field, when I was in there for the trench mouth I got from eating GI food; I used to see them go by the ward. That would help, not only now but later on. The officers in indoctrination, in the course we had to take called The Nature of the Enemy, told us that a lot of Japanese wore those things all the time, even when they were not in an air raid.

And, again, I knew that would help, and that there was more advantage I could give myself once I had picked out the door.

And there it was, so deep it might have been an alley. I slid and slanted and jumbled over through the women, and then made my two steps, one big and the other more or less ordinary, and I was in. I backed up some more to get the shadow, and got it all, all I could use. There was plenty of time now. Plenty of time, and good conditions.

I felt my face. I had shaved before the mission as I always did, because the oxygen mask fits a lot better that way, and my beard hadn't even begun to grow out. But that was not what I was thinking. I ran my fingers along the wood next to me and looked at them, and the tips were black; the smoke had sooted up everything. I took a good smear of soot off the boards and went across my forehead with it, then more down my cheeks and nose and around my mouth. As the color of my face disappeared and went to another color, there was something inside me that changed, too. It moved, and then sat still. In my mind there was a shape I couldn't exactly make out, but it seemed to be in a crouch, pulled up into itself and ready, and that was the feeling I got from the soot, the stronger the more I put on. I did the back of my hands the same way, and then concentrated on the crowd going by, screaming and moaning, and not one of them even giving a flicker of a look toward me. Millions of them could have gone by, and none of them would have seen me. I was dark now, the same as the shadow I was in. Some of the people were pretty smudged up, too, but I had not made myself like them in any way; it was just that now I wouldn't stand out. I was not like them, I say again; like something else.

I had another thought. Working with little moves, I pulled out the blood chit, the silk handkerchief with the American flag on it, and all the languages — Japanese was one of them, which I couldn't get over — that said that my aircraft was destroyed, I was an enemy of the Japanese, that my government would pay anybody who'd help me. I turned the flag and the writing to the inside and tied it around the lower part of my face. Almost everybody I saw had on a mask or cloth, and now I had mine.

It was time. I zipped down the flight suit and took the .45 out of the holster. I hit the clip with the heel of my other hand to make sure it was seated, and then let the safety off and charged it, and at the same time I brought the crouching shape up front in my mind, and had what it wanted me to have. There was not a flicker of light on the gun barrel. I put my free hand on the wood next to me to get steady, and all at once it jumped and shook. I figured the second story had caught fire, or somewhere up above me had, but I couldn't see for the smoke. On the other side of the street the fire had already come down to the ground floor; I could tell by the crowd edging toward me. In there amongst the people, and close to me, I looked for my size.

About five yards from me a man, I think, went down. The crowd went over him. He tried to get up, but before he could make it to his feet somebody else tripped over him, and this time neither one got up. Out of the smoke another man stumbled, and in a second I knew he was about right, about what I needed. For some reason the two that should have been on the ground were not there, maybe had been shoved off to one side by all that panic, all that pressure, but the one I had my eye on was still stumbling where they had been, correcting, you might say, trying to get his feet all the way under him, and I let him have a couple more steps. He came right to me, like every animal or bird I'd ever shot, or like the Nip fighters sliding

down the string of the pursuit curve. If you want to kill something, have it coming toward you. If it comes without knowing
you're there, it's the best way of all. I stood up in the doorway
and came up with the .45 and shot him right straight into the
face, at the same level as mine. I didn't want any blood on the
clothes, or any holes. The sound of the gun was hardly any
louder than the general noise, and the muzzle flame was just
one more little bit of fire, exactly like all the rest of it, and gone
quicker than you could think.

The blast knocked him back, the shock — a .45 at close range
is like a hand-held 30.06 — and he went down, with the two or
three other people behind him. I doubled into a crouch, watching hard. The others scrambled back into the crowd and left
him, all but one guy who pulled him to the side, and then
moved with the others again. The clothes I wanted were lying
about half under the feet of the people on my side of the street.
He had been dragged a yard or two by his feet, and I couldn't
see his head; the others were swarming all over him, to get on.
Nobody turned back.

I holstered the .45, stepped out, and then went down on my
knees amongst all those feet; they were going by me like they
were going by the dead man. I took him by an arm and a leg and
hiked him up on my shoulders, like I was maybe going to carry
him on with the rest of the crowd, wherever they were going.
But all I did was take two or three steps and lurch back into my
door, then rolled him off and rolled down beside him.

I stayed there still as I could, then reached a hand. The
building was roaring over us, and pieces of wood, some of them
big and heavy, were falling faster and faster, and I thought that
maybe the whole thing was going to come down on us in the
next few seconds. I hoisted up to my knees and took hold of the

middle of myself, under the throat, pulled down the zipper in one sweep, came out of the flight suit in a couple of moves, and started pulling off the dead guy's coat and shirt. They were all right by feel; even wearing them over my dungarees was not too tight. The pants were good enough, too, but the shoes were too short. I couldn't come near getting one of them on, sitting in the door frame now like I was doing, not too much different from the way I would have back in the Quonset hut.

I stood up and took one last look at the guy. The top half of his head was gone, but with the fire flickering on him and the ground smoke swirling in and out of the door, he didn't look too bad right then. His hat had been blown off with his head, so I would have to do without it, but I had a crew cut anyway, and my hair is black, so it didn't make all that much difference. It would not be a bad idea to have a hat later on, and some other shoes, but I knew I couldn't stay where I was any longer. The building was going to go any second, I was sure. I balled my flight suit up and flung it into the fire. Nobody was going to look at my feet. Breathing through the blood chit, the American flag, I stepped out.

It didn't take me long to pick up the kind of shuffle-stumble the crowd was moving with, screaming and moaning. For some reason all of us turned a corner, away from the docks, and just as we did there was a crash inside all the other noises — a terrific crash inside the big moaning sound the whole city must have been making — and a building fell in. Whether it was the one I had been in I can't say, and it doesn't make any difference, but I think it probably was. People kept shoving in from the side streets, and we were pushed closer and closer together. It was hard enough to breathe through the smoke, but all that being pressed on made it a lot harder. For a spell there I didn't have any doubt that I could raise my feet up off the ground and the rest of them would just carry me along. It would be better for me to work myself out to the near edge, on the side I had come in from, but still stay amongst them, and not separate myself out, even if I'd been able to.

I managed it, and could breathe better. There was only a little fat woman between me and the buildings, and a short, screaming man in front. Whoever was behind me I didn't need to know.

Over the knife and the emergency kit and the .45, I had on somebody's old shirt and coat. They were loose and comfortable. The pants fit all right, too, but they had a pocket only on the right side and no pockets in the back. I was holding the extra clip for the gun in my hand, and I put it in the pocket, which was deep, real deep. I had everything but shoes, and I planned to get some before I cleared the city. Shoes, and a bag like the ones a lot of people in the crowd were carrying. I was going to have to take everything I needed with me, and when I got out of the fire and into the cold, I'd have to be able to keep warm enough to stay alive. But even when I got to the real cold — the cold like the Brooks Range — I wouldn't need clothes as heavy as most people would have to wear. Still, it would be better if I could find some heavier than the ones I had on. Actually, I looked forward to getting hold of a parka somewhere; that would be like home, sure enough. As I shuffled along with the little screaming people, breathing through the blood chit, the American flag, my eyes almost shut with smoke, I thought about the parka. I'd like it to be one with wolverine fur around the head, because ice doesn't hold to the hairs; all you have to do is brush it off. I didn't have any idea whether there were any parkas in Japan, but if people lived in the northern part, on the big island the map said was up above the one where I was, they'd have to have the clothes for it. And if there were animals up there, they'd have to have fur, and the humans would've found a way to get it. But wolverines? Again, I didn't know.

Wolverine fur was maybe too much to hope for, but it wasn't costing me anything to think about it, or how I would get it if I found it. I hadn't counted on any of the other stuff that had happened, either: that my B-29 would get the ass knocked off it, or that I would bail out, get hung up on a crane, or that I would hide in a sewer pipe full of half the shit in Tokyo, or shoot somebody for his pants and coat, or join up with a bunch of little people trying to keep from being burned up by American incendiaries. So . . . who knows, I said to myself. Who knows I won't find a wolverine parka up north of here. Who could want anything better?

I thought of my father then, too. He was good for me; he had taught me everything I knew, until I was old enough to teach him. The day that happened was the best day of my life, I can tell you. It was not when I took off my snowshoes and ran the flat of the valley, but the day I put them back on, and knew there was going to be nothing but snow for a long time.

I hadn't been keeping track of the direction of the mob I was in, but just moved along with the others. After a while, though, I started to notice something I couldn't see any reason for. The crowd seemed to know where it was going, like way off in front there might be somebody leading the rest of us. I couldn't see how that would be possible, but there seemed to be a general direction we were headed in. Twice buildings fell in front of us, one no more than fifty or sixty yards off, and both times we turned into another street, and then back toward the way we had been headed. I thought we might be trying to get out of the city, but we just went on and on, and the buildings on both sides were just as close together as they had been down by the docks.

And then things changed all at once. The wind was steady now, coming from behind us, like it was pushing us along. The smoke was as bad as ever, but it blew forward, past me. People stepped away from both sides, and I could tell that the shape of the crowd that had been made by the streets and buildings was not the shape any longer. There was not a whole lot more room, but there was some: nobody was shoved against me. I was still with a lot of others, but they had fanned out, as near as I could tell, and they were moving a little faster, like something they had been looking for was in sight. I couldn't figure how any of this could be, or how any of them could see any better than I could, so I fell back on what I could hear, and tried to tune in on any new sound coming through that low, long moaning that just went on and on.

Sure enough, there was something. I thought it couldn't be what it sounded like, but when I saw the man in front of me get shorter and shorter, and not fall, I knew that he was moving downward, and that he was walking into water. I followed him down, and in.

The water was not much cooler than the air, but the crowd had quit moving, most of them. The people around me were just standing and screaming. If they had walked into that lake, or whatever it was, to do nothing but stand there and scream as loud as they could, for money or some prize, they couldn't have done it any better, or any louder, or got more breath out of all that smoke to keep it up like they did. I waded through them, with the idea that the water farther out might not be as hot. Some of them were trying to hold the others up — not all these were kids, either — and some were trying to push the others down and get on top of them. There were piles of people everywhere. They'd build up a little and then everything would fall apart and go under water. I didn't believe that many of them could swim, but some of them were moving out from the shore like I was, hoping for water the fire wasn't so close to.

The water was about up to the middle of my chest when I stepped in a hole and went under. I came right back up, though, and leaned forward to go on. There was something, a woman, in front of me, and not turned the same way I was. She was looking right at me, right into my face. I felt myself: the blood chit had come down and was around my neck. The soot had maybe washed off me, too, or most of it. It was the first face I had looked at since I'd bailed out, and the first person who had looked at me close up. Even through the smoke there was plenty of light, and she couldn't believe what she was looking at; my face must have been real pale in all that red glow. Her mouth opened and she screamed, and started to raise her hand to point. She did scream, but the sound was not any different from all the others, and she didn't scream but once. Under water I ran the knife into her with my move. The blade hit bone and traveled around it, and the only thing that stopped my hand was her. I pulled the blade out and put it back in the case, and was holding her down pretty hard as quick as anybody could have done it. But after a second or two I could tell there was not any reason to hold her down, and I turned loose and moved on, pulling the chit up where it belonged.

The water was not cooler, no matter where I went. When it got up to my chin I stopped; there was no use to swim, just to be swimming. Besides, I was worried about the .45. I might be able to use it again before it had a chance to rust, but I had better do it in the next hour or so. The bullets were probably all right, but

I wasn't sure about them, either. If I had to depend on a gun, I wanted to know that it would fire when I used it. If it wouldn't, or even if there was any doubt, I would get rid of it and use the rest of what I had. I was not sure I wouldn't rather do that, anyway. Not having a gun wouldn't bother me at all. I wouldn't miss it nearly as much as I would have the knife, or the compass, or even the fishhooks. I started working back through the stacks of people, and the ones just standing and screaming, toward the shore, and the crowd who thought that water would do them any good.

I had got used to panic. It was what I had wanted when I was in the pipe, and was what I had to go on from the Colonel's briefing, and all his talk about what three hundred 29s were going to do to Tokyo, as he said, within a week. I remembered my time in the pipe, and the Tokyo shit going past where I was hunkered down thinking about the caribou clearing the tree line into the winter range, and the ice calving off the berg in a slide, freeing up that blue window that didn't have anything behind it, but just showed the inside of the ice, a color that's not anywhere but there, I would bet anything on earth — all that time, all that time hunkered down in the pipe, with the shit going past me and falling into the bay, I had been pulling for the fire raid, the firestorm, and the panic. Wading out of the water now — the bay or lake or river or whatever it was — I felt that panic, that whole city-panic, and in the water it was different from what it was in the streets and the smoke. It was heavy-electric — and to tell the truth, I don't know what I mean by this, but it was a feeling, and maybe one of those that don't have words — and in the legs: in my legs but it felt good, coming from all those other people. It was in the guts and the balls, and that was the best of all.

While I was in the water, I didn't do anything but enjoy it, but when I got closer to shore it was like having to get out of bed when you don't want to: sleep holds to you, and your position and your feeling is so good that it seems wrong to change it. But I needed shoes. I needed some shoes like theirs, and a bag, and I started to think again.

It didn't bother anybody that I was moving the opposite way from the others, going toward the fire. I probably didn't need to, but I stumbled a little, even waved my arms like I was drunk, or maybe like the fire had got me in the lungs, or that the whole thing, the firestorm, was more than I could cope with and had driven me off my nut. I went face-forward through the crowd coming toward the water, going back to the main smoke and the fire like I'd lost something there — something or some-body, some damned thing.

I made it back into the streets, went up a block through the bunches of people, and turned up another street from them. This time there was hardly anybody there, maybe because it was so goddamned hot, hotter than anywhere else I'd been. While I could, I figured to blacken up again, and I did, from the closest house to me, just wherever I happened to be. I took my time and made myself up pretty good — better than before, if I do say so. I didn't need to see a mirror; I could feel how thick the stuff was on my face and hands, how heavy it was, how much of it I put on me. I kept slathering on the black, the soot; I kept putting on the smoke. It was like getting back into something I knew, something that was right for me, only a lot better version of it than before. All I needed now was shadows, because I was as much like them as I could ever have wanted to be: shadows I needed. I would get the shoes from them.

I held still in all the smoke, trying my eyes this way and that way up the street. But the pipe kept coming back to me. I couldn't shake it, or the feeling that what I had said there, said to myself, and on out the black-blue opening of the sewer out into the ocean, had been picked up, picked up by the crews and everybody who was connected with putting those B-29s up there over the town. I had called for that fire from a place where I was as good as buried. I had called that fire down. Damn right. If I didn't, who did?

I kept looking for people, for somebody with fair-sized feet and a bag. It was so hot that it was just possible to stand it. I thought that maybe if it got any hotter my clothes would burn, wet as they were. But nothing like that happened, and I started forward into the smoke and the bad — the worst — heat be-cause I figured I could catch somebody there who couldn't help himself, who would just be trying to get away. That was the right street, if I could stand it.

The buildings on the left were burning worse than the right — my black left hand was a lot hotter than my right — and all at once, like some acrobat — a clown maybe; clumsy, but an acrobat — a man shot out of a second-story window on the right, went across the street over me, and crashed through a window on the other side. Nobody will believe this, but it happened. In all the noise and smoke this guy just appeared in a blast of sparks like about fifty shotguns at midnight, like the kind of thing you see made into slow motion by a movie, and went right over the street into another building. The window he went through buried him in sparks — other sparks, but the same. I can't get over the way that happened: he turned over in the air, like he was just learning how to do it, and then hit in through the window of the other building. He really went. For a second it was slow, when he made the turnover, but really how he moved was fast, real fast and interesting, unexpected. It was not something you'd see every day. Hurtled would be the word; I can't do any better.

I went on under where he had been, and I couldn't help smiling, under the chit, the American flag, when I caught myself looking up, to see whether there'd be any more coming over: the rest of the act, the other guy shot out of the building, the gun. Gun, you bet, that was it: coming over me in the sparks of a shotgun.

It was bad, though. I thought about heading back, maybe picking up another street, but the good happened, right then. Two guys, one bigger than me and one smaller, came toward me. The clothes of the little one looked like they might have been on fire. I believe now they were; the sleeve of his left arm was burning. I let him go by, and then stepped out right in front of the other one. It was important to do it that way, with just him and me. I pulled the .45 and leveled it right into his chest. Shoes, you son of a bitch. Shoes. I squeezed off.

Nothing happened. I didn't even bother to try again. I was on him with the knife in a second, hit him once and hit him right, and was already dragging him before he was dead.

I wiped the knife off on his pants and unlaced his shoes and mine, sitting there in the shadows cooking, both of us, like meat not quite close enough to the fire to get done. But it was not bad, either, in a way. There was something coming through me that the fire couldn't touch, and a lot of times later on I've thought about it, remembering that it was true; I'd been a guy sitting on the hot rocks — or maybe cement — of a street, pulling on the shoes that were going to walk all over hell, and walk right out of it, and on — and on and on, up into the snow. I wanted that tree line, I wanted that move into the winter range with the caribou. There never had been such real snow as was in my mind right then, pulling on those shoes. Snow, man, I said: snow and the North Star, Polaris. Snow and the icebergs, and the ocean when it's what it really is, like I had told the guy, the recruit in the barracks. The ocean is not the ocean unless it's got ice in it. That's the real one. And that's the truth.

I stood up to see whether the guy had anything else I could use. I had forgotten about the bag I needed, but damned if he didn't have one, a fairly big one. There was nothing in it but some kind of musical instrument, I guess it was, and a short knife with a long handle, which I didn't figure to use but kept anyway. I put my GI boots in the bag, picked up the water-logged .45, and pitched it and the extra clip into the fire. I was glad to see them go, to tell the truth.

I went on up the same street. It had had what I needed, and I pushed on, though the heat was so terrific that I didn't really see how anybody could live. I didn't hear any more bombs, and figured the raid was over. Tokyo didn't need any more fire, and probably wouldn't see any more until the end of everything. It was so hot that I kept looking at the arms of the coat I had on to see when they'd take fire. And then it got hotter, goddamn it, and hotter than that. I didn't think my clothes would catch; I didn't think that anymore then. I thought I would take fire myself, inside the clothes, and that the clothes, shoes and all, would burn up after I did.

The street ended in a wall, and that's what saved me, I guess, because I would have gone on. I know I would have. A strange thing to say, but I was more or less happy with what I had, and the thing that made me the happiest was that I had got rid of the .45 and the clips, and that I had an excuse for getting rid of them. At the wall I turned to the right, which I figured was more or less north. The pull that way was not real strong then, but it was definite. I could have checked the compass, I guess, but I went by the feel. Like I say, it was definite; the smoke and fire couldn't touch it. I moved along for a couple of blocks and things got cooler. I sat down in my singed clothes and my new shoes and opened the bag again: I opened the bag I had.

The knife was a pretty little knife, there in the flicker. The handle was long, and with a kind of string weave around it, and there was carving at the end of it. It was strange, though. For such a short blade, the handle was a lot too long. It was more like the handle that should have been on a sword — one of their swords that they swing with both hands — instead of a blade that size. The steel was stiff, which I didn't like, but the blade was so short that flex probably wouldn't have done any good: you need a long blade for flex to do its stuff. I had put down two people with my bread knife, like I knew I could, and neither one of them had made a sound, or at least any that I could hear. That ought to tell you something.

I moved on through the streets, according to the pull and the feeling. I guessed some, too; I won't tell you that I didn't. As near as I could tell, I was working crossways through the main push of people, all of them going for the water. It made sense to them, I guess, though I'd reckon as many drowned as were burned up. The water seemed to turn them against each other, and a lot of them held the other ones down and tried to get on top for a second. That was a bad mistake, I could have told them — those poor bastards trying to stand on top of their own kids, just for one more breath of smoke. What if they'd got it?

I was surprised at how tired I was, there on another street, and then another one. I knew I had better get out of the city and hole up somewhere, because I felt the worst of the panic, the part that was best for me, more or less begin to die out — felt it from where I was now — and I thought that maybe I should try to sleep some, and build up. You watch any animal hunt — look at a lynx, for one — and they come right out of sleeping into hunting. That's the time to do it. You don't want any tiredness to get into it, because it all has to happen so fast. I wanted that quick, that quickness. I wanted the quick whenever I could get it.

But I sat down again anyway, and opened the bag. The instrument, whatever it was, was round, round as a wheel, and the strings, which were real tight, caught the fire, caught off the flames in the low part of the building I was sitting against, and I thought, what the hell, why not see what the thing sounds like. So I hit one of the strings and bent over to listen to it. You'd have thought I was caught up in the way the thing rang, in a low way, off those black bricks and boards, and there might have been something in that, I admit it. I hit that string, and then the next one to it, and then both of them together. You could tell that that was not the way they were supposed to sound — or I more or less supposed that anybody who knew would be able to tell, because I had not ever heard anything like it, quite. It was a tinny kind of noise, and it had something in it — if I can put it like this — that was like the singing somebody would make way back in his mouth, between his throat and his nose. It was like that except the person would have to be young, like a kid, like a real young girl. Well, I hit all the strings at once, one after the other, and this time it bothered me, because it was a sound — whether it was music or somebody's voice, or maybe more than one — that didn't go anywhere; it just hung there and made you dissatisfied. I put the thing in the bag, but when I did, I knew that I would probably fool with it again, somewhere between me and the snow, and that maybe it would not be such a good thing to be doing, so I took it out and leaned it against the place I'd been sitting, to add one more thing to the night, one more thing that there wouldn't be any way to explain. There were going to be a lot of things like that in Tokyo after the fire quit burning. But it would have been the strangest of all, I reckon, if somebody had seen me sitting there in the smoke, twanging on that little white wheel. They would have told the others, maybe — whoever lived — but nobody would've believed it. Or maybe somebody would have. Like they say, it was one of those nights.

I got up and went on, and I won't say that I didn't make, or try to make, somewhere in my throat, something like that last sound, the one that could have been a lot of voices, all young, and maybe all girls. They were in me somewhere, and wouldn't have been there except for that little wheel with the strings on it, round as a full moon, with a rack of tin along through it. I couldn't get that sound, but I could hear it. I knew it was there, and maybe I'd get it later on, when I went through the tree line, or saw the ocean with ice in it that made the whole thing the truth, as real as it could get.

❖　❖　❖

It had been night so long, in some places with fire bright as day, that I had got used to the idea that there wasn't going to be anything else. But in the way I was going, the fires were definitely less than they'd been — less bunched up, less high, and less hot. I kept moving according to my gut feel, even though I had to jog this way and that way amongst the streets. I did change streets a lot, but the people were all just like each other.

Nobody said a thing to me, and my main trouble was in trying to look as confused and aimless as they did while I held on to my heading. The smoke was still bad, and there was no way I could get a look at the sky. It was probably clear, if I could've seen it. The 29s had cracked down and hit the city where they wanted to, and must've had all the visibility they wanted. But for me there wasn't any sky, yet. I checked the compass, and I had been right, more or less; my guts had been right. Sailors and Eskimos have the same thing, and it's probably stronger with them than it is with anybody. But the hunters are next, next to the sailors and Eskimos, who are next to the fish and the birds.

As well as I could, I kept looking through the smoke to the east, to see where there might be some orange in the sky that wasn't fire. A new situation had come up for me now, as I got clear of the worst of the raid and most of the heat. I had to decide whether I wanted to stay amongst people — whatever people I could find — and work north, maybe, from one group to another, or more or less to go along by myself. The worst thing that could happen would be for somebody to say something to me, because there was no way I'd ever be able to make any kind of an answer. If I grouped with people, that might happen. No, it was bound to happen. But if I kept to myself I would stand out, and would have to depend on my clothes and the blood chit, and on getting away from anybody who came up to me. I decided to stay with people for as long as I could, not with small groups but with the largest ones I could find heading north out of town. Groups had paid off for me pretty well so far, and I still had a situation in which everybody was confused and scared to death. I still had panic going for me, and I thought I probably should use it till it ran out and I had to try something else.

I was almost clear of the main city now. The fires were low —
you could have stomped some of them out with your feet —
and the smoke not nearly as thick. Instead of the houses being
jammed up on each other, and all burning, there were some
now with spaces between them, and not all of them were on fire.
But I had never seen such an arrangement of houses in my life.
Even an Eskimo village would not have been so weird to somebody who had never seen one before. The houses were little
and squarish, and the yards, as near as I could tell, were kept up
pretty well. But between every three or four houses was a Nip
fighter aircraft sitting in somebody's yard like a car would've
been back in the States. That was a hell of a thing. They must
have had some way the fighters could taxi down the streets and
on out to the strip, wherever it was: some easy way to the strip,
because there were sure a lot of fighters.

Walking past the houses and the planes, which I got clear of
after a while, I was with a small group of women, two with little
kids, and three old men. I kept my head down, and decided that
if one of them said anything to me, I would just mumble and
shake my head, like all my words had been struck out of me, or
burned out by the fire. The squatty woman right ahead of me
was carrying her little girl on her back, and she didn't seem to
be bothered at all. I would look at the road for a minute, and
then, in the low fires that were still around us, at the little girl,
and her look was always there, waiting for my eyes to come up
from the road, come up from my feet, and meet with hers again.
I must say she was very pretty; with those bangs, nobody could
have invented a Jap doll that'd be any prettier. We must have
gone on a couple of miles that way, and all the time the panic
was leaving the people I was with. I thought that when more of
it left they would begin to talk, and I hoped to be able to pick up

a word or two and memorize it before any of them said anything to me. If the worst happened, I could handle this bunch,
and maybe even without having to kill any of them. I didn't
want any of that to happen, war or no war. This was not the
time for it.

I drew in what was there. I drew in a lot of breath, and I could
have it. I could *have* it. That's the way it struck me: I could have
it without gagging and coughing. I straightened up. I took my
eyes off the road, and away from the little girl, and looked east.
There was orange there. It showed through the smoke, but it
was damned well orange, and not fire, and it was big. Not the
sun, the Fireball Mail yet, but just before. The Rising Sun, I
thought. I'm in just the place for it. The Rising Sun. There it
was, sure enough.

And if I could see the sun, I ought to be able to see the other
sky, too: the last of the stars. I was almost afraid to look north,
but I did. The Dipper was there, canted way up, and Polaris was
there, off the two front stars. I pulled out the compass, and the
needle and the star trued up. I grinned at the baby, right into
those bangs. It was nice. It was all right there.

But I left them, and walked on by myself. There was almost
no traffic on the road. Every now and then a military carrier would come by — a truck or something that looked like a
jeep — going away from town, but I didn't see more than two
or three civilian cars, or even more than a few bicycles. You'd
have thought that people would be getting into everything that
would run and heading out, but it might have been that the
crowds in the streets kept anything from getting through, or
maybe most of the cars in town were burned up — I saw the
gasoline in at least one blow sky-high, with somebody in it —
or were where the people they belonged to couldn't get to

them. Anyway, I had to give up any idea I might've had about a ride, either by stealing a car or truck or by stowing away in a heavy hauler with a tarp in the back. I might do something like that later, if I could, but it was not going to be possible for a while. I had to walk.

The light was coming now. The sky was clear. There was even a little chill, and that changed my blood, and I began leaving the dream of all that heat, that night with all the crowds and white phosphorus in it, and the shithole of the pipe, and the water where whole families killed each other for one more breath of smoke. I say dream, and not nightmare, because I didn't think about it that way. Sure, it was bad enough, the worst heat I was ever in, and the firestorm killed a lot of people; I didn't know how many, but it must have been in the thousands. But for me there were things that were worse, things that I reckon you could say would be like nightmares. Not having a weapon was one of them, and being in a situation I didn't have any control over would be another. But that hadn't happened yet. In the aircraft, when it was hit, I got out because I had taped the chute to the bulkhead. I had got down off the gantry and into the pipe. I had outfitted myself the best way I could, and now I had got clear of the city, and the night was over. The night, not the nightmare. A dream, maybe. But if you say nightmare to me, you don't mean a fire raid on Tokyo. You'd have to be talking about something else.

More light came, and now you could see the sun behind the houses. I looked at the backs of my hands, which were as filthy black as I could have wanted, and I knew my face was the same, or maybe even blacker. But the people I had looked at, the ones I had walked out with, even though they were pretty smudged up and streaked up, were not — not one — as black as I was, and I was afraid that the job I had done with soot from the buildings was maybe too good, and might make me stand out even more than I would have if I hadn't done it. It was a real problem now that I was out there by myself, with no fire and hardly any smoke and no panic around me: last night's big city-panic that felt like the breath of life to me, in all that smoke. There was a lot of weight in my body now. I was tired and I had to find a way to get some rest. My black face began to bother me more and more, and I did what I could to streak it with my fingers, but I was not sure that that wouldn't make me even more strange looking, make me stand out more, and that was the last thing I wanted. But still, nobody said anything to me. I kept my head down, thanking God that my hair is dead black and that I had it cut almost as short as the Japs'. I felt like that was part of my luck. But I was nervous right then. I'll tell you the truth, I was. I was between plans, and I needed to move on to the next one I could come up with.

It was a time I wouldn't want to go through again. I tried not to get the full force of where I was: the whole, real situation. Even though I had been through the firestorm the B-29s had made, the idea of the war — of any war — had more or less left me when I was in there shoving through the streets with the people trying to get out, or in the water with them, or even when I had hit the three of them I'd killed. War was in back of the things I'd done, sure, but when I'd done them, the war didn't seem to have anything to do with it. I was not carrying out anybody's orders, that's for sure. But now the war — the idea, the fact, of the war — came back, and for the first time, really, I admitted to myself the worst I could, which was also the truth. I went over the truth from that side.

I was in the enemy's home country. Everybody was my enemy. Even if there had been one person in Japan friendly toward me, one who would do anything to help me, there was no way for me to find him. I didn't have any way to speak to anybody, even to tell him I would kill him if he didn't do what I said. I had tried to pick up a word or two from the crowds, and thought I had one there for a while, but I forgot it; and anyway, I didn't know what it meant. I needed a few words, just a few, and I needed to know what they meant. There must be ways I could work this out, but I didn't know them yet. Right now I was hungry and tired, though the little chill was just right for me; if I could find a place to lie down, I would sleep for a long time. And I had two high-energy candy bars in my survival kit. If I could sleep, I would eat them when I woke up and got going again. But in every direction, in everybody I saw or who saw me, death was there. My own death was all around me, and there would be a lot of torture connected with it. Everywhere I looked there was beating, fire torture, mutilation, castration. Getting my head chopped off would be the easiest part.

What did I have, myself? I started outside and worked in. I had my knife, still right where it should be, and the emergency kit; I had what I had brought with me. In the kit I had a compass, fishhooks and twine, and a little short blade. I had a silk map of the area, like a handkerchief, though it only showed up to the tip of Honshu, the Tokyo island. I sat down behind a low wall between houses and took it out and looked at it. Hokkaido, the northern island, where I wanted to go, only showed as a little nudge of land right at the very top of the map, but there was one place between the two islands that was fairly narrow, about fifteen or twenty miles, as I judged, and I might be able to get across there in a night, if I could find a boat. They had told us in briefing that fishing was a big thing in Japan, and I figured there would be all kinds of boats, because there is always a lot of fishing when two islands are close together, no matter where they are, if people live on them.

That was the outside stuff. I didn't have anything in the bag but my issue shoes and the short-handled knife, and I didn't think of anything in the bag as being nearly as important as what I had on me. Or in me. It's harder to think about that than it is about knives and fishhooks and maps, but when I got down to it I started to feel better, a lot better. I knew what I had done, and I knew what I would do. Sure, I didn't know everything I'd do, but I didn't feel like I had any limits on me when the right situation came up. Like I say, I had something that didn't have any limits on it. I would do what many another wouldn't, and the best thing was that I knew I would do it; there wasn't any doubt. It was funny. The idea of the war came back in with this other thinking, but it came in in a different way, not on the bad side but the good. I looked up over the wall to get a fix on somebody, some other person, and make a kind of concentration that way, but there was only an old man walking by, up the road, with an old woman about ten feet behind him, all bent over with carrying a bundle of sticks and logs that looked to be about as big as she was. They would do, though; they were there. I said this to myself after I ducked back down: this is my war as much as it is theirs; what they can do to me I can do to them. But I had to admit to myself that that notion didn't come through to me with the power that it ought to have had, that it probably would have with somebody else. No. The war was there, and I'd have to deal with certain things connected with it, certain situations, and they'd come up. But the war was not the main thing. It might have been to them, to the others, to the

Japs, but not to me. There didn't need to be any war. There were not any rules, except the ones I made. Everything would ride on that.

The north was the big thing I wanted: the biggest there could be. When I got out of the Air Force, if I ever did, I planned to go back up there as soon as I could, any way I could. I didn't belong anywhere else, even behind the twin fifties in the tail of a B-29, where I was pretty good, if I do say so myself. But you can't live there. I didn't belong anywhere, really, but above seventy degrees north, on the north slopes of mountains like the Brooks Range. And, I said to myself, what is the difference between going there after the war and going there now — like I say, however I could get there? Snow fields are all the same. Snow in the air and on the ground is the same, and water is the same, and ice in the water is the same. Ice, big ice, which is the best. But ice, and the same.

And there was another thing that came from there. I hadn't lived most of my life up above seventy degrees for nothing. There were things you could do. Up there, some things were natural, part of the skin and feathers and fur and eyes of the animals that lived there, the birds and the fish. And there were ways that you could do what they did, not by being natural but by thinking about it, by figuring what might work: what might keep anything, anybody, from seeing you, and ways in which you could stay in that situation till whatever it was went by. And ways, too, you could come out of it: come out on their blind side and be on them and done with them before they ever knew you were anywhere around, or even if you were in the world. I had seen the snowshoe hare lie down, lie down in a bunch of low bushes, and make an outline of himself. First there's an outline in the snow, and then there's not any outline. I've seen that. The only thing left is the eyes, and I've seen the hare close his eyes, and I could have walked over the place where he was, and unless I stepped on him I never would have seen him, or known that he was in the world, either. Most of the time I never saw the hare close his eyes, and I couldn't find him. But once or twice — once, to be honest, when the hare was in open snow and not in any bushes — I saw the eyes closing, I saw the whole thing, the whole disappearance. I've seen that; that's what I had. I had it. I was there with it.

And I've seen the lynx work, too, with his long legs moving slow, not wanting to touch the snow crust but going over it just the same. I've seen him move through dead limbs, and the shadow spots on his sides would make you think that the limbs of the trees, the bushes and twigs, were moving too, going somewhere without breaking the snow. You could do that, I told myself down beside the wall. You could do it; you can do it. You can use the snow, but you don't need the snow. You need just one thing. One. You need the color of the place you're in. Even in the big rush of good feeling, when the colors came over me and I felt like I could be any of them, any time of the day or night: when I felt like I could lie down in green or yellow, in purple or red, in the moonlight or the sunrise, and I could stay until I got ready to get up and go on, and nobody would know, or fall out of any of them, like a hawk: fall on somebody's back, or right into his face like a blaze of light flashing through him, or doing anything I wanted, I knew that it was only part of the truth, only part of the truth that would be, from here on. There would be lots of colors between me here and the snow fields there, between me and the ocean and the bergs, and there was not any way I could take advantage of everything between the place I was now — this wall — and where I was trying to get to.

But there would be long stretches — there were bound to be long stretches — where the color was more or less the same, and if that was true, I could find some way to tap in on it, take advantage of it, make it work for me. If there were colors in Japan, if there were colors in the world, I could go with them; I could get into them, be with them, be what they were. I could, damn it: I sure could. When I came on a long stretch of color — stayed in it for a day, maybe — I would try to make the best way to do it for the next day.

But right now, with the air clearing, and people coming out of the panic, I had to deal with the right now. More than anything else, I needed to be able to come up with an answer of some sort to whatever might be said to me. I needed to get where I could hear people talk, and pick up the thing they said the most, no matter what it was. The Tokyo raid was bad news, and anything I heard would most likely have to do with it. There might be plenty of other things to talk about, but it seemed to me that if I heard sounds out of people, and some of them were the same, then they would almost have to do with the raid. I could keep to my black, tarbaby look for a little while, and my head-low mumbling, and myself as somebody who had been so hard hit, so burned, so fucked up by the raid that I couldn't say anything anybody could make out. I could do it long enough to get a couple of words, maybe half a sentence that I could use, and then use it when I had to, keep going on and on with, over and over, like a man made into an idiot by fire and smoke, by American B-29s. I wanted people to feel sorrier for me than they did for themselves. That would help, until I got to the colors. At night I would look over the colors: the color where I was, and then get ready to go through it, go through it to the next one.

I decided to stick to the roads as long as I was let alone. The sun was up good now, but we still had the chill. I looked out over the wall. Three or four little women were walking toward me, but not looking in my direction, and I went around the end of the wall and, when they went by, fell in a few steps behind them. One of them turned her head, but I saw that she was going to do it, and I put my eyes onto my shoes as they went along. "*Taihen, taihen,*" one of them said. I went over it in my mind. When another one said it, or the same one said it, I would branch off. I stumbled and made like I was going to fall, and the same one who had looked before, looked back, but didn't do anything. We walked on, and she said the same thing. She said it: "*Taihen, taihen.*" I went over it again, and again. None of them looked back, and I was gone.

Whether it was food first, or sleep, I didn't much care. The farther I went, though, the more sleep came to me, came forward at me. I had been tired out on the Range, on the snowshoes, when I could hardly lift one off the snow and put the next one in front of it, but in some ways this was just as bad. I kept looking for somebody who was as tired as I was, and who nobody was bothering: some poor guy, an old guy maybe, lying in a ditch, who nobody cared about. I would have gone down in a ditch without any argument if I thought nobody would come up on me, but that was not really the kind of sleep I wanted. Some sort of hole, I thought, some dark place. But where was there anything like that around? The road was open, and in another half mile went up among some hills, but that didn't do me any good, none that I could see from where I was. I went over my word — *taihen* — or maybe it was a couple of words, and tried to make them like I remembered the sound, but I didn't have any real confidence. I went on, toward the hills and what looked like it might be a little bunch of stores, just where the land started to climb.

When I got next to the buildings there was a crash, something that sounded like a crash of glass, and that's what it was. A bunch of women were breaking the window of the store, and I waited to see if there would be anything for me. The women who had busted the glass went in, right through the splinters, and in a minute they were throwing things out to the others. I eased up to the bunch catching the stuff, but didn't make any try to get what was coming out; I thought I might go in when the rest of them left. Finally they did leave, and I went in.

There was not much, but I found some rice in a bowl and parts of a fish — the head, too — like you might feed to a cat. I ate it, all I could get, and licked the inside of the bowl. Right then a woman — maybe one of the women who had broken the glass — came back in and grabbed me by the coat. I turned around with my hand going across me, ready to come up through her if I had to, but there were eight or ten others behind her, and I mumbled my word — mumbled my words, mumbled something — put my head down, and staggered out. I let her and the others beat me clear of the store, and not one of them got a good look at me. I was pretty sure of that, because they all kept screaming at me, and I could more or less tell that it was the same kind of way they would have treated any bum. I didn't mind all that much. I had got a little something to eat, and even while they were kicking me and beating me any way they could, the fish and rice were doing good, and after I was on the road again, I felt like I had got hold of some new blood, a transfusion or something. With some sleep on top of that, I could make it a long way.

I went around the first turn up off the flat, looking for a ditch or bushes. There was some scrub and weeds, but nothing deep, nothing dark. There was junk along the side of the road — paper boxes and a can or two — and all kinds of paper with Japanese writing on it. I kept moving in the orange sun that was getting higher and turning yellow. They had told us that Orientals didn't have any respect for life, and wouldn't even help a man who fell down sick in the street, or who they just came up on, lying out in a field or in somebody's yard, but there was not anything like that where I was walking.

And then there was. I saw the sun, very yellow now, not at all orange anymore, slant up and off glass, which just as soon as I looked was a bottle, and beside it an old man was either dead or unconscious or asleep. I stood off from him and waited for some other people to come by, to see how much attention they would pay him. I sat down like I had some business with him, my head down on my knees. Every now and then somebody would walk past. I would look up just enough to watch them pass by, but nobody even glanced toward either the old man or me. It was bright winter sunlight now, bright and yellow, and I got the feeling, stronger and stronger, that nobody gave a damn who I was or why I was there.

The old man didn't move. The most important thing about him was that he had a hat, canvas, and I took it and put it on, because it had a good brim, and it would make it easier to hide the shape of my eyes, which I couldn't figure how to do anything about. But there I was, right out there in the yellow open Japanese sun, with Japanese clothes and shoes on that I'd got from killing two people, and a hat from one who looked like he was already dead, with a bread knife and a survival kit and a bag with wet shoes in it. From under the hat I could look out a little better, and what struck me then was what I had noticed before but hadn't thought about as much: there were hardly any young men around, or even teenage boys. The only male people I saw were little kids and old men, and that was not bad for me, not a bad sign. I wondered what they did for police, because I hadn't seen any. In the trucks and jeeps there'd been a few men in uniform, but they were in service. I didn't know what a Japanese cop might have on, but the military had the only uniforms I'd come across. And that was good, too.

Out of the smoke I could see the women better, and honest to God, I don't understand how even the Nip men can tell one from the other. They all had flat dish faces and round shoulders — maybe from carrying all that cordwood — and walked with little steps, so little that I don't see how they ever got anywhere; a mile would've taken them all day. I pulled the hat down, closed my eyes, and stretched out by the old man. I listened to the women tiptoe past on the hard road, and, even though the day was warming up by now, brought the tree line to myself just for a minute, and then it went, and that's all I can remember from that first day out of Tokyo.

❖　　❖　　❖

When I woke up it was chilly again; I sucked in the air before I opened my eyes. Then I sat up, pulled the hat down low, and looked around. The old man was gone. I don't have any idea how he left. Maybe he hadn't been dead, or if he was, somebody who knew him might have found him. Either he had been alive or family had come after him. If people'd just been cleaning up the streets, they'd've got me, too. Or that's the way I figured, anyway.

It was coming on for night, so I'd been down a long time. I

was really rested. For one thing, I like to sleep on the ground, and I'd slept on a lot worse ground than that was, ground where you have to keep clearing rocks out from under you. I hadn't felt a single rock; I was just a little stiff. Nobody else was coming past, though there was a light in the house next to the place where I had eaten the rice and the fish. I got up and walked past it, on up into the low hills. I figured to walk all night and, if I could, go for a place to bed down that was darker and quieter. I wanted to be *under* something the next time: to find rocks, where there'd be overhangs. That way, I wouldn't be hemmed up. I'd have some cover, but I could scramble out either way. Always leave yourself a way out, my father used to tell me. Fight with something to your back, especially if you're fighting more than one guy. But sleep where you can go the other way from whatever's after you.

The old man had left the wine; I had it in my bag. When it got dark enough, I uncorked it and took a long swallow, and then another one. It was like sour water, and kind of bitterish for wine, but my head began to work faster right away, and the good side of things started to show up. The nights were when I would use the roads, as much as I could. Any car would have to show a light, and I would be where they couldn't see me before they could even think, before the light got anywhere near me. If people were walking on the road I could hear them, and even if I happened to run into somebody, some guy walking the other way, maybe, the advantage would be with me rather than him. I wasn't worried about one guy, or even two or three of them, especially at night. I hadn't seen any one person I couldn't handle, and handle pretty easily. I just had to keep the situation like it was, and find food wherever I could, and a place to sleep during the day. Those were the main things. In daylight, whenever I wasn't too tired, I could get off the roads and take out through the fields, or woods if I could find them. The middle part of Honshu was not supposed to have many people — or so the briefing officer had told us — and was even supposed to be wild, with a lot of woods and lakes, a lot of rivers. Maybe there would be some snow in the mountains, if I could get up into them. Snow, but not enough. For that I was sure I'd have to get over onto the other island, and move due north whenever I could. It was going to take a long time.

I had another shot of wine, and finished the bottle. The houses were farther apart now. The lights in them were low, like everybody was telling secrets. I started to think about another house, not one of these.

I took the blood chit down off my mouth and breathed the new dark, and the cold that didn't have any smoke in it. I was going to need something heavier to wear before long. No matter how much you like the cold, it'll still freeze you. You've got to keep your feet warm, or the ground will get them, get your toes. And you've got to look out for your hands or the air will make them things you can't use. It's against my way of doing things to take along too much stuff, but if you're going where I wanted to go, there are certain things you have to have. I could get by with my Tokyo shoes, and could switch off to my old GI brogans whenever I had the chance, or if I wanted to, but I needed socks. Socks and gloves. And a scarf, a heavy one. If you can find a way to keep your neck warm, it helps everything else, even your feet. I don't know why that is exactly, but you ask any trapper and he'll set you straight, right quick.

The farther you go, the more stuff you pick up. If I could, I wanted to get hold of a bigger bag and make myself some sort of backpack out of it, one I could also use for a sleeping bag, so I could lie down anywhere and get some rest. The idea of a house, one off from the main roads, or from any road: some farmer's or woodcutter's place, in the fields or back amongst the hills, would be what I was looking for. I thought about the house, what would be there and how I would get it, and worked on my words. As far as I was concerned, still, the word or words I had picked up had to do with the fire raid; with the napalm and white phosphorus; with the people choking and scrambling in the streets and the long moaning noise that came out of them; with the buildings falling in and the guy turning a somersault over me and crashing into the building; with the shoving and the stumbling and the smoke. All that seemed a long way off now. There were some things about it that I could hardly remember. What mattered was the road I was on, and that I could use something else to eat, and maybe some more wine. There was a house somewhere that would give me what I wanted. There was one. But it was probably two or three days off, maybe a week. That's the way I reckoned, but the more I thought about it, the more I knew it was somewhere, and that I'd find it, one way or the other. I wondered if I would have to use the word there. I couldn't tell, but I thought probably not. Still, I kept saying it as I walked along, not knowing what it meant, trying to get it right.

Except for me there was not a sound. The moon came up, and I could see where I was going for maybe fifty yards ahead. The later it got, the farther I could see, until I could look across the open fields that were on one side now, and make out the low hills bulking up on the other side of them. I don't know why it is, but every big space I had seen in Japan seemed to have the same kind of stitched-up look about it — a big piece of silver sewed up with black thread. The bay where I'd come down in the parachute looked like that, and now these fields did too, moving out on my left off through the moon: that silver and black, that sewed-together look, that sewed-together feel of it, was the main Japan that I had. It took a real hold on me, and was realler than anything I'd seen or been through. And blood: I thought about blood, too, and couldn't reach it. I had killed three people, and I couldn't remember that I had seen any blood at all. I had stuck the woman under water, and she never came up. I had shot the guy for his clothes, back in the fire, but even though I'd blown the top of his head off, there was not any blood that I'd noticed, and the same thing was true about the guy I'd gutted for his shoes.

I thought I would stay with the road I was on, which was going a little east of north, until the moon got higher, and I could strike out across the fields by compass. I was not having any trouble this way, though. At first I was worried because the road had so many curves in it, and they were so close together. Every time I could see far enough ahead to make out the curve, I would wait and be sure that no light was coming. Then I would move on up to the bend, look around it, and wait again. I did this for around two hours, but I wasn't making much distance that way, and as soon as the moon got up so that the shine was straighter down, I hit off across the fields.

The ground was soft but had some giveback to it, too; I thought that there was probably a crop in it ready to come up. What did they grow in Japan, anyway? The only thing I had ever heard of was rice. They even made whiskey and wine out of it, which must take some doing. I sighted on Polaris, and moved where it said. The hills were more or less parallel to my track, but if I maintained due north, I would be sure to run into some more, and then mountains, which suited me fine. I didn't believe I would be walking in the open fields all night, though I couldn't be sure of that, either. I was going along pretty well when I made out a house in front of me and off to the left. There were no lights in it, and no sign of any people. I angled out to go around it before another notion hit me: maybe the big open spaces after all those crowded streets, maybe the cool and quiet after all the screaming, changed me and caused me to do things a little different. Whatever it was, I swerved my track again and went toward the house, closer and closer, quieter and quieter. It was not the house I wanted — I knew that — but I might learn something, anyway.

Learn what? I stopped in the soft of the field to puzzle it out. Even in the dark I could get to know something about a Japanese house: how it was put together, how you got into it, and maybe a little about how the rooms were — where the kitchen was, and so on. I moved in closer, up to the nearest wall, right up to the window, which was not glass, but from the look of it was like some kind of heavy paper. It cracked a little, just a very little bit, and I steadied with my hand against the wall, and leaned to look.

I would have bet there were people in the room, but when I first put my eyes where they should've been, I didn't see anything, anything but the other wall. But the wall was not steady; it moved one way and another and seemed to back away, almost to disappear, and then settle down again where it was. A low light was making that happen. It was on the floor, which was maybe a foot higher than where I was standing: a candle in some kind of frame, and around it there came to be three people sitting on the floor, an old man and a woman and a little girl. They were either eating or just about to eat, or had just finished. I made out some bowls and dishes, but I couldn't tell what was in them, or if anything was. Then the old man reached for a bowl, and I knew they were going to eat. The girl passed the bowl, and bowed almost into the flame. Except for the people and the bowls and dishes and candle, the room was bare. I reached across and pulled the knife slow, slanted it and held it close to the crack. I wanted that light, the light of that one candle, to flash off my blade — to flash just once, whether they saw it or not. I never knew whether they did, but the flame couldn't have missed the blade, because I angled it so that the light would hit it, no matter how it was shining. That was my mark, and I left, jumping out of my tracks in the field, with the tracks springing me up.

After a while I looked back at the house, and even thought of going back, because everything had been so easy for me. I had forgotten to do one thing, which was to try to catch their talk, mainly to see whether they would use the word I had been practicing, and to check how I said it against the way they did. It would have been some satisfaction to me to know that I had at least one word I could bring out if I had to. But it didn't seem worth it, and I went on. Really, though, I didn't want to take any chances with my sign, or try to make another one, or do anything that might tone down the strike of that candle on the blade. That was a pure thing, just what I wanted, even if I hadn't seen it. If they had seen it — and one of them, at least, must've — they wouldn't have known what it was, which was all right with me. They might not know what it was or what it meant, but it had been there. I was in Japan, and I had leveled my sign, and put it in.

I came up on a fence, and went over it into another kind of ground, harder but not real hard. The moon glowed off it like it hadn't off the first one, and the going was a lot easier. Tokyo and

Tinian Island were in the same time zone, and when my watch said three-thirty, that's when it was. I could go for about an hour and a half, and then I had better look for a hole. There weren't going to be any high rocks on this night, no overhangs or caves.

I went on for an hour, an hour and fifteen minutes, and there still was no shelter. I was wide open, the only man in the fields, and I didn't want the light, even the first light, to catch me. If there'd been anything growing high enough, or just growing at all, I might have made do in the fields, but there was nothing anywhere. There were no more houses, no more barns or sheds or hog wallows where a man could lie down and shove the animals out. But the animals would have him if he came in. The animals would usually have him. They would come back around him.

I was getting tired again, and I went due north against the big dark black, where there were not any stars. I went right for that.

There was that time, I can remember it. My foot kicked straight into something, something that felt like a bank. It was not a hill, exactly; it was not a mountain; there was not any feeling of rock; no bone.

Soft. I went from the soft fields to the soft bank, and kicked into it again. My foot buried.

I could climb it. I could scramble. I could get up.

I got up, and the moonlight hit me like saving my life. The moon hit me when I leveled, when I quit climbing and leveled. The ground underneath me was level, by God, and I hadn't climbed up but just a few feet. I stood where I was, and turned around and looked back, looked out.

Crops were growing at the levels; they were growing with me? That must have been the answer to it. A level was underneath me, which I had just come from, and there was another one up above me. And another, on above that one. If I could come up the first one, I could get to the other ones, and on up. I could top out, I could crest. I could crest with it.

I turned around, from the sewed-together moonlight down on the flat fields, and started to climb in the other moonlight, the one in the levels.

God help me. I went up. I went up and up them.

But I didn't want to clear the top. I sat down high, high up, and now I looked back again, and the whole sleep was there, the sleep of the other people. The house was down there, where I had made my flash. My mark was down there somewhere, amongst the people: three of them. It was down there with the little candle, and I was up on the levels, big levels, the levels of the world, like they were in that place. That place, and not any other place. The levels were the levels, there in the moon; they were the only levels. That's where I was, and I opened my mouth and said it. I had the word, and I was ready to give it to them. Everything was silver and thread. Everything was levels. I was ready. I was ready for some other levels, just up behind me, and I was ready to sleep all day in one of them. Terraces, that was the name of them.

I sat down. I was getting used to sitting down in Japan. What worked in one place would work in another one. I had laid down by the dead man with the bottle of wine, and he had gone off from me, and maybe lived, gone off with his folks and left the wine. I sat down solid on the level where I was — the level somewhere amongst the other levels — and felt around. Was this a place I could sleep all day? When would they come out to work? Could I hear them, when I was asleep, climb up the levels — the hard climb in the soft dirt, and then the straight foot, the foot that wasn't climbing but was yours, and the flat you came out to be standing on? The flat above the flat you had just come from? That made you think about the flat just above you, and the one above that?

I was bushed again. I had come up through the levels underneath me; the ones over me I would leave for later. Right now I felt the sag. But at the same time I felt the old flash in the candle, and I knew that the three people handing the bowls around would know; would know that something they were not used to had gone by them, that they hadn't suffered; had gone through them; had held the candle in their house for just a second. After them, there would be a lot of others.

Like I say, I felt around. There was a lot of straw, and there were sticks all over. What about sleeping in the sun, I said to myself. On just this level. What about covering up with this stuff and waiting till you hear them? First hear them, hear them climbing. And then make your move. Were these flowers, or what, they were growing?

There were twigs and stems all over the place. Nobody had cleaned up the levels of the hill, or at least not the one I was on. I figured to get a little night sleep, when I had my mind right, and get out over the top of the hill before anybody came to work, if they were going to. Farming was something I didn't know much about, and farming on terraces was so far from anything I could imagine that I didn't even try. I ought to do something, though, about being spotted if I overslept; I didn't want just to be lying there. I looked around and felt around, and I could pile things up, pile up sticks and twigs and leaves if I wanted to, and I did; I did that. I made three long low piles like bundles, not right together but about ten or fifteen feet apart, and I figured to get down behind one of them and stretch out and sleep when I felt like it, when I felt more like it. My idea was to work kind of like the man at the fair who my father took me to one time in Barrow when I was a little boy. He had three shells and a pea. He put the pea under one of the shells and moved them around, and you were supposed to guess which shell had the pea. If somebody thought there might be a man behind one of my piles, he wouldn't know which one, and that short minute of confusion might be just what I'd need. I stretched out behind the last pile I'd made — not the middle one — and settled down to get my mind like I wanted it, so I could sleep deep and strong.

I got out my knife and my sharp-stone, and my two flints. I wasn't going to light a fire — I didn't need it — but I wanted to feel them: to feel the shapes, and know that fire was there, and had always been there, in the ground, in the hill or the mountain, that didn't know anything about fire but had it for the one who knew, and would give it to him.

I started working on the knife, holding the stone in my left hand and running the blade down it at around a forty-five-degree angle — that I knew better than the color of my eyes — like I was trying to cut into the stone, trying to shave it, you might say. However sharp it had been, it got sharper. Knives are big with trappers, and every one of them will tell you he can put on an edge finer than any of the others. The ones who haven't been up in the north for a long time think it's a good edge if you can shave with it. I even knew a logger who could shave with his ax. But shaving is just the beginning of it. I can put on an edge that will cut gauze, a long piece of it, if you hold the blade edge-up and just pitch the gauze in the air and let it come down across the knife. It'll come down in two pieces, and you can win bets with it. I couldn't do that well, up behind my pile, because

I didn't have any oil, but I could get the steel to the shaving stage without any trouble, and I thought about shaving when I finished.

But I was having a good time with it. I kept turning the blade one way and another in the moonlight, and I won't say that didn't make it a little bit sharper. Like I say, you have to know how things are: how to get what's there for you, that maybe most of the others don't know, or maybe nobody knows but you. I must have a feel about knife-shine. I must have had it all my life. I never really knew how strong it was until I held the blade in the window of that house so it'd pick up the candle. On my level of the hill it was good to compare the strike of the moon off the blade with that other strike — the gleam, it must've been, which is a word I don't use but I know the meaning — the house gleam down there in the field under the terraces. That gleam caught in somebody's eyes. It was in somebody's head right now, trying to understand what had caused it. It was in that house, and it would stay there. I ran the blade down the stone five more times on each side, sharpening by feel and by the moon.

❖   ❖   ❖

I slept pretty well, not cold except for my feet, but they bothered me, numbed out; I had to stomp on the ridge to get them going. When I killed the pins in my toes I moved on. It wasn't as far to the top as I had thought — a couple of hundred feet and six places where the hill tabled off into smaller and smaller flats. And I found a little path switchbacking on up; it was right there for me, and easy. When I got to the top, I took a good long look back down the way I had come. For some reason I wanted to see people, even one person alive, moving. I can't tell you why. It might have been that it would be better for me to know where the closest person was, and even what he was doing, which meant I would have the advantage, if it came down to that. Even if it was just in my mind, I needed the distance between, whatever the distance would be.

There was not any point, though, in just standing there waiting for somebody to show, and I turned to the other side, where the terraces stepped down north, into another valley.

To one side I heard a dry, stiff hustling sound. I had heard it plenty of times before, but not below me. Before I saw the birds, I knew it was feathers moving fast, hissing like a hot iron. The sound was not above, like I say, but I glanced up anyway, as I usually did. Then I looked level, and then down and off, the way I had come up the night before. There were two birds, big white ones, mostly neck and wings, barreling straight for the top of the ridge about fifty or sixty feet from me, under the crest and going for it like they were trying to hit it, cut through it, take it clean off, and for a second I thought they would, that they had the speed to do it, and their own reasons. They were dead white, and big. Their necks and wings were longer than anything I'd seen except tundra swans, white-stretched and going all-out like dogs to take the hill apart.

Without a feather changing, they lifted and went over the crest, clearing it by a foot or two, and then were back down at the same level they came from. It was something you'd like to see happen more than once, but if a thing is strong enough when you see it, once is enough. It was flying that would make any airplane look ridiculous without any trouble. Later I tried a lot of times to see the top of that ridge, not like I did see it, standing there, but like they saw it, coming right into their eyes head-on, bigger and bigger, and knowing that they could go right through it if they wanted to, but something in them — or in the air that knew what they needed — right at the last second lifting them just enough, and back down, and on. I watched them make a line away from me, very straight, and then go out of sight. That was all, but they went north and I followed, down the terraces and into the flat of the next valley.

I used a road part of the way, and passed people now and then, going along talking to each other. I tried to walk like they did, with short steps and my head down, and nobody even looked at me. To tell the truth, I was off the road more than I was on it, going through fields that were about half grass and half sand, and it wasn't till later that it came to me: I was doing what I could to make as straight a line as the birds, the tundra swans, or whatever they were. I looked up every so often to see if any more would go by, and they did, though higher than the first two.

The business of being in the open bothered me, though there really didn't seem to be anything for me to worry about, at least not right now. But as I went, I kept looking for places to put in, and more or less grading them by how much concealment they could give me in how much sun. It is easy to hide in the dark; anybody can do it anywhere. But in daylight you've got to know what you're doing. I wanted to travel any time I could, and take my chances. I couldn't make nearly the time I'd like to have made if I just moved at night, but since nobody was bothering me, I figured to make as much distance as I could any time I could do it. And if I struck inland as well as north I would be in mountains, my map told me, and though the going might be harder, there wouldn't be as many people, and there'd be more places to stay out of sight. As long as I could make it in the flat day and night, I was that much better off. Birds went over, and I was as much on course with them as if the long neck of any one of them was the needle of a compass.

It was cold, and though I could control that if I could find what I wanted to wear, I was still not as comfortable with the temperature as I wanted to be. The sun was thin, with a few high clouds, and a wind blew across me from the northeast, the sea side. I moved up to my left onto another terrace when I saw there was nobody on it, and sat down to think things out.

In front of me, far off and down, was a heavy stand of trees. There might be something for me there, and I decided to go down and have a look when I could make out a way that was not too obvious. I had forgotten about the birds in my mind-move toward the trees, but now they came back before I even had to think about them. They were going by at a great rate, dozens of them, and as I sat there I saw more, coming from all over like they were homing in. From every which way they were getting there, and I saw more than one lift its head and rear back, setting its wings like flaps, to go down out of sight on the other side of the trees. A curved line of bushes was between, and if I could get on the far side of it, away from the road, it shouldn't be hard to work on into the grove. I eased down the side of the hill, and with my new short enemy steps slanted along toward the bushes.

It was almost too easy, but when I slid through the bushes it came to me that if I happened up on anybody now, I would be in a rough place, because being behind the bushes would have more the look of somebody trying to keep out of sight than if I had been in the open or on the road. I quickened up a little on my Japanese steps to get into the trees, where they would be hard put to deal with me, because trees and I have got an understanding, especially when it comes to hiding from something, or getting after it.

The trunks were very close together with a lot of low branches; a lynx would've loved them. I could have got up into them and moved along the limbs from one to the other, but there didn't seem to be any use in that; no one knew about me. Here I was in a place in a country that seemed to have all the land cultivated that it was possible to farm, and it was like timberline forest, or just a little farther south of that. I stood still, listening for a scratch. Where I come from, if you hold still long enough in woods that thick, you will hear a scratch — bark making a sound in some way — and then you can locate what's making it: a pine marten, a squirrel, maybe even a fisher, because everything that lives in trees or uses trees has to deal with bark, and no matter how quiet the animal is, the bark will give it away, sooner or later, if it's dry. Or if your ear is good enough and there's no wind or rain, even if it's not dry.

All I heard was the whistle of wings, though, and the change in the sound of them when the bird would brake back and settle down. They were coming down on water, I knew before I saw it. I went up a tree about ten feet, put the needles aside just enough, and looked out. I thought of a fisher marten, which is just about my favorite animal: how he would look out. I did that.

The lake was about thirty acres, with swans all over it, hundreds of them. I had never seen so many birds at the same time, even when the geese were migrating, up home. They were actually *crowded*, and that's something you don't expect birds to be. It was surely not all that hard to get food, wherever they had come in from. It's true enough, any animal or bird is glad to eat food it doesn't have to work for, but it seemed to me that there must be something else here than food, though I never did find out what it was.

The fisher faded off me, except for his eyes and the fact that I was hungry, like weasels always are, and I got back into myself to figure out what might be the advantages. It was just the middle of the morning, and there wasn't much I could do until the sun went down. But seeing all those swans convinced me that I had business there, and I needed time to make out my next move.

It was a park, and while I sat in the tree a few people, women with little children, came in and walked part of the way around the lake, and fed the swans pieces of bread. Neither the mothers nor the children seemed any too enthusiastic about what they were doing, and most of them didn't stay long. I was not interested in them. I was looking for somebody who was there all the time, because there was a fence around the lake, and a little shack at the side of it nearest me. I figured somebody must live there, or use it in some way. Probably there was only one guy, and I waited to find him.

It didn't take that long, or anything like it. A little girl and her mother went up to the shack and knocked on the door, and an old man in baggy clothes came out. He bent down and gave the little girl something, and then went back in. I didn't have any way of knowing whether anybody else was inside with him, but I didn't believe there was. Or if there was, it would likely be only one. I came down out of the tree, stretched out behind it, put my hands under my arms, and went to sleep. I was hungry, but your mind gets sharper when you're hungry, and it was a good feeling in its own way. I felt good and strong, and fast, and quick. My time as a fisher had done me good. My eyes burned through the leaves and needles when I opened them.

I slept a long time, curled up and not too uncomfortable, and when I woke up the sun was just leaving. I couldn't see the lake from the ground, so I went up the same tree until I could. There were no people in sight. All I could hear was the rustle of feathers as the swans brushed against each other, and the whistle of feathers on the ones still in the air, changing their beat as they pulled up and settled in. A dim light was in the shack, and I planned to wait until I knew the park was closed and empty except for whoever might be in the shack. With the dark I felt my strength grow until it was better than any sensation I or anybody else has ever had — a million times better than fucking or being drunk. The breath in and out through my nose had fire in it, except that it was cold, colder than the air. I slid down and stepped clear of the trees.

It was no trouble getting past the fence. The top rail was smooth metal, and I just put one hand on and vaulted over. The swans nearest where I came down made a shift, a little flurry, and then were just like the others, crowding, a few of them dipping their heads. I moved along toward the shack, in the shadows; there were plenty of them. I got to the one window.

There was nobody but the old guy, with light shining on his bald head, in the middle of short bristly hair. He was bent over, and I waited until I could make out what he was doing. After my eyes came good I saw he was working on something on a table, and when I could see even better I could make out it was a swan with its wings spread. The neck was in some kind of a clamp, and when I moved a little I could barely tell — but I could tell — that the old man was fixing one of the swan's legs, putting a splint on it and wrapping it with string or tape. The swan couldn't bring its head up, but the light caught its eye; there was nothing in it that had any interest. People in hospitals have the same look. I tried the door, and it was not locked. Then I pushed on in, little by little.

He never heard me. For a second I stood right behind him and watched his hands work on the swan's leg. I pulled the knife and took the step, the one step. I had him under the throat, lifting him off the floor, and ran the knife through him right to left, all the way through. I held him until he quit kicking — both legs kicked together — and then let him down slow. He was close enough to my size, and I pulled off his coat and shirt and pants. There were some bags in a corner, and I took the biggest one and put the others over him. Then I went back to the table. I cut off the swan's head and started pulling out feathers and putting them into the bag. When I had got one side plucked, I cut out a piece of the leg and ate it. People have a hard time getting used to the idea of eating raw meat, but it is not really much different from the way it is when it's cooked. I ate all I wanted, and then plucked the rest of the feathers. I aimed to fill the bag before I left. Then I could work for cold weather, sure enough. There were a lot of things I could do with feathers.

I needed more, though. I would have to go after them on the lake, grab the swans out of the crowd they were in, any way I could. My notion was to panic some of them and force them out of the water, and then take what I could get.

I left the bag in the shack and went out. The swans were just like they had been, a big shifting blur on the water, making those strange noises they make, all neck but still sounding like they were a long way off, no matter how close you were.

I worked the shadows, then let them see me as I came nearer. There was a corner to the lake, and some of them bunched up in that. When enough of them got in, I picked up a stick and

pitched it. Three or four slapped and flapped up out of the
water, and I hit the shadows again, and worked around. There
were two left on land when I got close enough, and I grabbed
the nearest one. I made the mistake of catching it by the wing
and one leg, and it turned and bit me right below the eye. That
thing really clamped down, without making a sound, and
wouldn't turn loose till I tore it off. You couldn't believe a bird
could be as strong as that one was, not even a bird that big. It
bashed me with its wings and it was like being hit with a soft
hammer, but one that had a whole lot of power in it, soft or not.
To tell the truth, I was afraid to turn it loose, afraid it would
come after me if I did, and maybe the whole lake of them would
hit me then, from the water, the land, the air, everywhere. I
dragged the swan into the water and held it down with everything I had, held it and kept on holding it. After a long time
it died, and I was left with that long neck in my hands and
the wings down limp: all that power, and the thing so light. I
couldn't believe it. I went for the bag, dragged the swan into the
dark, and plucked it. And ate a little more, too. Then I went
back into the water and found the stick I had thrown in, and
from then on I used it. I found out I could get close to the swans
without all that stalking, and when I did, I could level a hard lick
along where their heads were, and I'd hit one or two of them,
and one of them really hard, usually. It wasn't easy, and I missed
some, but I was at it nearly all night, plucking them and then
slitting them open, letting them fill with water and sink. I raised
a lot of hell with those birds, and if I'd been able to carry more
sacks I could've had more feathers. But by the time I finished I
had all I really needed, and I put the bag over the fence, went
back through the trees, then through the bushes, and was in the
open again, and on the road if I wanted it. My face was bleeding

pretty badly — flowing right on — and I kept trying to sleeve it off as I walked. But then I got to laughing, not a whole lot but really, when I thought of the old guy back under the burlaps. He could say that I killed him for his feathers, which is the God's truth.

The bag was great. I hefted it and shook it around, and the feathers made a sound like they did when they were flying by on the real birds.

All the time I've been alive I wondered at the strange things that come to my mind when they don't have any reason to come. The trees had made me think of the fisher marten, and a big wave of love went over me when I thought I might be like it was, and have the eyes it had. Now it was the swans I had killed, and also the ones I had not killed, and would never kill; they were all the same bird. I shook the bag and the feathers scraped and whistled, and I laughed again. I looked up as some more birds passed over, going to the lake. Seeing the swans in flight, hearing them, it was hard not to think I could fly myself, and I didn't turn my thoughts, because on that particular road, at that time, they were right.

❖   ❖   ❖

I wanted to lay up for a day or two, and sew. I had some thread in my emergency kit, though I didn't think I had enough. I could come on more thread, though, I believed; there would have to be some wherever I went. I had two coats and two pairs of pants, all of them more or less the sizes to fit me. I might have to cut a little in one place or the other, but that was all right. Though it was not cold enough for it where I was, I wanted to make an insulated suit, with feathers between the two layers of clothes, and then carry the suit in the bag until I was ready for it. That meant I needed one more suit for the weather until I got up into the snow, and if I was going to make the suit any time soon, I needed the extra clothes before I started sewing. When I thought it over, I decided not to do it until I had the other suit, which I would find some way to get in the next few days. That was good enough, and I went on, shaking the bag now and again, for the sound.

The last part of the night I stayed on the road, checking my compass now and again, ready to get off into the fields if the road swung too much from north. I was pretty sleepy after a while, and went on not really paying enough attention to what I was doing. Then I heard somebody yell, and out of nothing three or four people were running straight at me. If they came up to me and talking developed, I was out of luck. I looked right and left for shadows, and hit the ground next to a dirt bank with my feet pulled up under me until they got close. They came right on, and I got ready.

Then they stood there, and one of them said something, and then something that sounded like the same thing. I stood up slow and put up a hand like I might be asking for something, or even begging: begging maybe for them not to hurt me, hit me, maybe for them to understand me. I held my hand flat between his eyes and mine. He took half a step in, and I straightened up with everything I had and took him in the middle of the chest with my shoulder, lifting at the same time. Before he even hit the ground I was past him and the others, running like the first day the snow had melted and I was clear of snowshoes: like I was on the floor of the valley, and enough weight taken off me and my feet to make me light enough to fly. I had the bag of feathers and the other stuff, but that didn't slow me down at all.

They were yelling and going on behind me, but there's never been a one of those little people who could catch me when I had the summer-valley feeling. I let my stride out, and I have to say that I was really moving, and not afraid of a thing. When I turned a corner of the road I was gone, not where they probably thought I would go, into the grass to the left, but over a wall to the right and behind a little house, and around on the other side of it, and then down flat in what was probably a garden, long stems all around.

I put the bag of feathers and my other stuff under me and waited. I had seen a lot of rabbits wait, and marmots, and mice and even lemmings. The snowshoe hare can stay all day in one position, all night, as long as he wants or thinks he's in danger, or even *could* be in danger. I can make out a hare when a weasel can't see one. I've done it. I've seen a white weasel go by a hare when I was looking right at it; a lynx might've seen him, but I'd put myself up against one of those, too. I was still: still like that, and kept my eyes closed, and listened. Nobody came. I couldn't hear anybody search, and I couldn't hear any sound from the road, either. I listened to the other side then, and heard something I didn't like. The sound must have been there all the time when I was concentrating on what was close to me. There was a far-off noise of cars — trucks maybe, most of them; they kept shifting gears — and though the sound broke every now and then, it always picked back up and went on and on. I wouldn't have been surprised if it was a truck convoy, and that meant I was not only fairly near a highway but maybe another big town. I didn't remember that there'd been one on the map, and it was maybe more likely a military base of some kind. With my attention on the birds for the last few hours I hadn't taken any notice of aircraft, though there must have been some, would

have to have been. Lying in the long bare stems on the bag of
feathers, I listened for them among the far-off trucks and other
cars, jeeps, whatever they were.

I stayed an hour, and in that time I heard two aircraft. Both of
them cut their engines, which had to mean they were landing.
Putting things together, I read a strip or even an air base somewhere around, maybe not too far. That meant I'd better get
back up on the terraces, or any other hills I could find. A few
civilians I could get around; a whole lot of the military in one
place, most of them armed, I couldn't. I got up out of the weeds,
the stems, picked up the bags, and headed out over the wall due
west, which was quite a concession, but sometimes you have to
make them.

There was still some moon, going down fast, and I went
up three terraces, then four, then five, and walked along the
last one. The Japanese didn't seem to keep any lights in their
houses, though I saw one every few hundred yards — I was
heading north again; Polaris was right in front of me — and
even though I didn't make very good time, I was going more or
less steadily toward where I wanted to go. I looked for a place to
hole up and sleep, when it began to get light.

There was something in the way, and it didn't move. I went to
it real slow, with my hand on my knife, what I called my bone
knife. It still didn't move, and when I got next to it I saw it was a
rock. Smack there on the terrace; I hadn't seen a rock that big
since I'd been in Japan. Back on Tinian they used to brief us on
Japanese customs, their food, their habits, their religion, and all
that. I never paid much attention, but I did remember the thing
they have about rocks. They were supposed to have whole
churches — temples, I guess they call them — where they have
rocks put around in a certain way, and they sit down and look at

them, as still as a snowshoe hare that thinks the lynx is after him. What a damn lot of foolishness I could never have thought up in a thousand years, but this big rock in the middle of the terrace was maybe something like that; if they'd wanted to farm that place, they would sure have got it out of there. It was big — as tall as I was — and rough, and I wondered how they could have got it up there. It must have weighed tons; it would have taken a good many men to push it over.

But I didn't want anybody to push it over. It was what I needed, just like it was. I got down behind it where the terrace shelved up, and when I got in a little under it, I practiced a couple of moves. I could roll out either way, to the north or to the south, depending on what I had to do and how quick I had to get up. When I was satisfied, I stretched out as far under the rock as I could get and still roll fast and move, and relaxed in the rock dark, as pure as dark can get. I put one hand on my knife in the position to draw it, and touched my dick with the other. It was the same as it had always been. That was good, real good. Nobody had done a thing to me. I pushed up under the rock a little farther, even, and thinking about the one or two low stars to the north, but mainly about Polaris, which was not going to move, I went to sleep.

It was a good long sleep, for I had let myself get tireder than I should have. Lying with my head on the sack of feathers, I had the feeling that the rock got warm along with me, and that I was in the place I'd rather be than anywhere else in the world. Just before I went all the way into the dark — my own dark, inside the rock's dark — I kept thinking of the snowshoe hare and the lynx, and the stillness: the stillness of two kinds. In that picture — image, whatever you'd want to call it — I saw the way, or I think I did. Camouflage, when you look at it right, is one of the most interesting things of all. I'd seen a lot of it up on the Brooks, seen it in birds, seen it in animals of all kinds up there, feathers changing colors, fur changing colors, to hide better, to hunt better: both sides.

To be invisible and still to know what was going on, that was something. I wondered what it would be like to be a ghost. When I started thinking about camouflage, like I say, I knew what I wanted to do — no, what I *had* to do. It was going to be the way. Not the way out of Japan — by now I had almost no notion of ever leaving Japan. If I had had to go back to the States or to the Territory, I wouldn't have any idea what to do. I was so much involved in what I was doing now, the interest of it, the possibilities: the way up to the north, the other big island the maps and the briefers told us was all mountains and snow, where there would be the kind of animals and birds I grew up with, the kind of cold that cleans out your insides like fire, where there's ice in the water and I could live like I was used to living, like I wanted to live. There ought to be places between me and the mountains and the snow fields where I could more or less pick the colors, and take them on, at least in some way. If I took my time — and I had plenty of it — I should be able to fit the color of some of my situations — hillsides, fields, woods — and tune to them: tune myself to them by color. Maybe this wouldn't always work, and maybe I wouldn't always be able to do it, but I planned to try. It was worth it, worth a lot. It might be worth everything.

I drifted into sleep with all this on my mind, and there'd been very few times when I'd been happier.

What happened then was what should have happened, and it clinched the thing for me. I was in snow, and bushes were over me like the rock was over me. I was dead white, and still, stiller than the rock, than the bush. I was waiting, and I knew I would wait for as long as it took. I guessed that the field around me was wide open; the danger was there. Plenty of fear I had, and in the dream — daydream at night, or whatever it was — I was afraid to move. But then, too, I was not only afraid to move, but I knew how *not* to move. I closed my eyes and knew that I was dead white, and might not be found. But as I lay there everything slowly started to change. I was not afraid: the main sensation I had was terrific hunger, more than I'd ever had. The stillness translated into that, turned into it. I was not under the bush anymore. I was outside, but I was just as still. My muscles, though they were crouched, were not pulled up to make me small, but gathered, and I could tell they were longer. I looked for the breath of the other thing; I looked for the eyes. Breath, breath, I held my own, there in the open field with one bush. Something was there. All it had to do was open its eyes and I would be on it. It would not have a chance.

I woke up in the same position. When I turned my head the feathers crackled. I gathered myself up and rolled out in the same way I'd practiced the night before, but there was no need. I crouched, stayed in the crouch for a moment, and stood up. The light before the sun was coming on; I could see the roughest places in the rough rock.

The snow field and the two kinds of stillness left me, though they had told me what I needed to know, and I began to listen and look for more aircraft, the reality of them. The traffic, though farther away, was still there, and I was more sure than ever there was an air base somewhere around, maybe even over the next hill.

The hill curved, the terrace curved. When I came around I looked down into the valley on my right, and stopped. There were houses close together, and in front of three of them were aircraft, parked in yards. They were Jacks, the big new barrel-shaped fighter the Nips had just brought into combat. I had never seen one in the air, but we'd been briefed on them, and told to watch for a plane that looked like the P-47, the Jug, but didn't have as big an engine. The Jack is a clumsy-looking crate, even more than the Jug is, and it looked even clumsier standing next to those Japanese houses where civilians lived. They weren't camouflaged, and one of our fighters could have got all three of them on one pass. It didn't matter all that much; that was somebody else's problem. What it did tell me was that I had been right about there being an air base not far away. The Jacks would have to get to a strip to take off; they sure couldn't use the dirt road they were parked next to. The likely thing was that they would use the road as a taxiway to the strip, and it wouldn't make sense, even to the Nips, to have their roads cluttered up with aircraft for long stretches. I was close to a strip, I was sure, and when I came around the next curve it was right there in my face.

It was a big field, real big, going out as far as I could see, but there were no aircraft up. Around the tin hangars, which were starting to catch the sun, a few people moved around. I would have to make a big detour to get past the place, and I was beginning to put my mind to it, watching the hangar area because there was not anything else to look at except rows of parked aircraft — mainly Bettys and Zeroes, with a few more of the big ugly Jacks — and empty field going out to the horizon, when my eyes concentrated before they knew it, and I went down on my belly, wishing I had field glasses or the kind of sight a hawk has. A bunch of men were with one other, and were walking him along. Even as far away as I was, I could see that his hands were tied behind his back, and that could mean only one thing. Or it meant two things: he was an American, and what they told us at Tinian about being captured was the truth — the Japs were going to do what we'd been told about. I wondered if it was somebody who'd been shot down in the same raid I was, or in some other raid, but it didn't really matter. They came out through the rows of planes to an open space just off the near end of the hangars, and stopped.

The wind picked up, coming from there over me, and I listened, listened hard. There was nothing I could get, and I put more strength into my ears, and cocked one, cupping it. But I didn't need to, and I probably wouldn't have needed the wind, either, though with the wind there was not any doubt. The guy screamed, standing there with his hands tied, and screamed again, something that sounded like a name, but if it was, I didn't catch it. The others shoved him down onto his knees, and he fell over to one side, moving his legs. One of the Japs pulled him by the hair back to his knees and he screamed again, and this time it was not a name — just a sound, high and carrying. There was a lot in that sound, and if I hadn't known what made it, I would have been hard put to believe it was from a human. It was not like any animal, either; it was different from all of them.

The sun was pretty near blinding, now, off the tin roofs of the hangars when you looked that way. The shimmer of it spread on the tin, and in some way seemed to stand up off it into the air and curve, one wave bending out toward the ocean and the other over into the hills. It went into the bunch of men, too, and for a second it seemed like some kind of magic that the blaze from the roof had put into somebody's hands, there in another curve, short and flashing in and out of the dry cold light that should have been hot. The rest of the group stood back, and there were just two of them then, at the edge of the cement, on the grass this side of it. The man on his knees was still. The Jap with the light in both hands bent his left knee like somebody getting ready to hit a baseball, and brought the sword around in a fast lick like a man who knew exactly what he was doing, had done it before. The American's head fell forward, but not off. Blood jumped in front of him at least a yard, and before he went down the Jap with the sword hit him again, and this time the head came off and rolled over. The body jerked and lay there pouring out blood, and one of the other Japs came over and kicked it a couple of times, hard.

❖   ❖   ❖

There was nothing more to see. Before they picked up the body and the head I was already moving off, keeping low, and over the crest onto the terrace on the other side. I leaned against the bank with the feathers, checked my compass, set my mind forward, and started west, to spend however much time it took to get around the base.

I made a wide detour, very slow, going ahead a few steps at a time like I was on a stalk; I would probably be on a still-hunt before long. It was cold but not too cold. I had been looking forward to sewing my suit of feathers, but I didn't really need it yet, and besides, I wanted some other clothes to wear while I did the sewing. Right then I concentrated on making time — slow time — around the air base, and gave it as much room as it needed. This took me back over a good many ridges and terraces, and on some of them people were working, but I moved so they were all far away from me. From what I could tell, the Japanese, the men and the women both, like to spend a lot of their time crouched over. More than half of them wore glasses, and it struck me that all of them, or most of them, were near-sighted and couldn't cope with anything unless they could get their eyes right up next to it. I could see them working with whatever they planted on the terraces, bent way over and stay-ing that way, moving around little by little, or down on their knees peering at something right in front of them. Only once did I see anybody turn his head and look anywhere else but at the ground. The guy saw me, but I just stood there and then bent over like they did. When he looked back down at the ground, I was gone.

When I had been traveling on the terraces for two hours I slanted, not due north yet but northwest, and by that time I was off the terraces and into real hills, steep ones, like foothills are, some places. That suited me a lot better, because there were not likely to be people, or only a few now and then, since there was no work to do on the hills, amongst the trees, except maybe picking up kindling, and no food.

It was very quiet, and as I topped out over one hill after another, and never came on anybody, I decided I would knock off the traveling and rest up. I still had a little raw swan meat, and knew I had better eat it before it went bad from carrying it and sweating on it, and I pulled up in a corner where that par-ticular hill made an angle, and figured to have myself a picnic and rest my feet. Whenever I could quit the sweat-out of mov-ing in daylight I was cheerful, and felt like I'd spent the day pretty well, and hadn't got caught or had to fight or run. Since the night before, and my notions about camouflage, I had got more confidence than ever, and I looked forward to being still and turning my mind on that subject again, for the good feeling.

I did all that. First I thought about camouflage, but I couldn't add a whole lot to what I'd already come up with. Even though it was cold enough, there was not any snow yet. I wasn't expecting it here, anyway; I wasn't ready for it. I was moving through hills and short fields covered with needles — spruce needles, though not the kind in Alaska — and I thought brown had to be the good color, an easy color to pick up from. The dirt was almost the same color as the needles.

❖   ❖   ❖

But I wouldn't do that tonight, I told myself, chewing on part of a swan wing. I wouldn't. I'd give myself a vacation, and think forward, on up to the other island where the big snow was, where it always was. When I got to the deep snow I would roll in it, roll in it like a bear. I could feel every sense I had get better just thinking about it. The light went and the moon came, and another light. I put the bag of feathers over my feet, and then opened it and put my feet in amongst the feathers, which was great. When my feet got warm the rest of my body did, too. If you know anything about cold-weather people, you'll know how true that is.

I got up before dawn and traveled, slanting a little west again as the sun came up over the hills. The land was higher now, and the hills were steeper. There were no roads at all. When the sun was about level with me I topped out over the highest rise yet and there was a lake below me, a fairly big one, around a hundred and fifty acres, as I judged. I thought about seeing if I could get down into one of the coves, where I could hide in the bushes along the edge and try to fish with my emergency hooks and line. I was almost out of swan meat and would have to have something to eat soon, to keep going.

I had never seen a lake so empty since I left Alaska; there were people and boats swarming all over the ones in the States. The blue of the water was sure an interesting color, and as the sun came up and hit down and across it, the color deepened and brightened in a way that would really hold your eye. I'd seen the sun on water lots of times, and always liked it, but there's one thing I always look for that I haven't seen but once or twice, in summer after the ice melts on the Brooks and there's water standing in lots of places. The sun on top of water is one thing, but the sun *in* it — down somewhere under the surface where it makes a kind of a box shape, you could say, a box that changes, that goes in and out like it's breathing — that's something else again, I'll tell you.

This lake had that for me. It might have been my angle from it, or the angle of the sun, or maybe both, but I saw that gold box with the sides thinner than any paper, alive down there, alive with itself. It was big, too, the biggest yet; it would've had to be big for me to see it from that far. Then the box was gone, but I took it for a good sign, and knew I could go down and do whatever I wanted, near where it was.

I made little steps down through the trees — mostly needle trees but also a small kind of oak with wide, stout branches — watching all the time. There was a cove right under me where the trees grew down to the edge of the water, and I slid into it and looked around. I'd thought I would fish, but now I wanted to use the time another way. It was warmer, and I could have sewed my cold-weather gear together if I'd wanted to, got the feathers into the clothes and not have to carry the bag anymore. But if I did that, I would have to wear what I made, and if there was even a chance that it would be warm anywhere, I would sweat bad, lose a lot of strength, and not have anything I could do about it. Wait, I said; wait on the cold and the weather that would make a suit of feathers feel like it was something that God made just for you. Wait for the other island, I said. Or the full north of this one.

I sat down in the bushes to rest my back. The lake took on a different tone this close: it was a lighter blue. What I wanted was to get another glimpse of the sun down in the water, under it a few feet, or way down, maybe. I wanted the conditions to put the sun in a box, in that red-orange box that went in and out, that beat like a heart in a way nobody could ever have thought of, but was there.

I couldn't find it, though, no matter what, no matter how I angled my head through the bushes. But I had seen it from the hill, in a way that must be like you'd see a ghost, and that heart, that sun in a box, I had. It meant a lot to me. I kept thinking about it: the underwater cube, about half box and half diamond.

I peeled my emergency kit loose from my side, opened it, and took out the fishhooks. The kit itself was exactly like it had been when I taped it to me on Tinian. I had looked at it once, in the cab of the gantry on the dock where I came down, but I had taken the time to put it back together right, and it was still no different from when it came from the factory, or wherever the Air Force got it. The fishhooks were bright, with the kind of brightness that makes metal seem new, whether it is or not. They caught the sun, and with each of the four I held the shank and bent the curve out a little. When you get the hook in the fish's mouth you don't want him to be able to nose up against the shank and tear loose. It should be just him and the hook, and you pulling on it from the other end. That's something they don't teach you in factories, but the machines could just as easily do it as not, if they knew what they were doing. I packed the kit again and taped it back. The adhesive was still strong enough, and I could pull it loose two more times, or maybe three, before I would have to think of some other way to carry it. But that would be later.

I looked back up through the bushes onto the hillside, and then leaned over and picked up a handful of dirt. I could do it; I believed my notion was right; it would work. Beginning with my feet, I rubbed the dirt into my shoes and clothes, into the skin of my hands and face. It took me an hour to do the job right, taking off the pants first, and then the shirt — or coat, whatever it was — to do the back parts. I wanted the dirt dry, and kept it that way, and rubbed it in, heeling it with my hand to put on as much pressure as I could. Now and then, as the sun got higher, I matched the color of the clothes — my color now — to the slant of the hill. I kept doing this, and in the end the match was surely close. If I kept still I was sure I would blend with the hill, with any hill around there. Then we would see.

I worked on my face and hands again, looking into the sun on the lake, getting farther from its color, darker and darker, but not too dark. There was not a sound, except a little sift of air at the level of the water. Sitting there on my heels, I was quieter than it was, and I waited, halfway between the snowshoe hare and the lynx, enjoying both sides, hiding and still-hunting at the same time. Something flowed back and forth between the two kinds of invisibility, the two kinds of stillness, until finally — I couldn't help it, didn't want to — I bent forward on one knee and pulled the knife up along my thigh and out.

Light on things was different in Japan, I was thinking; at least it was for me. Especially it seemed to catch metal and water at another angle, and catch it quicker and stay longer, always quivering. I tilted the blade, running the sun up and down it. I wondered if anybody on the other bank would pick up the flash. It was a long way over there, though; nobody would come. If anybody noticed, it would be like the house where I had flickered the fire of the candle off the blade: the family had looked up and around, and then gone back to eating and forgotten about it. There had been a sign set in that house, and this was another one. I bent over close to the water and laid the blade flat on it, and then a little under, still catching the sun. I didn't run the light along it this time, but held it steady, making it balance like the bubble in a carpenter's level, branding the blade from inside. Very satisfying it was, for sure.

After I wiped off the blade and put it back, I opened the survival kit and got out the small GI knife and sharpened it. I washed the dirt off my face, sat on a rock where I could clean off the hair in the lake, and shaved. It was not so bad, shaving in cold water, by feel, the light cutting clean while the sun hit the fresh skin. I waited for a few minutes before I smeared on more dirt, just to keep the freshness feel longer and watch the light on the lake at the same time. When I'd done that, I put on a new face of dirt and was ready to try it out.

Going up the hill, I kept matching myself with what I came to, with whatever I passed. I would look at the back of my hand against a bare place on the slope, and if I had kept still, and there had been any distance at all between my hand and whoever was looking, it would have been hard to tell it was there. When I was about ten years old my father took me south, all the way down into the States, to Colorado, because he thought that maybe we ought to move there, get off the Brooks Range so I could grow up with more people around, not just Indians and Eskimos. We stayed in Colorado a week. Neither one of us liked it, and we went back north as soon as we could. There was nothing for us amongst all those cars and stores, where you have to ride everywhere. I did get off into some of the hills around Greeley, though. It was summer, and real hot, and I remember climbing down part of the trail, and out of the corner of one eye I saw a rock move. I went over real slow, and it didn't move; it was just a rock, a dull slope and the pattern of it. And then it moved again, like a wave of rock, coming to life and flowing, almost floating, over the other ground with the same marks. It was a big rattlesnake, the only one I ever saw, and when it quit moving again I got as still as it was, and took it in. We both stayed a long time, and then it started off again. When it moved the whole canyon shifted a little. This time I stayed where I was and let it flow away until I couldn't see it, because it had blended in even better than before or was under another rock or was just gone. From watching the animals and birds up on the muskeg, on the tundra, and on the Brooks, I've always believed that if camouflage is good enough, if it is right *exactly*, the bird or the animal will not just be invisible, it won't be there. When the rattlesnake did something so that my eyes — which can see what the others can't — couldn't pick it up, I knew I was right. My hand on the bare place on the slope, there in Japan, was like that. Like that or just about; it was almost somewhere else, or just not.

I moved part of the way up the side of the hill, and when I couldn't see the lake anymore I started to travel again, walking the slant and being quiet. My camouflage made a lot of difference in the way I was moving, like I had put on some other kind of dimension, you might say; that was the feeling of it. And because it was, the trees and bushes and pine needles and rocks that were on the slope were different, too. I used the trees in another way from what I was used to. When I came to a bare place the other dimension was stronger, like it even stood out from me, stood off me a little, and everything in me and on me got better. Where there were trees I slid from one to the other on the downhill side of them. Where there were spaces between I went over them, not hurrying, facing uphill, not just to see what might come down from that side, but to give my camouflage a chance to work, give me a chance to check it.

The only thing that worried me were the bags. I had done everything I could to make them the same color I was, but they were still loose from me, not right on me like everything else I had, and I didn't trust them not to swing or separate from me in some way that somebody might notice, if he was to look. But nothing like that happened, and I went right along, and must have made a couple of miles, concentrating on the different shades of brown — needles and bark — as my own brown came past them and through them. I was hungry. I'd been hungrier, but I knew that before long I would most likely have to be around people again, for their food; I didn't want to go another day without eating anything. It takes energy to walk, a lot of it, especially when you're walking the side of a slope and have to do a certain amount of balancing. I was thinking about this when I heard a shuffle, up from me and maybe fairly far off. I was between two trees. I stopped right there and waited. I could have got down behind the next trunk — it was only a few steps — but I didn't. If there were people, they wouldn't be close enough to see my eyes, no matter where they were.

It was people: four women and two girls, all in long black dresses. They were picking up sticks and tying them into bundles. I couldn't hear any sound from their handling the sticks: the shuffling was made by their clothes. Strange that the sound carried that far: about fifty yards, where they came out of the trees. I stayed where I was, and when all six heads were down I put the bag on the ground behind me and got real still again, waiting for one of the heads to turn.

That happened. One of the women, old and almost bald-headed, separated off from the others and came down the hill. One step she took, two, then three, looking at the ground all the time. I looked with her: looked for the same sticks she was looking for. Neither one of us found any. Then she raised up — Japanese women seem to have a lot of trouble raising up, but she did — and had her eyes on some place a few feet to the north of me. She turned to go back up the hill, and when she did her eyes went across me like a ray, the beam of a flashlight, if you can think of it that way in broad daylight, and then went right on by. Nothing about me registered at all, and I breathed and waited more, halfway hoping she'd do it again, because my invisibility was strong, the strongest yet. It stood off me like a wall, a circle; she couldn't break it. Come on, old lady, I said, almost out loud. Come across me again and not see me. Come back the other way this time, going north.

She bent down again, though, and went back to the others, doing as close to crawling as a person could and still be on feet. They talked a minute — me all the time standing right out there in the open between the two trees — and then got all the bundles of wood together in a pile, picked them up, and put them on one woman's back or the other, and in those shuffle-steps moved up the hill. When the trees closed in behind them I followed, out of sight but going where they were, at least for a while. When I got up over the ridge they were gone, and I forgot about them and just walked, staying on the ridge and having no more to do with them except to remember the woman's eyes going past me, around me, over me, like a flashlight beam in broad daylight: something inside the other light that couldn't see.

I didn't run into anybody else that afternoon, and I moved along more or less like I wanted to. There didn't seem to be any reason for me not to stay on top of the ridge, where it was easier to walk, and so I did. The notion came to me that I might try to work inland more, because from what I could tell, and from my map, it was steeper there, and I might not be as likely to run into anybody. But for now things seemed to be pretty much in my favor the way they were, and there was no sense in my changing them just to be changing. I walked the ridge, looking down both sides every few steps, until it began to get dark.

It had warmed up some, and was really not uncomfortable weather at all. I knew what I was going to do. First I wanted to make something unusual, so that if somebody found it they would look at it and not me. In the last light I piled up a lot of branches and twigs and pine straw, and shaped the whole thing more or less the size of a man, like I did before, though he would've been bigger than I am. I had the pile, my straw man, just under the east side of the ridge. I didn't want to put him on top, because there was not any reason to cause suspicion if nobody came along. But if I put him down under the crest a little, and somebody found him, I'd be sure to hear it when it happened, and I could move off in the dark. Sound was what I depended on. I had all the confidence in the world that this would work. I can hear as well as anything on two feet, and most of them on four. I can listen with any animal.

After I finished under the ridge, I went down about fifty yards and made another pile like the first one, but this time behind a tree; the head and feet stuck out only just barely. When I'd checked it from every position I got inside, put my hands under my armpits and my feet in the sack of feathers, and stretched out. I could still feel the ray, the beam of the woman's eyes, go past me. I left my listening on, wide open, but with the wood-woman's eyes going past me, and past again, like a lighthouse beam going around and coming back. I knew I would sleep, and I did. Never better.

❖   ❖   ❖

I got up at first light and went to check my man under the crest. Nobody had bothered him, and I left him like he was, with a friendly feeling for him watching out for me all night. I needed to eat, that was all. I hoped the day would figure that out for me.

I decided that it wouldn't be a good idea to walk the ridge all day, because I was almost sure to come on somebody on one side or the other, and I didn't want to stand out against the sky or the trees for a long time, either; that would be maybe putting more weight on my luck than it could hold. Besides, the ridge was dropping, getting closer and closer to the floor of the valley between banks, and when the land flattened out there'd be people, more than likely. I slanted down the bank and worked up and over the ridges to the west until I found one I wanted, then moved up to look down the crest, to see what was on the other side, and plan for it.

At first it didn't seem any different from the brown side of the hill, like the other hills and slopes I'd been on. But it was not exactly the same when I stayed with it, watching. About a hundred yards off, part of the hill was moving, and it was not with wind. There wasn't any wind, and the movement seemed to be going away from me, like parts of the bank stepping backward

and upward on each other, lifting one foot, one bunch of needles after the other, to climb, but not moving from the same
place. I had never seen anything like it, or felt anything like it. I
held on there, in the feeling, for a couple of minutes because I
thought I shouldn't break it. I didn't really want to know what it
was that was stepping backward up the hill in the same place,
going but not going.

The feeling left me, or thinned out some, and I wanted to
know. I moved, not toward the other hill but to one side, and
the shape of the thing came clear. It was a wheel of some kind,
turning backward, like a ferris wheel I'd seen in Colorado on
that trip with my father. I couldn't hear any sound from it, but
now and then there was a spark — a sparkle would be more like
it — from somewhere in the wheel. It'd flash out when I got
to looking for it, but hit me quicker or slower than I expected,
like a game, like something blind-siding me because it knew it
could. It was not steel, not glass or tin; it was water-flash, not
any other kind, and it was being carried up, backward and
around. The thing I was looking at was a water wheel. I went
toward it, tree by tree, then across the floor of the draw where
there were not any trees, then tree by tree up the other bank,
dead alone, the same color as the hillside and the wheel.

It was fed from a spring behind it, in a low position you
couldn't see from the forward side. I drank with both hands, and
watched the buckets fill and come down and forward and under,
then up backward and around, and top out over the ridge,
where people must have got the water when they needed it.
The wheel and everything about it — the rims, the spokes, the
cross-strips that held them together, the buckets, the pins they
turned on — was a job of work you wouldn't see every day,
going around on itself like it was, not making one sound you

could hear until you were right there at it, and with it, until you were as close as I was. Even then I could barely make out a faint splash as a bucket went under the spring, and a little wet grinding-swinging noise as it passed the bottom of the curve and started up. I hadn't known until just that minute how good the Japs were with wood. Everything about the wheel looked like it ought to have been made out of metal, engineered metal, but it wasn't. Wood was better; this way, it was. A real balance was part of the whole rig: I had the notion that air could have turned it just as easily as water was doing.

I went over closer, where I could see into the buckets as they came past. A tree was right behind me, and in every bucket as it started to lift, a reflection of branches and leaves was in it, trembling, rocking, being held and raised with a lot of care, like the water in each bucket that went by was worth more than the last. It was a thing I didn't mind watching, didn't mind getting in there with and staying for a while. The way the water was raised lifted something in me, too, that at any other time might have too much weight, would stay where it was and not climb, or even move.

When I turned, an old woman was looking right at me from about ten feet away. She might have seen a man made out of pine straw and dirt, holding a brown bag, but she saw me, eyes and all. I had got used to holding still when I thought somebody might be watching, and I didn't want to give myself away like the snake in Colorado, so that I saw the rock move and turn into him. I was already nailed now, though. Where the woman had come from, how she had got so close without my knowing it, I could never figure out because I never heard a thing. She was just near me, a rag around her hair, her head cocked and her mouth a little open. I couldn't let her go, or stay.

I had the knife through her before she could even blink, and then pulled it out and put it through her again. She hadn't had time to scream, but I got into my stillness again — deep — and from there went over the whole valley with my eyes. There was not any change. I picked up the body, which was hardly bleeding, and carried it over behind the tree that had made the reflection in the buckets. I looked back at the water wheel, and it gave me a notion of something to do. Behind the tree I sawed off the head and put pine straw and leaves over the body, making a shape like the one I had left on the ridge the night before, to watch out over me while I was asleep. Then I took the head and fitted it into one of the buckets, just as it came past. I watched it rise up toward the crest of the ridge, but before it got there I left, keeping to the lower side of the slope until the wheel was out of sight behind me. A head for a head, I thought. But really, when I'd done it I didn't have that idea at all. It was just something that came to me later, after I was gone.

❖   ❖   ❖

All the rest of the day I traveled west and north, moving over one ridge after another. The ridges were about the same height, but the whole land was climbing, me with it. I thought the country would probably top out and leave me on a plateau, and if that was so, I'd have to be even more careful than I already was. Walking the slopes, I was protected on one side until I cleared the crest, and I was more or less confident that my hillside brown would pretty much keep me from being seen, at least at a distance, though it still bothered me that the old woman had got up on me without my knowing it. If it had been anybody else, or more than one, it might have been bad. I went on, doing my best to make sure that nothing like that would happen again. Three times I saw people, always below me, picking up wood, all women and kids except for one man, whose voice, sharp and thin, was the only one I heard. They were far down from me, all the time with their eyes on the ground, and I eased by them little by little until I was out of sight, and could pick up my pace.

In the late afternoon wind started to blow, and when I came up over another ridge it didn't fall off to the other side. I had my plateau, and now I tried to figure what to do with it. Being as cautious as I could, I went along it, still angling west, and came to a kind of gully, with walls about ten or twelve feet high. I thought at first that it was a road, because it was getting too dark to see, but when I slid down into it I could tell it was not a road. But the gully was not natural, I could tell that, too. The bed, covered with leaves and pine straw, had been cut out for some reason. I walked it as free as air, near the west bank. I thought the middle would be just as good, and more room, but when I tried to cross, my foot caught on something and I went down.

When I was down I was already feeling, though, and in a minute knew what the situation was. The sides were cutbanks, and under the leaves and needles were railroad tracks, closer together than any I knew about, but tracks they were. I looked north along them, and in the new moonlight I could see a wink of metal forward from me, and then, now that I knew what I was looking for, another one farther on. I walked ahead in the moonlight, one foot on the west side of the tracks and the other in the middle, and even on the curves I didn't stumble again. I felt freer than I had in a long time, going along with no slope to climb or pull back against, with no trees, nothing to go around. I walked until I was tired out, and then climbed up the east bank — it was not quite as high — put my feet in the bag of feathers and my head on a pile of pine straw, and went into a good strong sleep.

When I woke up I was sorry the night was over. Walking the tracks in the moonlight had been a good thing; after every curve I would look for the glints along in front of me, and they kept springing up, white with some blue in it, like runway lights set to show you where to come down, to be safe for a little while on the ground after the night's raid. Finally I stretched, and slid down the cutbank. I knelt down then, and put my ear to the track. I had done this a few times before, in western Alaska where they have railroads, and also in Colorado, but I had never heard anything. I wondered what the sound was supposed to be. Somebody had told me that you can hear a train fifty miles off if you listen to the rails. I bent down, solid on my hands and knees, and listened again. Nothing. But I stayed there and thought about my listening — my ear, I guess you could say; my brain, my head — going both ways down the track, but mainly forward, through the woods, on over the mountains ahead of me, over roads and bridges, through towns, on and on, never getting where it was supposed to end up, but just going. The places I thought of — with my head on the track like somebody who was trying to commit suicide when the train came or who was just practicing for it — were only one or two of them in Japan: the city on fire, which I blanked out because it didn't interest me, and the road where I drank the bottle of wine. The track to the north — really, that's all I wanted — went up into the snow and over the frozen water. I believed that if I or somebody could've made a record of it and called it "Frozen Water," people would've believed that's what it meant. The sound was nothing, but the listening was level, dead level, like looking over a lake of blue ice that didn't have the other side. There wouldn't be any animal tracks on it, but maybe snow falling. I put snow there, and it was twice as good, twice as much as what it was.

I got up, and pictures of lakes and the tundra faded; the muskeg went, and I leaned back against the cutbank. I decided to follow the track, but not walk along it, where it would be easier to get trapped. I climbed out, and keeping the edge of the cutbank in sight, started to work forward through the trees. They were wide apart, and most of them were big; there were lots of cones and needles on the ground. As I went on they seemed to take on a shine, especially the cones did, and I picked one of them up. It was wet — not soaked, but wettish. I didn't like that, but went on anyway, checking the bark of the trees. They were all like that, wet on them when the air had condensed. And it was warmer, too. How could that be? The sky was overcast with light gray clouds, fast cold-looking ones, and the woods were not still, sumpish; there was air from behind, moving with me into the sick-feeling trees.

I went on, the land dropping. As this happened I began to feel like there was something ahead of me: something concentrated, stopped up, maybe, something I probably wouldn't like. The more the land dropped, the more I felt this, until what had caused the feeling came at me, almost not there, as dim as it was, but there just the same, shifting a little with the air as it climbed out of itself, spread, still climbing but thick enough to reach back down to the ground.

It was steam. No wonder the trees are sick, I thought, inhaling the stuff that had always made me queasy, and was doing it now. There was a town in the midst of it. I could see some low houses when the air moved, and something came back to me from the briefings on Tinian. The Nips like heat, the intelligence officers told us. They live from one steam bath to the next one, and they'd stay in steam and sweat all their lives if they could. I looked around then, and the situation made sense: the village, the steam, and the railroad. None of the trees had been cut. That meant the steam was made by either coal or wood, and I was fairly sure that it was wood, from the smell of the steam, which I should have noticed before but probably didn't want to believe when I first picked it up. How could anybody live like this, I wondered, half sick still but not getting any worse. Who would want the trees around him to be wet, unless it was rain? Or the leaves or the rocks? I knew it from what I saw, and from my breath. Nobody should have to live like this. It was all wrong, I was sure. They didn't deserve the world.

I put my eyes on into the steam, farther and farther, using the wind shifts that moved the heavy air to one side or the other. Whenever it happened I tried to get some notion about how big the town was and how it was laid out, how I could get past it the easiest. No matter how hard or how long I looked, I couldn't make out a lot, there was so much of that warm, feathery fog hanging down. There were no people in it that I could see. They were probably in the buildings, wallowing in hot water, hoping they never had to get out. If that was so, it was good from my standpoint, but I knew better than to trust the notion too far. The way I do things is to concentrate real hard on the first part of a problem that leads to another part, and then bear down on the next one, the same way, when I get to it. Sometimes you find yourself in a situation where it's better not to think, but just to let go of everything and ride — there's a split second when you tell your brain to go out of you and something else in yourself takes over. You don't have to worry anymore; it'll all work out.

This was not one of those times, though, and I boned down on what choices I had and what advantages I could give myself. I had to get past the town — that was first. I could pull back and go around it, which would have taken some time, but I could have done it. I could try to walk through at night. I doubted if there'd be an electric light in the place, and I might just ease on through and nobody say anything to me. But somehow that didn't suit me all that much. The situation might give me a chance to do something really interesting, something it called out of me, and that I ought to do. My mind kept coming back to the train, and I thought of open freight cars full of logs: logs laid in the same direction as the tracks. I thought about being carried along, too. I had been walking long enough; I had just as soon ride for a while.

I decided to give the train one more day. Even though there was a lot of stuff on the tracks and between them — cones, needles, leaves, branches, pieces of bark, twigs — there were some things you could guess about as a result; they gave you something to hash over. Either the tracks were not used at all, and the railroad had just been left there to the weather, or they were still used, but hadn't been for at least a week or so. The last notion seemed to me the best, because the banks hadn't crumbled, or at least not much, and even though it didn't look as though anybody had been to much trouble to keep them up, they had not just been let go, either. Again, one more day, I said. I really wanted the train to come. I looked forward to it, up there on the station platform of pine cones and wet rocks.

I slept most of the afternoon, feet in my feathers, and then went down and listened to the tracks again. Still nothing. The lake of ice went farther and farther in my brain, the far shore of it did, and never ended, because the no-sound of it never quit, and the sound of the no-sound.

I hadn't realized how tired I was, and went back to sleep as the moon, which had halved itself going through a cloud, or gave me the notion that it might have done it that way, rose over the woods and came down on the tracks, shining straight away from me toward the village until they got to looking like needles, points of light that would go through anything.

I woke up hungry. It was barely light, and I lay like I used to do, topping the Brooks Range looking south, when it got warm there, as warm as it ever got. There was something about Japan that bothered me, now more than before. In all these woods, among the trees, under them, in them, and over them, there were not many birds, and I hadn't seen any animals at all. The ones in my head got stronger, though; stronger because of the absence of the others. Luck or not, I couldn't tell you.

But I believe in luck, which sometimes you can push and sometimes just comes, even when it doesn't have to. Blind-side luck I don't count on much, but I did then, while I waited for the train. Once in the morning and another time in the early part of the afternoon I went to the track and listened to the ice stretch away. Then, when the sun got down far enough so you could look right at it without blinking, I bent down again, and it was different. Inside the ice sound was another one, a steady beat with a wire hum through it. Not music exactly, but near. I lounged out on my belly and put one ear to the track and then the other, making sure. I laid my hand to the steel: there was not a quiver. I waited, and the humming waited. It must have taken an hour for it to get close enough for me to go up the bank, kneel on one knee behind a bush, and get ready for what would come.

After a while it was there, the engine turning the curve real slow, like an animal at this time of day — heavy twilight — putting one foot after the other on strange ground, careful about noise. The engine went by, and I concentrated on what was unwinding behind it, moving past the curve into the straight. There were three closed cars, and the rest was open-car wood, some of it lashed but the logs of most of it stacked, the ends of the top ones pale as targets, coming under me and on by. I didn't think about it, but I knew what I would do. I picked up my bag of feathers and the other sack, waited for the engine to start around the next turn, took one long step and a short one, left the bank in the air and dropped to the logs, about ten cars back from the coal car. I landed solid, and sat down on a log, watching the bank and the trees on it ride sideways and backward, like I was sightseeing or something, even though there was nothing to surprise me; I had been there. I knew how far it was to the town, and I knew I had time.

But I kept on looking, anyway. I shifted around amongst the shapes of the logs until I got into a position like I was in a chair, and crossed my feet like I might have done if I was in one, and kept watching the trees go by. I've always been one to get comfortable, no matter where I was. I can take a piece of ground my size, or anywhere near it, a couple of rocks or branches or just my shirt or coat, and kind of arrange it myself, and if I'm the least bit tired I'll be asleep in five minutes. If, later on, the train went through the town and I stayed with it, I already knew which logs I would lie down between, and how I would put my feet and head, so as to sleep with the position, and add the train's motion to make it better and deeper. I looked forward to that, because I had been on a train once before, going to Colorado, and I remembered how good the sleep was.

But now it was treetops, after the sun had gone, but with a little light left in the high branches. We slowed, and must have been close to the town. I was going in amongst the logs when I glanced back up one more time, and something, some part of a shadow, moved, not catching any light, but with the shape of a body to it. I just caught a glimpse, like part of the new dark, a kind of a blot that went from one limb to another, but I saw it had legs and a tail, though I couldn't make out the head. Something like a marten, about the same size, from what I could tell. A fisher cat — it could have been that big. But that thing went through my heart like a charge of buckshot, I can tell you, and those logs around me, that whole train, lit up. You get those charges sometimes, and the charge has got more power to it — a lot more — when you know you're not fooling yourself, that the thing has hit you from a real place, that it's got the truth in it, and the whole truth.

The train slowed more, and kept on slowing. I went amongst the logs for real then, pushing this way and that way, finding which logs I could move, what I could make them do. It was like building a blind. The arrangement had to look natural, but for this it had to look arranged, too, like the logs had been put in the car that way — not too arranged, though, because nobody except maybe the Germans would have logs in perfect formation. It was lucky for me, in a way, that the logs were as heavy as they were, because I like to change things around when I get the chance. I go on the notion that anything can be better than it is; you can really make it better. But there was not much I could do or, really, that I needed to do. I wedged one of the top logs over onto another one, rolling it as much as I could, so that I could slide in and down and out of sight. I did what I could to make sure the top log wouldn't roll back and pin me in there, because if I got trapped and they tumbled the logs out I would be mashed up pretty good. But, like I say, I did what I could, and got down. It was not bad there, and I waited until the train stopped. It was dark now, and I turned my listening on full power.

I didn't have much idea about how you unload logs, but the station side of the car probably unhooked and let down, and the logs rolled onto the platform, or onto whatever carried them off from the station. I didn't think they would do my car first because of where it was, but, even though I didn't hear any grinding of steel or logs bumping or anybody's voice, I still thought I ought to lift up and glance around, maybe like a marmot looking for hawks. I eased up out of my wood hole, and then up over the side of the car, tilted, getting just one eye clear. Even that way it was warmer, blurred, still — no air, or might as well not be any. I hated to think what it must be like inside the houses: little people, mainly women and old men, most of the women dumpy and fat, slick with soap and sweat and pouring stagnant water on themselves and each other, dim lights flickering on them, chattering with a lot of teeth, most rotten. What an enemy!

Four or five men were down the platform from me. A vehicle like a weapons carrier was backing and angling alongside the train, and I ducked again when I heard metal on metal — a short sharp groan — and a load of logs rolled and bumbled down. It was time for me to move, and keeping as low as I could, I went up over the opposite side of the car, dropped to the gravel, and elbowed and slid under the train, coming out on my back, facing into the bolts, rolled a foot or so away and listened.

How long? I couldn't say, because I didn't want to move. I mean, I didn't want to move a little and stay where I was; if I was going to stay I wanted to be as still as I could. The thing that bothered me was that I didn't have any plan. I didn't know what I was going to do, either there or when I got up. I didn't like where I was, because there were too many uncertain things about it, but I couldn't think of any reason to get out, or any place to go if I did. I looked at the bolts and rods, and their arrangement, to see if I could get anything back. Nothing hit me from the way they were; they were just there.

Then it was all solved. The train gave a jerk — it happened so fast that I thought I was dead before I could move. It only went a foot or two forward, just enough to change the bolts and rods over me. It was fast enough, though. The next jump might do me in. Or if the train started and was dragging something along underneath it, that would be the end, sure enough. I rolled out the same way I had come in.

It was real dark where I was, and I couldn't make out a thing. I hadn't even looked on that side of the train when it was moving, and now I had to feel around, first along the car and then behind me. There was a bank about ten feet away, and when my eyes got a little better adjusted I saw that I could get up on it from that side better than from the other, and decided that's what I'd do when the time came.

But what now? I could stand there, I could sit, I could go back under the train. Or I could wait a while — how long? — roll under the train, check for feet and noise, and then, if things seemed clear, move out and look around. About then, there was a long scratching screech of metal — which I was sure had plenty of rust in it — and I heard the logs from a car down the line rumble and bash. They unloaded one car after the other, coming along toward where I was, but two cars down from me they quit. They were near enough for me to hear voices, and after the banging and wood-whooming of the logs going down into the carriers, everything got quiet again. This might be good. If they didn't come back it meant that the rest of the wood was supposed to be dropped off somewhere else, that the train would go on. Another thing: a feeling came through the side of the train that the business on the other side had been finished. I can't tell you how I knew, but I would have bet on it. I took the chance and went under the car again. I could see the wheels of the carrier and a few feet shuffling around it, like feet of people who are pushing something, and then everything was gone, and dead quiet was with me. I hedged out, edging on my elbows, cleared the train, and backed up against the car.

The carrier, full of logs too big for little men, was just going around a corner. The men were bunched far up toward the engine, but nobody looked at me. I separated myself from the train just then, before anybody could see me there, or see me leaning, walked by a couple of buildings, shuffling, and into a street.

Underfoot was dirt; there was almost no sound, either from me or anything else. A light over one of the buildings might as well not have been there. The windows had wooden shutters on them, and at least two were boarded up and nailed. A few people passed me, walking like shadows, going slow and bent over, and not talking or, as far as I could tell, looking at me or even at each other. I didn't have the slightest bit of anxiety, and hadn't had any ever since I got on the train. I went along like the others did, and as far as it mattered to the town, it didn't seem as if I was any different from the other shadows. I didn't feel as if I belonged there, exactly — that would have been hard — but nobody was interested enough in me, even as an enemy, to break whatever routine they were used to.

I turned another corner. Down the street, which had two lights on it instead of one, there might be, I believed I could tell, something a little more worth my time. Still listening for the train to whistle, or to grind its wheels or bang its cars together, I bent and foot-dragged along toward the lights. There was something different, sure enough. Part of the light, I saw, was on the ground, and came from one of the buildings. When I got to it the window was not boarded, but heavy-steamed glass. No one was looking in. No one was on the street anywhere. I went back and forth along the glass, trying to get my eyes through the steam. I couldn't at first, and then I found a place where the glass had been rubbed across from the inside, maybe by somebody's back or shoulder, and the heat hadn't had a chance to thicken up again yet.

I could make out forms there. No, one form. It was getting dimmer as I watched, dimmer and dimmer, but the energy of my focus on it made it last a little longer, maybe, than it would have any other way. A naked girl was standing on the other side of a pool, facing me. I hadn't seen a woman naked since I was a civilian, back at Point Barrow just before I came to the States to enlist: a college girl from Kansas working with the Unuluk Eskimos one summer who took up with me because she thought I could get her out into the country around the Brooks Range, and other places she couldn't make it to on her own. I told her she was trying to fuck herself on up through the tree line. That was all right with her, she said; better than all right. She was a good enough girl in some ways, strong and smart, with calves like a couple of kegs; she could walk. But I didn't take her, as it turned out. I was going into the Air Force, and didn't plan to go back out on the tundra before I enlisted, to keep from getting drafted.

As I say, she was the last before this, and she was not bad. A naked woman in a room with you, one who you can see from both sides at the same time — the Kansas girl liked to stand in front of a full-length mirror so I could see the back side of her while I looked at her face-on from an angle — is right there with you; she was double there, you could say. But the Japanese girl was dissolving, disappearing, going away for good into steam, but still in front of me for just a minute more. She could not have been stranger if she'd been standing in powder snow — snow as fine as flour; no, finer than flour — or in a cloud. Her face was toward me. Her eyes were more or less on a level with mine. There was not any way she could see me, but I bet she felt me; I was concentrating on her feeling me. She picked up a bucket, filled it with water from the pool, and poured the whole bucket over her head. I couldn't see the water run down. All I could make out was an explosion of steam without any noise where her head was. She lifted her arms straight up and shook herself — that was for me, I'm damned sure — as the water ran down into her bush. I didn't see that that was where it ran, but it would have. The dark place, there at the middle of her, was the last of her I saw before the cloud was solid with cloud, and I turned and went back the way I came. When I cleared the first corner and didn't see anybody, I had the thought to straighten up, and I did. Until the train came in sight I went along like I usually would, and didn't even change when I passed another bunch of shuffling shadows. I eased right on by them, walking American.

After the dark of the streets, I thought that the place where the train had stopped would be lighter, but it was not. It was just as dark: dark up toward the engine, dark under the wheels. It could have been stretched along one of the streets buried behind me, maybe where the one window was, but on back farther into the town, and it would have looked just like it did now. All at once, when I was about twenty-five yards from it, the train jerked. It settled, then jerked again. I thought fast. I might make it from the dark of the street to the dark of the train, then under and, when I started, back up onto it from the street side and in amongst the logs where I'd been. But if I tried to scale the side of the car from the near side, I'd be a lot more likely to be seen. If there was one eye in that town pointed even anywhere near my direction, that would be the end of it. On the other hand, if the train was getting ready to start out, under the wheels would be the last place to be. But if I wanted the train — which I did, because I believed I understood it, that in a sense it didn't mind me, and was even in favor of me — I had to take the chance, and I took it.

Crossing the dirt between the buildings and the train was only four or five steps, and in the last step I was already rolling. That's one of the good things you learn in Basic Training: how to roll. And I never rolled better; old Sergeant Brickley would have been proud of me. I was under the same car, staring hard at the bolts and rods again, when the train jerked — jumped, this time — and I thought sure I was gone. I wondered where the blood was spurting and why I was not paining yet. But nothing touched me, and the train was still again. I was paralyzed for a second, but I shook it off and scrambled out the other side. I took hold of the metal slats of the car, and it pulled on my hand — pulled and kept on pulling. I wasn't worried, though, because no train starts fast. I walked along beside it, holding on, then ran a little, pulled up and left the ground, hanging on to the car until trees came in around me.

It didn't take long for that to happen, but before we got all the way clear of the town, a guy I didn't make out until it was too late looked up from the roadbed and saw me. He pointed and hollered, almost close enough for me to kick him, but I didn't try, because we were picking up speed now, and there was nothing he could do about it. We were gone before I could have kicked; I could have caught him a good one if I'd of seen him in time.

When we were in the full night dark I climbed back up. My swan bag was right there, and the other. The log I'd been able to move, so that I could either use it as part of a chair or get in under it and stretch out, was in the same position; the only question was whether I wanted to ride sitting or go to sleep. I lay down, watching past the big friendly wood next to me out into the tops of trees, out into the sky, which was clear and flying.

The first thing that came into my mind, then, was how long this could go on. In my situation there were not many things I could be sure of, and it was good, every now and then, to check — to check in with — the ones I knew wouldn't change, and would be with me if I used them right. Up through the logs I looked for the North Star, but from that position I couldn't make it out. I broke loose my emergency pack, pulling the tape off my side, and got out the compass. I put it on a log and hiked around so I could look at it straight. As little as it was, the dial was easy to read, and I propped up on an elbow and watched the needle hold steady as the train went around one curve after another, and farther north. That was a good time for me, I can tell you. I still had a lot of the dirt and leaf mold I had put on me, back at the lake, to camouflage myself on the hills, the brown slants and valleys, and it gave me a very right feeling to know that the logs and I were the same color, or just about. Nobody was going to be fooled by it where I was, riding by myself through the woods; nobody else knew it. But *I* knew it, and took my pleasure, on and on, a long time for lots of miles.

I couldn't sleep, didn't really want to. I sat up in the chair position and watched the trees rush. If you put your eyes to one place and things keep flying by you, your brain starts to change. I've felt it happen before, on takeoff in the 29, or sometimes when we landed, though when you're tired it doesn't work as well; you're not interested in your brain.

But I was interested in mine now. In fact, I had never been more interested. That may have been because I was in woods. There was the mix between me and the trees that there always is. It didn't bother me that I didn't know which birds and animals were there, or even what some of the trees were. Back before the town I had seen a body move from one limb to another, and that was enough for me; I would come back to it. It would be better now, I thought, while I didn't have any problems right on top of me, to give my mind some kind of rest. Not sleep, maybe, but just by letting anything come into it that wanted to, anything I remembered, anything I thought was good or bad, anything I could make up or that had stayed with me for whatever reason it might have. I put the compass away and leaned forward into the rushing of the trees.

The riding itself was first. Rocking through the woods sideways on the enemy's logs, I admitted to myself finally that I didn't like to fly; I hadn't ever liked it. In a plane there is not enough of a sense of — well, what would you say? — of *riding*.

Not nearly enough. I had plenty of that now, which was maybe why I was happy. I was in the middle of a stream of trees, and out into the snatching blackness of it I could put anything I wanted to, anything of my life, anything of anybody else's. Where was the pull of the snow? I asked myself. Right where it had always been; I didn't even have to feel for it. We turned another curve, and the compass needle fixed itself just as much due north in my mind's eye as it had when I'd been looking right at it, on the log. We were going there. Which snow, what part of it? What was in it? I saw the caribou moving out of the woods, onto the barrens. The wind coming right into my face, staying on my closed eyes like another kind of fire, made the focus of my mind's eye — or eyes, maybe — a lot sharper than it usually was. I could make out anything I wanted to as the horns came out of the trees: first one big bull, and the others after him, giving up dark for open snow, their herd-heads going lower as they moved free, where the danger was, where the danger might be. I didn't have a gun, in my mind; didn't want one. I pulled in close to the lead bull and watched his eyes, as big as a buffalo's, to see what he might be looking for. I knew he couldn't see me, but just looked on through, onto the snow beyond. I stayed where I was and he walked through me; the rest of them, too; the whole herd went through me, and it was a nice feeling to know that I could come and go any way that suited me. Well, I thought, if riding on top of these logs can make me see things that are that pleasing, and with sight that strong, the train was the right place for me to be. I had all that pleasure of the herd going through, with those big eyes not having the slightest notion of what was going on. I thought that later I would bring up some other things I liked and knew about. But first I had to do what I could to solve a couple of problems, so I could go back full-time to the wind and whatever it would bring me. I had all night, maybe longer.

I pushed back and down into the logs, and brought up the good and the bad. The good, or part of it, was that the train was going north, and every minute I was getting closer to the snow and the mountains. It sure beat walking, I can tell you, even though I liked walking and snowshoeing better, when it was time for them. But I planned for the train to carry me as far as I could manage. How far would that be? And how long? I didn't have any idea of where any of the other towns were, the ones that the train was supposed to service. But there was plenty of wood on board, and I thought it was more or less reasonable to believe that the towns were not real close to each other, or else the people would all have got together in the same place. I doubted if we would unload any more at night, though of course maybe we would. That was the thing that bothered me most: I would go to sleep and the train would pull in somewhere and people would come climbing all over the logs and find me. I needed sleep, though, and it was warm where I was. I put my feet in the feathers again, and tried to see if I could bring up any more problems. There would be plenty later, but right now, with the train pointed through the trees toward Polaris and making around forty or forty-five miles an hour, I felt like I could go to sleep with the motion of the train, hoping I would wake up if the speed slacked off, and get down onto the ground again and into the woods before they gave out and cleared away for a town. I put all the good and bad out of my mind, kept all pictures out, and was gone in a minute, not dreaming.

I woke up in four hours, and it was still dark. As far as I could tell we hadn't stopped anywhere; that part of things had been lucky. I felt very good, even though I was a little hungry. But I was rested, and we had made a lot more miles, all of them north. I decided to keep my head down and try to think more forward in time. I had made up my mind to get to the north island, Hokkaido, and I would have to cross at night, working hard all the time. Twenty miles of water is hard to make, rowing or paddling a kayak or whatever I would be able to find and steal. There wouldn't be any kayaks, but I can make better time paddling than rowing: paddling on both sides with a double blade. I could see something like that happening, but I needed the wind. I wanted to call up water for just a second, to make sure of one thing. Then I would go back to it for what I knew it would bring me, that I wanted more than any water that ever was.

I raised myself up, and the air hit me with that one big, ongoing cold push, and I was hunkered down in the snow in white fur with my eyes ready to close if anything I didn't like showed. This surprised me, because I thought I would be in the air somewhere, up over a mountain or maybe a glacier, like something in a dream, something that needed meat.

But I stayed, and watched. The wind was coming in over the snow, and over me, and there was no way to tell, except for the feel of the wood bark under my hand, whether I was moving through trees with the thing I was on making the wind, or whether I was still, with the wind running toward me over the snow, and maybe the snow making and sending it. I could see the snow of the tundra just as well as I could make out the trees of the woods in Japan — or maybe could see it better, for it was closer to how I felt and what I wanted. I gave all I had to the snow, and it was there, in a long slope lying forward from a foothill, with about two hundred yards of level ground between me and the beginning of the slant. Marmot? No, hare. That would make me white, in my waiting. There was no lynx any-where I could see, but the possibility of one somewhere around rayed out and around me like electricity. I can tell you right now, it is exciting to hide. And there are ways of doing it that are better than others. When you hide without any cover, with-out any concealment except the way you are, and the country around you is like you, and there's not any difference that anything but you could tell between you and where you are, then you're in another place from where you seem to be: a place that's completely yours, and will be as long as you lie still. You amount to more than color, there, more than your fur or your skin the color of the country, because when you close your eyes — all you have to do is close your eyes — you're gone from that place, too, not in it anymore. You're the same as it, the same as it is.

I didn't close my eyes, but slitted them down to be as near to being completely gone as I could and still see, and waited in the wind for the lynx I could tell by my skin was somewhere around.

I never saw him, though, and the wind died, then came up again and was water, and ice was over me. I was still again, but in another way, with the wind in the form of a current. I could feel the curves of it in front of me and behind me — where I had been and where I was going — and I was hanging in a kind of hoisted standoff with it, holding what I had, keeping my head into it, maintaining. It was not as good as hiding in the open — white in white — but it was good in its way. I was in the dark, almost dead dark, but I knew that ice was over me, and snow over that, and there was a place right at the forward limit of what I could make out that looked like it might be a hole, and I moved up on it.

Moving was easy; the resistance of the current made it easier;

all I had to do was move my body a certain way and my face split
it to the heart. When I got under the hole I took up my kind of
hanging-there again, and looked up past the jagged edge of the
ice straight into the blue sky. For a second the other sky came
back to me, the one that had been on a level with me, that I
watched change into a round hole with two stars in it, at the end
of the pipe where I had hid on the Tokyo docks before the big
raid, damn near dying of shit gas, of waiting for the fire to fall.
That went away, and I was clean again in the current, my eyes
on the blue through the ragged ice. I went on, like a bullet with
a long jaw, on and on, bending with the curves, straightening
and hunting, hanging when I wanted to, where I felt like it.
There are a lot of things people don't understand about fish:
how everything in the world looms up, looms until you can almost see through it, and how a fish's eye cuts it out sharp when
the thing just wants to be a dim shape, and loom, and you won't
have it that way. A fish's eye cuts things into clean outlines and
then lets them go back to being dim when he's through with
them, when he goes on past. And there's always the feeling of
slotting through, but you never touch the sides of the slot. As I
say, there are a lot of good things about it, but hard to talk
about.

And then I was back on land, and had flowers on me, gray-
and-black flowers all over, and claws as long as a man's hand. I
had weight again, but not as much as you'd think for my size: if
I'd been any lighter I would not have left any prints on the
snow.

I went over it, looking for eyes. I ate almost nothing but
hares, hares on their big feet like snowshoes, when they forgot
to close their eyes in the middle of white. My ears tingled in the
wind, and the air above my ears, as I carried my gray flowers,

one foot after the other, looking for something in the field to disappear, two things together, to go out like candles. I was waiting like floating. My marks were like a ghost had made them, or the next thing to it.

The wind did all that, made it for me — the snow, the water, and what I was in them — when I gave myself all the way into what I wanted most, in the places where I wanted it. For the longest time, maybe most of the night, the train didn't make any sound, or I couldn't have told you if it did. Every now and then, while my mind and the solid air were still making the snow, I would watch the trees with nothing there but them, no pictures in between. Then the sound of the train would come back, and the feel of it moving me, and splits and the wavers in the track would rise up through the logs, and the logs would be real, the way they were sliding longways through the other trees.

What I really wanted was to see the shape, the shadow, move through the branches, like it had done before we stopped in the town. It had been there. It was, I can tell you, a real animal in real trees, and not one that I got out of the wind and laid over the woods and the dark sky. Mostly the trees were just a black wall going by, sometimes almost close enough to touch, I'd have bet, but a wall that quivered like it had an engine behind it, or something that was trying to get through. Whatever the animal was, I couldn't see it in that wall. It was when there was a break in the trees, and the sky showed between them, that I looked the hardest for whatever it was to take the leap across the free space. I had just caught a glimpse of it, back there, but believed I remembered that it was bigger, a lot bigger, than a squirrel, and bigger than a marten, but not as thick in the body or heavy as a wolverine. It might have been about the size of a fisher — a black cat, like my father used to say. I was watching for something about that size. I don't know why I thought I would see it again, but I did think so. I even felt like the whole situation owed it to me to show me whatever it was in a long jump — a short one would have done — where the trees got loose from each other for a second, and I could make it out. I felt that if that happened there was nothing in the world that I couldn't do, no place I couldn't get to, nothing I couldn't eat or fuck or kill, whatever. Finally, though, I let the wind give me back the snow, and I went into it with everything I had, like before.

It was night now, another night. Snow again, a slope down to a long valley almost like a tunnel. Caribou were in it again, moving through the valley, but I was not one of them. I was on a hill with some others like me, watching them, waiting for the time to move about a mile to the floor of the valley, going down in twos and threes when the stragglers fell back, and we knew it *enough*. We went when it was time, faster and faster down the slant, the snow not breaking under us, eye-first into the wind we made, and cut out a calf. The others came up, and we sat around looking at each other while the rest of the herd disappeared. I didn't call up the eating part, because it would have made me hungry, there on the train, and I didn't want that when I couldn't do anything about it. Even though it was night in the other place, and I was in the Japan wind, I felt the stillness we were in, sitting in the snow with the blood and the down calf in that valley in Alaska, and finally I did what the others did, and howled. I thought, Why not do the same thing here? Why not join up with what I had in my mind right then? Who would hear me? And so there, on the train, I howled, putting my head back like I should have done. I don't know how long I kept it up, but I was raised on that sound, and even though I don't remember that I'd ever tried it before, I'm sure it was not too much different. Nobody would hear me, and it might do some good. I believed it did, anyway, and I kept it up for a while.

Then I was white, and hunting again, but for something smaller. I was not like the lynx anymore, but was after something about my size. I had a taste for blood in my mouth, in my whole body — my body that borrowed something from snakes — that was stronger than anything in life, that had more power than the sun and the moon shining together. It was not just being hungry; it was way more than that, a lot more necessary. It was the taste, it was the color of it, the heat. It was what it came from: something alive and now not, the steam rising out of it before you tore it apart to eat. Everything about it was enough to drive you crazy, but you like it and want more, have to have it and will do anything to get it, will go for the color and the heat and the steam a long time after you've eaten all you want, and more. As soon as all the blood was out, you go looking for the next one, to do it again. You? I? Who? What had me was more than I was. I couldn't help myself and didn't want to. All I could do was what it said.

The dizziness didn't leave me, and the need didn't leave me, but I was bigger, and not white anymore. I was as strong as a bear and could climb like a squirrel. I was climbing, was not in the snow anymore, looking for mice and rabbits. A dead tree this time. Most of the branches were gone, but a few at the top, a nest.

I climbed up and looked in. There was a big bird, dead white, live white, with black speckles on his chest. He pulled back to the rim of the nest as I pushed in. I saw he couldn't fly — was too young maybe, as big as he was — but the wings went out anyway, a spread that covered up everything in white feathers, and I fired my head at him.

I stumbled into the air, because it didn't matter whether I could fly or not. The last thing I saw up there, with the swaying, was the eyes over the teeth, and then they were gone, and so was the nest.

In Japan the trees rushed clear — rushed, swept, I don't know — and one more time I looked for a four-legged shadow to cross the open air, to show for a second against the clean sky. If there was ever going to be the right time it was now, when I was falling in Alaska, tumbling, like when I bailed out over Tokyo, and yet not like it. Nothing crossed, and the trees flashed solid again. But in Alaska I was still falling, and hope was going. Inside the hopelessness, though, was something else that had just come into it, but had been there, too, in some kind of way. I jolted, a little like when the parachute had opened, but it was better this way. The chute had saved my life, but this was better — better, believe me, there are better things than life. I was whole in the air, long wings left and right, the color of snow, the color of cloud, and I was not falling but riding, riding over the whole frozen earth, whiteness everywhere under me, the land pushed up in hills and mountains, the rivers like white roads made out of white, going through white, the woods covered with snow, all hanging, all hanging with me, and pure, the whole earth as pure as it could get, and still, real still. All I heard was the air I was in, the wind holding me up in myself, over everything. Pure air: pure: pure. Pure riding. I looked up, and white cloud was there. Where I was, the clouds didn't have to be dark to snow, and these were not dark, but it was snowing, and I climbed up through it on air that was doing it for me, riding, rising, not moving a wing, to be inside the cloud. The wind was making another kind of sound, and I was everywhere, wanting to fall on something and kill it, fall all the way down, maybe thousands of feet: fall but not yet, because I was riding. I was riding in snow and on snow, in the whiteness where whiteness counted for the most it could. It held me that way, and I was riding.

Something under me — everything — jumped, and I woke up. Somehow or other I had got down amongst the logs again, and even had my feet in the bag of feathers. The train was jerking and slowing, and there was a little light, more than I should have let come. I didn't have any idea of when I'd gone to sleep, but I must have settled down without knowing it, and one of the logs had rolled part of the way over me, balancing on others, so that I had to struggle a good bit to get out. The train had slowed down even more, was jerking and bumping, and I knew I had better get off, because I didn't want to risk another town, and this one in daylight.

I hated to leave the train, in a way, and I hoped I could remember some of the things that had come to me out of the wind. Before I dropped off I lifted my head and tried it one more time, but I could hardly feel the air move past; that part of things was over. I did get one last flicker, though, just before I jumped. It was of a whole lot of deer heads. Just the heads, either because the bodies of the deer were buried in the snow or because the heads had been cut off and lined up. They were in a long row going out of sight, and if I had wanted to put a name on it, or maybe had the notion of making a picture out of it, I would have called it "Deer Head for Infinity," or something else just as crazy. I dropped off onto the ground, fell, rolled, got up with my bags and headed into the trees, feeling great.

It was rocky where I was now; everything for me was uphill. I went up over the rocks, big ones and, in between them and on top of them, a lot of little ones that would move and slip if you so much as touched them, seemed like. It was a place where you had to pay a lot of attention to what you were doing, where you put your hands and feet, and I did pay it, because a fall on that stuff would have been bad. I didn't mind skinning my knees or elbows, but I damn well didn't want to break anything. That would have put me out of commission, sure enough. At the beginning I was careful — more than that. Since my bailout I had lost some weight from all the walking, and from not having much to eat, and I could tell it, going up the rocks. I could jump farther if I had to, and when I landed my knees didn't bend as much as they would have before. And I believed I could run faster, too. For some reason, on those jumbled-up rocks the thought came to me of the flat land on the south of the Brooks Range, and the way I would run in the late spring, the first day I got off snowshoes. That was a wonderful time for me, when it seemed like half my weight was gone, and I could just fire out full blast down the valley with nothing to stop me, nothing to keep me from going faster and faster, until there was not any limit to me, and my feet damn near left the ground. Going up the rocks a little at a time was like that, though I couldn't tell you why. It's just the way you think at certain times, I guess, and the way you feel when you're doing it. After a while I noticed — it was kind of a surprise — that I wasn't paying all that much attention to where I put my feet anymore, but was going along just the same, with the rocks more or less cooperating with me, if you know what I mean.

I topped out, and stayed low. In front of me was a poor-looking valley, more like a gully or a draw, and then another ridge of hills, probably pretty much like the one I was on. Even with the rising mood I had, and the advantages of the lighter weight, I was fairly tired from all the climbing, and it came to me that I had not been scanning what was around me nearly enough. I took a good sweep now, before I started down. Far off to the left a small shape with legs, probably not a woman, was moving along the floor of the draw, and I sat down behind a rock until it went out of sight, carrying a bundle that bent the man almost double. He went, and after him I looked for the south side of the Brooks Range. It could have been the last of May.

But it was not quite that late in Japan, and that would work for me where I was going. I was in the valley left and right, though, and the main need I had was to run, because I couldn't believe I hadn't just stepped off snowshoes. A few steps, maybe. I did it, and was picking up speed. I had what I wanted, and was getting more. But my own speed scared me. I didn't know what I was doing; a few more steps and I would have really been gone. But I didn't give my speed a chance, a real chance, to take me out of control, and slowed down in time. I was breathing hard, harder than the running would have caused, and I looked right and left again, and then onto the next slope, rocky like the last one, and steeper.

I couldn't help it: I ran at the bank and went up over the first few boulders like they had been put there for me, and would stay, so that I could do the same thing again if I ever came back. From those first rocks I lifted, springing like, on and on, not looking at the top or anywhere around me, or even at the next rock that would come to my foot, and for a little while, I swear, I did it with my eyes closed. But then something told me that this was like running on the floor of the draw, that it was dangerous, and I ought to cut it out: slow down, not be crazy, at least not here.

When I slowed and stood on a pointed rock, my feet holding toward each other like pliers, but slanted, I was pulling in the air again by the buckets. It filled me to the brim with that place, and I was happy to be there. But when I got hold again and took a sight on what was in front of me and above me, I didn't feel all that good anymore. The rest of the slope was more like a mountain, and it would have been hard to do any jumping from then on. And, believe me, I didn't plan to close my eyes again, either.

So I went up. It was cold and overcast: pleasant cold, not the real stuff, and I started to sweat a lot. I was having to use my hands as well as my feet to climb, and though the hill didn't get any steeper, after I was about halfway, it did seem to stretch out and get higher, and it took me most of an hour to get to where I was, even near the top. I had hold of myself real well, though, and kept looking back and down, and tried to keep behind the biggest rocks whenever I could, so that I wouldn't be visible for more than half the time. The notion of what might be on the other side of the hill started to get stronger, because if I had to keep climbing like this for two or three more days without anything to eat, I would end up in bad shape, and might have to do something I ought not to. I couldn't make more than a couple of miles a day going along like this, and I couldn't do anything at night at all; I'd just have to hole up. But I was getting close to the top of this particular hill, and that buoyed me up some.

The light had changed, and it was afternoon, the sun out now and headed for the level where the top of the hill was. It kept striking off the rocks I was climbing, or was about to climb, like it was brushing over them, and then would come around and brush over them again. But on one it stopped, and even though

I was ready to go by, I stopped when the light did. It was not on a big rock, either, but on one that stuck out of the yellow dirt at a strange angle, not like a rock would have done. I straightened up, took some more air, bent down, touched it, and pulled on the part that was showing. It came up without any trouble, and I sat down and went over it, brushing off the dirt. It was a bone, a human pelvis, and there was not any doubt about it. That's a damn strange thing to be inside of somebody, I said to myself. And it was, and is. What I know about skeletons has to do with animals and fish, and I had never seen anything like this except in the medical and first-aid books my father kept in the cabin. But there the thing was, with the sun leveling onto it and then into it and through it, and it hit me that I could turn it — I was right there, and no one else — so that the light would come down through the hole in it and make a shape on the ground, on the slant yellow dirt of the hill, and it did, though not just like I would've thought.

Bone, damn sure. It had the feel, as it was in my hands, of something that had belonged in life. Where was the head? Where was the rest of it? I couldn't see any other parts, but that was not really something I was interested in. I took a good long look at what I had, and at the sun through the hole, which seemed to burn up a point on the ground. I saw something there, felt something. I remembered, at Barrow, the Eskimo women pounding for needles. Would this be possible? Bone, all bone; bone is bone; I would need to be able to do it. I positioned the pelvis. There was a rock — it could have been any rock, anywhere. There was another rock, and there was not anything to say I couldn't put the pelvis down and hit it with another rock, or that the whole thing wouldn't splinter into needles I could sew with, using what I already had, and what I could get:

winter clothes for where I was going to go, no matter what. Most of the things that live have got bones, which was a good thought.

I socked it. Nothing. Crumbs. And one half-assed piece, a kind of triangle, that I couldn't help thinking was telling me to fuck off, it was no use.

And it wasn't. I had a bad time right then. I could remember, but I couldn't remember enough. It was in that dim light, through the ice — the ice window, the ice panels, an igloo with burlap — that I could still see it: the old woman Ungalikuk, I think her name was, sewing what she was sewing, but I didn't have what she had. My attention, my interest, had not been strong enough. There was no use trying to bust up a pelvic bone, it just wouldn't work. I was ashamed of myself. Needles it would have to be, though, somewhere up north. But I had learned something I hadn't thought I'd learn, even so. It would have to be the long bones, where the grain ran right, not the center of things, not where the body hung together. Leg bones. Or arms, maybe. They would carry the needles.

I got up and dusted off my hands, climbed over the ridge and a little way down the other side of it, and picked up my heading. I went on like that, not making very good time. I slid a couple of times, not bad slides, or long, but bothersome, because I had got so self-conscious about breaking a foot or a leg, I would have done just about anything to keep from it. Finally I went down on the road, because there was nobody around, and I didn't see any reason not to. I walked on the flat road for about two hours, and made maybe five or six miles, when I heard something I didn't like, the sound of an engine. No, more than one, because the noise had that seesaw to it that you get when more than one engine is running. I went up the hill again to the next curve and got down behind some rocks, not big ones, but when I stretched out I was sure that nobody from the road could see me, especially with the up angle.

It was a truck convoy, all the way out of sight and moving very slow. The trucks, about the size of a GI six-by-six, were covered with dust, and if the soldiers in them had wanted to camouflage them to look like the road, they couldn't have done any better. When they were about halfway around the curve, the lead truck stopped, then all the others, one by one. A man got out of the first truck, went back to the second one, and said something to the driver, then to the third and on down the line. Wherever he had been, soldiers got out of the cabs and beds and stood around, waiting. They were as dusty as the road, but even with that, I could see that most of them were either old men or kids, though they were all in uniform. All the time I had been in Japan I had never seen a Japanese soldier whose uniform looked good on him. They were always too baggy or hung wrong in some way, and none of them was ever too small; they were always too big. What that might mean I didn't have any idea, but these were worse than most, even. As far as I was concerned there had never been such a bunch of sad sacks in the world, trying to be an army.

The original guy, the one from the lead truck, was taking his time, and I knew that until he came back the convoy would sit where it was, stuck in the dust. I was stuck, too, but like I usually do I tried to get some notion of what might work for me, if I would have a chance to steal a truck or some other type of motor transport, and it would be an advantage if I knew the setup from the driver's standpoint. I scouted along the line, and fixed on the truck where I could see into the cab better than into any of the others. I could barely make out the gears, and would have to see the driver shift when he got back in, though I didn't think, really, that I would be able to pick up that much information, because the driver's body would be in the way. I might get a glimpse of his hand shifting, and that would be something. Thinking that way, and waiting as the sun went on down and nothing happened, I tried to connect some of the few things I could remember that had to do with the Japanese and machinery. I didn't have to go far. I didn't need any more than anybody with good sense would have known: the Japanese love machinery, and they try their damnedest to be like white people, especially Americans. If it weren't for us they wouldn't have any factories, any cars, much less any airplanes. I would have bet that the trucks had the same gearshift as an American make.

Finally, after about an hour and a half, the head guy came back, got in the cab, and the convoy started to crawl. I kept my eyes on the one truck I'd picked out, and sure enough I caught a flash of the driver's hand as he upshifted, and it was exactly like I thought. He put the truck in third, and as far as I could tell kept it there. In a few minutes the end of the line went around the far curve and rolled through all the dust that the other trucks had stirred up. After the whole line had gone, the dust still hung there, lifting up little by little, though it never got as high as I was. Because I thought that maybe other traffic had built up behind the convoy, and might be coming along, I kept high and made what time I could, though it didn't amount to much.

There was always the problem of night, and I didn't have any plan this time except to keep going as long as I could. I'd always be able to bed down on the side of the hill, even if I had to dig out a place where I could lie level, and sleep with my feet in the bag of feathers. It was not something I looked forward to, but if that was the only way to go, I would do the best I could. I had been in worse places, because it was not really cold, not the kind of cold that I liked and could work with, but just kind of chilly, as people back in the States would say, and I would be able to sleep all right without any cover.

It was coming on for dark, but I could still see well enough to move, and I went up to the top of the ridge to get as good a view as I could. As soon as I topped out, I was surprised. There were some lights ahead of me, not many, but definite, and split in the middle. If the ridge went on as it was doing, I could, when it got a little darker and if I took my time, go past the village on the slope, and then, if I wanted to, go down and see what was there. I was looking for certain things, wherever people lived. One of them was food, and in the last few days, based on what I had been doing, and bringing back the years on the trap lines, I had got more and more into a state of mind telling me it was best to look at myself like I was a machine that needed to be taken care of in certain ways. Sleep I could manage almost anywhere. But eating was different. Every day it was a new problem, and every night. I didn't want to lose too much weight, for if I did I would be too tired to do some of the things I might have to do, and some I might want to do.

I came up on the village. The road ran through it and separated the groups of little lights, split them right in two like a river would have done. In about an hour I was past the town, and it was almost dark. The moon was just rising, and it was full, really beautiful. There was no need for me to try to stay under cover where I was, and I stood up straight, shook my swan bag until it evened out, checked the equipment taped onto me, saw that my knife was loose and hanging right, and went down toward the last light to the north.

It wasn't really the whole of dark yet. That would be in around fifteen minutes, or so I judged. When I got to the flat, I expected that there would be some people around, but that they wouldn't bother me if I didn't bother them. There was not anybody, though, and I came on toward the house, the one house I had picked out, little by little. This time I didn't have any notion of flashing my blade on whatever light there might be inside; I had already done that. I ducked behind a tree and tried to spot what I had an idea might be there. In the rising moon, a man came out of the house and went into the ground. That was what I had been looking for. The Japanese are big on caves. They had told us back on Tinian that the Japs can dig like moles, and will do it whether there's any reason for it or not — the old men, the women, and the kids. They store all kinds of stuff in caves, and where that man, as quiet as his shadow, went out of sight I knew there must be a cave. When he came out a few minutes later carrying two sacks, I knew this was a right guess, amongst the wrong ones I had been making. Again I waited; I was used to it. If the man needed something else, he would come back after it fairly soon, and when he didn't I would make my move, keeping low, in whatever shadows I could find.

I would have to use my flashlight on this one, though I hated to waste the batteries or risk somebody seeing it. When I got to the hole in the ground, I saw a short ladder going down about three or four feet, and that under it the ground was level. I hesitated for a minute, because a man can get trapped in a place like that. I had to get in and get out fast; there couldn't be any fooling around. Following my beam down, I got to the floor and looked around.

Sure enough, there were stacks of things, bags and big square tin cans. I didn't want to fool with the cans, but there was probably rice in the bags, or some of them. I picked one up, and could handle it. I tried another one, and it wasn't any heavier, but made some kind of sound when I shook it, like leaves, dead leaves, and I thought maybe dried fish, the scales and all. That would be enough; I would take whatever it was. I turned to the left and there were two human heads between me and the moon. I dropped the bags and put my hand on the knife. Someone was talking, and then someone else, and I could tell that they were kids, probably young ones, and they were looking right at me. I turned off my flashlight, left the bags, and started up the ladder. When I got to ground level, they had backed off, but they didn't run. That was good, real good. I went down the ladder again. The bags were made out of coarse thread, and if you could find a loose end, you could pull off however much string you wanted. I pulled loose a section and knotted the ends together, then went back up where the kids looked as though they hadn't moved a muscle. The moon was rising behind them, and I put my hands into the string and began to weave.

I made the moves with as much motion, slow motion, as I could, like I was a magician or something, making passes over some kind of object or person, casting a spell, you might say. When you have lived as many winters as I have with no place to go except out on the sides of mountains and in fields full of nothing but snow, nothing but a few trees when you're down low enough, and the only walls and roof you know are those in your own cabin where you live with your father, you pick up lots of ways to entertain yourself. My father had taught me how to make figures with string, designs and games. That was one of the things we did when we were not trapping mice, harnessing them to milk bottles with string, and making them pull the bottles around the floor. We even had teams of them, and ran races.

But right now I was weaving a complicated design we called Jacob's ladder, where, if you know how to do it, the string twines around itself, loops in and out and around, and comes out as a real interesting kind of ladder, like something that a combination of an engineer and an artist might have dreamed up.

If you watch somebody do it, you can't tell what's going on except that it's a tangle of string, until right at the last; that's the best, and I was saving it. To get steady, I sat down on the ground so the kids could get close to the string, and as I got ready to make my last move, their breath was warm on my face. The moon was big now, real big, and I glanced up at it so they would do it, too. Then I turned my hands over and there it was, the big silver-blue moon caught in the ladder. The kids came closer, so they could see it just like I saw it, and then little by little I changed the position of my hands, so that the moon walked step by step from the bottom of the ladder to the top, and then out into space again.

I got up, and without any fuss pulled the kids up, a boy and a girl. They were real little, not more than four or five, and I don't know to this day why they had come out to the cave, because they couldn't have moved anything in it. I put my finger on my lips, then went down the ladder and brought up the two bags. I took the string from around my wrist and put it around the neck of the bigger kid, the boy. They were both looking at me, and before they had been standing there too long, so that I would have to figure too much, I turned them around toward the house and, shushing one more time, gave them an easy push. I watched for just a second or so to see if they would run, but they didn't. I saw the boy reach for the string, and just as that happened I turned back to the road, walked on very fast with the bags until I was out of sight of the house, and then started up the hill, using my flashlight whenever I thought I ought to, and making good time for the conditions. In about half an hour I topped out over the ridge and went down the other side about twenty or thirty yards. When I came to a flat place I sat down and opened the bags with my knife. Sure enough, one of them was rice and the other was dried fish, cut up, heads and all. I ate a few pieces of fish, because I was damn hungry, and then some of the rice, raw. I wished I had had something to drink, because eating makes me thirstier than it does most people, but there wasn't anything, and I chewed the fish as much as I could to make it juice, but doing that made things worse, because of the salt. I put the bags on the downhill side, kicked open the sack of feathers, put my feet in, wrapped my arms around me with my hands in the pits, and went to sleep fast. The moon was like heat on my face.

I don't remember that I felt much chill that night. As the light began to come I woke up in a sweat that seemed to have been caused by the temperature in some way. I felt fairly bad, and I wondered if I was beginning to catch a cold. I didn't like that, because it meant that I would tire out easier. But the worst thing was the thirst. I was really very thirsty, thirstier than I had ever been in my life, except for the time when I ate some snow before my father could tell me not to do it. I was about four or five years old, and I thought the snow would just melt in my mouth and I wouldn't be thirsty anymore. You've got to melt it another way, however you can find, he said. I knew now that I had better not eat any more of the fish, so I closed up the sack. The two bags were too heavy and bulky to carry for any distance, so I spent some time getting a reasonable amount of rice and fish slabs into one bag, sorting out the heads and putting them in with about half the rice and a good many of the slabs in the other bag, which I kind of half buried in the dirt of the bank. Then, from the top of the ridge I went over the whole landscape, concentrating on whatever might tell me how to find water. My mind went back to the water wheel and the old woman, and I saw myself dipping out double handfuls from the buckets as they went up past me, diving into bucket after bucket, drinking all I wanted. Everything in front of me was dusty, though. The only possibly good sign I could make out was that the hills to the west looked like they might have some trees, because there were darker patches that I didn't believe could be made by anything else. I decided to cross and try that side of things, hoping for what might be in the next valley over.

It took me most of the morning to get across the valley. It wasn't all that far, but my heaviness was dogging me bad, and even though I just had the two bags now — fish and rice, feathers — it was still hard going. Some people — women — passed me on the road, and I trudged along behind them like I was going the same way, but when they went around a turn I started up the bank.

I had been right, for there were trees, small ones like scrub oak, and because the slope was steeper than the one I had just come from, I pulled up, some of the time, on the trunks and lower limbs, and when I got to the top I was really sucking wind, really tired — "joe'd," my father would have called it.

I blew a minute and then started down, because there was a big flat at the bottom and no road that I could see. I worked along the lower slope, where there were more trees than had been on the other side. Underneath, the land kept falling away until, as far off to the north as I could see, something flashed through the dry leaves of the trees. In an hour or so I came out over a big flat lake. I say flat because I've never seen a lake that wasn't flat, but I mean something else. As I got closer to it, it seemed to me that the lake must be very shallow all the way across, and when I scanned out through the trees, and made out a man standing two or three hundred yards from the shore with the water not even up to his knees, I knew I had been right.

I stepped out where he could see me, but he didn't even glance my way. He was fooling with some sticks or stakes that were rickety and kind of pulling on one another, which probably meant that there was a net run between them. I knelt down and drank as much as I wanted, then moved on, because what I was looking for was not the lake itself but what fed into it. If there were fish around I aimed to have some, and I like fish that live in water that's moving. I've fished in lakes a lot of times, and through the ice a few, but what I really like is a good stream. Water over rocks has got a private understanding with me, and if a creek has one fish in it, we'll get together, no matter how long it takes.

I spent the rest of the day going up the lake, taking all the time in the world, and as the lake tailed off I found exactly what I wanted. Woods on both sides closed down on a creek, and I got out into it and moved up it, not on the banks but on the rocks. My cold had not come on me, and the rocks in that running water took all the heaviness off. If there were fish in the lake, there would be some in the creek, but they would be more alive, and would taste better. The best thing in the GI survival kit was the packet of fishhooks, I remembered with a lift of blood in the stomach, and went on up the creek sure enough, but in the good sense — there is one — jumping from one rock to the other, my soft bags banging at me, not worried at all, where I was, about breaking bones or spraining an ankle; it wouldn't happen. I felt so good, to tell the truth, that I didn't see how anything could stop me, but the one thing that did stop me was perfect, it made the world right. A waterfall about fifteen feet high was there in front of me, and I stood on my last big rock and looked at it with the low sun striking gold across that pure white: whiter than cloud, whiter than egg white, whiter than snow, whiter than an eyeball, whiter than anything.

There was a dry thicket downstream a few yards from the falls, and I set up a kind of camp there. I could really take my time, and I wondered if I might not want to stay maybe a couple of days and rest up, make things comfortable, eat and drink as much as I wanted and really get myself recharged. I could fish at night as well as in the daytime, and I could make a fire here, and cook. I didn't see any reason in the world why anybody else would come here. I couldn't see any signs that the place had ever been visited, and I was sure I could stay as long as I had a mind to. I put off that decision, though, and broke out the survival kit, with the packet of fishhooks and the nylon twine that went with them. I wanted to work by the last of daylight so as not to use up any more of my flashlight, and even though I was going to make a fire later, I didn't want to tend a fire and fish at the same time; some things ought to have all of your attention. Besides, I wanted to fool with my rig, make it right, and see myself doing it. I cut off a short piece of the string and tied it onto the main line, then found a rock and made a sinker out of it. I cut off some more twine, rigged two hooks, and baited them with pieces of the dried slabs. I sat back in the thicket and cast out, just this side of the falls and almost under them.

The light was down now. The gold had been pulled off the falls, and the whole of that straight-up water was turning blue. The sound was the best sound on earth, and with that, and with pulling the line until the most sensitive and alert area that existed anywhere, in anything alive or dead, was in the forefinger of my right hand, where the string went across it — I could have felt it if a fly had lit on the line — everything locked into the good.

For a while nothing happened. The line going out of the thicket seemed to shorten; it was just that I couldn't see as far along it as before. But that was not important. I might just as well have been blind, because what mattered was somewhere in the water, and my finger would be the only way to know it.

A difference, then: not a strike, not anything you could call a strike, but more like a change. Not much change, but there. I pulled some and felt it happen just a little stronger, then turn into a real fluttering tug, and I pulled, not too hard but quick. Something was on.

I brought it in, and risked my flashlight for a second to look. It sure wasn't a trout, which for some reason I had expected it might be. I had never heard of any fish in Japan except the carp, which they told us was supposed to be magic in some way — the Emperor's ponds, so they said, were full of them — and this might have been one. It had a fair amount of meat on it, and not a whole lot of fight, and I laid it down on some leaves and baited up again. The same thing happened twice, and I quit, because I didn't think I could eat any more. I raked up some twigs and leaves, and made a circle with some rocks to keep the fire closed in on itself, and then took out the flints.

Ever since I was a little boy I had used them, and it had been a long time since I couldn't raise a spark on the first shot. That was still true, though I couldn't get a leaf to burn with the first one. But on the third or fourth try a leaf caught. I lit another one from it, then another from that, cross-stood some twigs over them, and when they caught, some more over those, and in a while I had a very nice fire there, with the rocks wheeling around it. I pulled in as many twigs as I could from where I was sitting, slit the fish open, gutted and filleted them with my issue knife. To do things right I needed to boil the rice, and thought I might use the lid of my survival kit; it was not supposed to break. I made a kind of grill of branches, scooped up some water, and put the rice on and let it stay long enough to absorb the water. Then I stuffed the fish, sharpened some twigs, ran them through the sides to hold things together, and did what I could to cook, keeping the fish over the flame with a couple of branches.

It worked out pretty well, if I do say so. It may be that I was hungrier than I thought, and the smoke smell got my glands going, but I never tasted anything better, and was so anxious to get the next fish going that I spilled a whole handful of rice into the fire while I was doing it. With the last one I thought I would try something else, so I cooked some more rice but left the fish raw, and ate that way. I must say it was better cooked than not, but it was not bad the other way, either. When I finished and raked up leaves to make a bed before I put out the fire, I felt so comfortable and secure, with the waterfall standing like it was watching over me, looking out for me, that I made the decision I had been putting off. I would stay one more day, and two if I felt like it. I would get cleaned up in the creek, and even shave, though I didn't have any soap. When I went out of there I wanted to feel like I could take on anything.

❖   ❖   ❖

Two days it was, strange and good. I didn't see another living thing except the fish, which were easy to catch and tasted better and better. During the days, I went out and ran on the rocks, almost down to the lake and then back, breathing deep and sometimes almost singing, but I couldn't tell you the tune. If anybody was to try to think of having fun in a place and a situation like I was in, with not a whole lot of a chance to stay alive, he would have a hard time believing it. There was no friend anywhere, only thousands of people who wanted to cut off my head, castrate me, do anything they could to me. But fun it was, anyway, those two days and three nights. Before I left I knew every rock, from the waterfall to the lake, and the last afternoon I went up and down them twice, trying for some kind of personal record, running with the current and then against it, with the banks, and racing downstream with special leaves I set going. The leaves were dry, and there were some big ones, and I picked them by how much they curled up on themselves and rode high in the water, going through the rapids better than anybody'd have believed. These things happen, you know; all you have to do is watch. When I won the last race, just by a hair, I turned back and went all-out for the waterfall, racing the bank shadows, the branches and spikes alongside.

In between races I swam and shaved. The water was cold enough to turn your skin a bright blue, but it was worth it, and when it got dark enough so that there wouldn't be any chance of my smoke being seen, I heated some water and shaved by feel as the dark came on, whetting the blade of my GI knife every now and then, and getting the hairs off as close as I could. Clean and dry, I lay down on the leaves by the fire and watched the thicket grow almost solid over me. Almost, but not quite, because between the spikes I could see stars, some in the places I wouldn't have expected, and some where I would, as though they were made to be there. I was too happy and lazy by then, and full of fish and rice, to look for Polaris, but I knew where it was. I wished I had had sense enough to find out more about the stars, the names of them and where they were at the different seasons, when I had the chance. The navigator of my ship, Lieutenant Stennis, was a real shark at all that, and he would have shown me about the stars, the constellations, and anything else I wanted to know if I had just taken the trouble to ask him. It would have been fun to pick out different stars through the twigs without moving from where I was, to know their names, to feel the difference that knowing a name makes. But I was left with what I had: being able to find Polaris and pick out two or three of the biggest constellations, like the Dipper and like Orion, which is the prettiest thing up there. It didn't take much of this to put me to sleep, and I have never slept better in my life, as safe under those spikes and crooked branches and twigs and stems as if I were lying inside a rock, one that let in air, and through which you could see stars whenever you opened your eyes.

❖ ❖ ❖

I was not happy when I left, though in a way I was, because I knew the feeling couldn't last, and that I couldn't make it last just by staying there, even in a place I felt so right about. It had done its job. When I climbed up past the waterfall, clean, with my legs feeling about twice as strong and sure as they had since I left Alaska, I had the confidence I needed. I was moving with plenty of new power, as though I had eaten something magical, or swum in water that had radium in it, or had a transfusion of something that was better than blood. No blade could penetrate me. A bullet fired right at me would have curved and gone around.

I worked back east, a little east of north now, because by my silk map it looked as though I would have to do this to come out on the north coast where the strait between Honshu and Hokkaido was the narrowest. It would take me some time to find the right place. If I was lucky I could do it, because I would be able to see the other island from this one.

When I came out of the woods there were long fields with terraces on the other side of them going up the hills, and the sun was warmer than it had been for the last few days. There was some traffic on the road, so I stayed fairly far west of it, and went along pretty well, moving close to the trees in case I needed to get back amongst them for any reason. A few people were in the fields, but nobody bothered me. As I noticed before, the Japanese spend most of their time looking at the ground, and they don't even seem to like to look at each other. The heads stayed down, every one, or at least until I was gone.

The woods gave out, the hills flattened some, and there was a lot of open space now, which bothered me. I sat in the last bushes and looked out over the terraces in front of me. People were working in the lower ones, though only a few. I had had to deal with the terraces once or twice before, but I'd climbed up at night, and I felt that if I kept on operating that way I could not make the distance I wanted. This seemed like it might be a good time to try to work out some way of getting across the terraces in daylight, if I needed to.

I had come far enough east, I believed — though I was just guessing — and could work back to the west, at least a little. I seemed to have better luck that way, better conditions, better going. I didn't have any particular plan for getting through the terraces except to pretend to be working like the others were doing, and just maneuver to the edge of the next terrace and scramble up onto it when nobody was looking. I didn't think my bags would bother any of them, because they all had stuff around them, wherever they were. Just before I left the trees I had a notion that stopped me for a minute and gave me something to look for; it was always better if I had that. All these terraces, all this land, this work in the fields — who got the benefit? I didn't know anything about the government of Japan, and didn't care, but I had the idea that the government didn't own the land, that it probably belonged to families, to people who had inherited it or maybe bought it, which meant there would be rich people somewhere around. Rich people, and the houses they lived in. I might have passed some of these but not paid any attention to them — or enough, anyway. This would be different.

I made it across the first terrace by keeping as much distance as I could from any people, and climbed up onto the next level, where there were only a few workers a couple of hundred yards away, bent over like always. On the third terrace a man stood up, put one hand on his back and the other over his eyes, and hollered something at me. I bent down and wondered what I would do if he came to me. He didn't, and edging over a little slower than I had before, I got to the bank and went up. It took me all afternoon to work into the top field. I came to a path there, and even though I was on the ridge and anybody could see me, I went along it until it dropped and led through a clump of those same little trees that grew around the waterfall. They were spaced different, though; I didn't have the feeling I was in a real woods or among trees that grew like they would have if they were wild. I probably knew more about Japan already than I thought I did. I had noticed, for one thing, that the Japanese like to arrange whatever they can get their hands on, to have as much neatness as they can; arrangement is big with them. I had never been in a forest of arranged trees, but it was easy to walk there, and not bad. After about half a mile I came on the house. It was bigger than most of the houses I had seen in Japan, and to the side it had one of those weird arches of wood that look like they might be big doors or gates, except there's never anything behind them. They just sit out in the open.

My way is to wait, as long as I have to. I got fairly close to the house and set up behind a tree that lined up with another one between me and the house. Arranged trees are good cover, I could see that. As it was just beginning to get dark, about quitting time for everybody and everything except the predators, a bunch of men came along the same way I had and went to the house. A door opened — slid open — and another man stood there, not coming down, and talked to them. There didn't seem to be any excitement in the talk, and nobody moved his arms around. The Japanese are very excitable, and if the slightest thing bothers them, whatever is not exactly what they're used to, they talk fast and loud and throw their arms. There was not any of that, though, and I took it to mean that none of them had thought there was anything strange about my being in the terraces, if I had even been noticed at all. I didn't recognize any of them, but they must have been some of his workers; there was nobody else for them to be. Finally they left, and the night kept coming.

About the time the first stars started to show, a dim light changed the house. On my side was a window, a big one, and there must have been a blind over it, because the light was not only dim but had a haze to it like it was shining through cloth, the kind bandages are made out of, or maybe slats real close together. I moved up.

I saw things like this as being no different from a stalk, and used everything that was there, going from shadow to shadow, and from my toe to my heel on every step. Nobody in the house could have heard me, even if he had been listening. Looking, maybe; listening, no. I stepped up on the one wooden board that took my eyes to the level of the window, and started to try to penetrate. At first I couldn't make out anything, but when I got used to it, I could see a couple of shadows, and they were sitting down. I moved side to side, and up and down, until I found a chink that gave them to me. There was an old man and a woman not quite as old. The man sat near a corner, and the woman was putting things on the floor, probably getting ready to eat. She moved very slow, and after a few minutes got up and went into another room. To do this she had to slide a part of the wall, or panel, and she didn't make any more sound than I had. Everything was so quiet; it was more quiet than anything in the woods. She came back with some bowls and dishes, and the man, without any hurry, came and sat cross-legged where the food was, and near something that looked like they probably cooked on it.

I went over everything I could see, which was not a whole lot. There were three sets of panels, and before I went in, I thought it would be good if I knew what was in the other rooms, if I could find a way to look in. I moved to my left and around the corner, but there were no windows on that side. I went around. In what I took to be the back, there was a window but no light. There was a door, too, and I pulled on it just enough to see that it would slide. The other side of the house didn't have a window either, so I came back to the door, pushed it open just enough, left it that way, and went in. I could have waited until they went to sleep, but there might not be any light then, and I would be at a disadvantage I didn't want.

I was at one, anyway. I thought I had better not try to make out just by feel in such a dark place; I would be sure to hit something, trip, make a noise. I risked one step, feeling with my foot, then another, which should have put me in the middle of the room. I needed to find the other door, and there was nothing to do but use the flashlight for a second, let the setup brand on my brain, move a couple of steps, cut the light, and take hold of the panel. I should come out behind the man. I figured to take them fast.

I got set for the light, and hit the switch. The door, with a big red dragon design on it, fire out of his mouth and all, was right in front of me, and out of the side of my eyes I could tell that this was a room used mainly for clothes and stuff that hung up. There was a bed almost flat to the floor that I had just missed in the dark. I could have busted my ass, might even have pitched through the screen flat on my face. Luck, sure. I pulled out my long blade, made for American kitchens, and put my hand on the door. I knew which way it slid.

I moved the panel. It didn't make any sound, but he heard it. He was on his feet in a crouch before I could even take a step, and was halfway to the wall before I tried to cut him off. I couldn't get the shot with my knife I wanted, but I tried anyway and missed, and drove through the panel, which was paper, or something like it. By the time I pulled back, he had a sword that he held with both hands, like a baseball bat. He came at me flat-footed, and then with a loud low scream like an explosion swung the blade. I backed off and held up my knife, and it was gone like a bell had rung and made it disappear; that was his blade on mine. I heard my knife hit the wall, the panel, and for the first time since I had been in the room I made a good move. I faked and went around him, as fast as he was. I jumped faster than he could turn, and was down the panel and through it, closing it before he could get to me. It was dark in there — not completely dark, but almost. Now, I thought, now. And then: No, not now.

I pulled my issue knife, my short one. The panels were closed at both ends, and even if I couldn't hear them move, I would know it as soon as one of them changed. I had my hand on the one I had just closed, my fingers as sensitive as they were on the string when I'd fished by the waterfall. If he moved the panel at my end I would hit him through the paper before he knew it. If he tried to put the sword through the paper, hoping to hit me blindside, he would miss, and would have given himself away. I'd be all over him, too, if he did it. I had my eyes on the panel at the far end, and if it showed any new light I would ease my own panel, look out, and locate him.

Nothing happened. He knew I was there, somewhere along the panel, and he knew that I would try to kill him if I could, and probably his wife as well. I felt building up the need to take a risk, maybe just a small one, to find out more than I knew, standing there in the dark with half my nerves in my hands and the other half in my eyes. That couldn't last for long, and I knew it. I believed he would not think I had stayed at the same place where he saw me disappear. I slid the panel a crack, didn't move my feet, and looked out.

There was no one in the room. Now what? My first thought was that he had left the house and gone to get some other people. He might have gone out the back, the way I had come in, and taken his wife with him. But I was willing to gamble that he hadn't. One of the other things I had noticed about the Japanese, besides how excitable they were, was their pride, especially the men; the women didn't have much say. And this old man with the sword was a soldier — a samurai, or whatever the name is — and would have that pride. He would defend his house. He would not let some stranger run him out. And as I kept looking into the empty room, more came to me. If the guy was a warrior, from the warrior class, like they say, he would not only fight, but he would *want* to fight. He was the quickest man I ever saw in my life. He had probably been using that sword, in one way or another, for fifty years, and this would be his last chance to use all that training. Quick, he was quick. I didn't say fast. Fast means running; I didn't know whether he was fast that way, but it didn't matter. I didn't plan to run.

The only other possibility was that he was still in the house, behind one of the other three panels, and if that was so, he had me in the same position that I'd had him in. He was invisible; I had to go look for him. I had to move the other panels, and he would be in there in the dark, and he would be able to see my silhouette as soon as I let the light in. And that was not all: he could move from one paneled-off room to another. We could keep this up all night, until somebody made a mistake, or guessed wrong. And I was at one other disadvantage, too. I was up against somebody who could hear better than I could. I hated to admit it, but it was true. I would never have believed it in a million years.

Disadvantage; advantage, maybe. Most of the movies I had seen in my life were cowboy movies. I hadn't seen many, but in

171

at least three or four of them was a scene where two guys are shooting at each other from behind rocks, and the hero pitches a rock over behind some other rocks, the other guy raises up and fires in that direction, shows himself, and the good guy mows him down. Why not? I thought in the dead quiet. Why not something like that? I felt around and pulled some silk stuff off the wall — a gown or a dress of some kind — and balled it up very slowly, using one hand against my side. This would have to be a soft sound, not a rock making a big clatter, bouncing off other dry rocks, but soft, real soft. I leaned out a little and pitched the silk so that it would fall close to the middle of the room. I slid the panel down to a fine crack and watched. This was my bait.

Up in the cabin I used to read a lot. My father was a good hunter — pretty good, anyway, but not as good as he wanted to be. He had a lot of books up there in the cabin with the one red wall, with the snowshoes and rifles, and the mice pulling the milk bottles. More than half the books were about hunting: hunting in Africa, and India, and places all over the world. There was even one story about men hunting each other, like big game. The thing that struck me the most of anything I read was about a man who hunted alligators in the Everglades swamp in Florida with an Indian who took him around and showed him where the big alligators were. The hunter was going for the biggest trophy in the swamp with a bow and arrow, and the Indian had to get the alligator to come in for a close shot. What stuck with me was that the Indian touched the surface of the water with the end of a pole, just barely touched it, and the alligator came, and the guy shot him with his bow. This was something like that: my touch on the surface of the silence was the roll of silk out in the middle of the floor, and I watched the other panels, one after the other, and then back. Believe me, I watched.

And finally one moved, just a hair. It was not the one I would have expected, the one opposite me, but the panel I had first come through, in the room that went to the outside, where I had left my shoes.

Things had narrowed down, but I was still up against his ear. No matter how quiet I was, he could hear me. The logical thing would be to move down to the end of my room, which was like a long dark hall, open up real sudden, and jump him through the other panel as hard as I could and as fast as I could. But if he heard me — and he would — he would then be able to make a move of his own, would hit me with that fantastic speed, or would be gone. Or I could move out into the center of the room and dare him to come at me, but right away I knew I wouldn't do that. He had too much quick, too much training for me; the life I had behind me would not stack up to his, at least in hand-to-hand.

I could step out, let him see me, cross the room, and go in behind the other panel. That way, he would have three choices. He could change panels and come into the dark hall where I would be, and we could have it out there. I would be able to see him come in, and he would not have all that much of an advantage in the dark. I liked this. I wanted to pull him in, like the guy did the alligator. The sound of silk had done part of it, the sound of silk falling. It might be that the dark would do the rest. I believed he would come in there with me. I had the image of him staying outside, in the main room, and stabbing back and forth through the panel, and I knew that wouldn't work, and he would know it. And he would know, also, that I'd learned enough not to stand up against him in the open. It was my notion that his pride would bring him into the room behind the panel on the other side. I felt this so strongly that I didn't believe there could be any other way to go.

I stepped out and went over. It was like crossing water so deep there was no bottom to it. The depth was the danger in itself. There is that pull, you cross on top, and you know what you've been over. I got to the other side, opened the panel and closed it, knowing that he had seen me and would have to deal with my new position. It wasn't like on the side I'd left, where I was sure I couldn't stay very long. Here, on this side of the depth, I was not worried about that. I would stay as long as it took.

Not long, not too long. The far panel opened, the light came in and stayed on the wall of clothes, on the bed between. The old man flat-footed forward, his sword at something like port arms, except that both hands were on the handle, the blade across his body, hip to shoulder. But this time was new, he was new: his head was forward, peering, in a way it hadn't been in the main room. I could maybe risk some sound, and I hit my bare heel on the floor. He took another step and swung, but he was at least ten feet from me. He swung again, backhanded, and then went into his crouch — his defensive position, must have been. It was clear; it was clear, slow, then right away. Sound was his, but mine too, if I could use it. Sight was mine, and in the almost-dark there was no way he could use it.

I hit the floor again, the mat. He began to fight, but he was fighting a ghost, or maybe more than one of them. He still had that marvelous quick — I had never seen anything better — but it all went into the dark, and into his form. The moves of that long blade in the dim light were like a weave of steel, a net of metal and light. He thrust out, he pulled back, he swung the sword like a ball bat, he came forward, he backed up, and all the time his balance was perfect. I didn't breathe and, almost caught in that net, for a second I thought I had everything. I thought I did. But I couldn't wait, and I didn't. I would not ever forget, though. He must have been almost blind. But still quick, too quick. I led him with sound, he came in, he came onto my knife. I held it for him, just so. Even though his jugular must have been cut, judging from the fire-out of blood, he stayed on his feet, still making his moves, holding his form, holding on to his ancestors, who must have been soldiers, sure enough. Then, with the blood coming weaker, he went down, rolled, and I hit him through the back of the neck, cut the cord, and finished him. He was still from then on out, but for me he would always be the one who made that weave of steel. Any lick would have cut through both forelegs of a bull elk, and I would always be just outside, but watching; that was the best. "You're a good one," I said. "You sure are. I can use you."

❖   ❖   ❖

I went back into the main room, got my knife, which was just like it always was, except the relation was not quite the same. I needed to find the woman, and started through the rooms. She was down behind some clothes, near the door where I had come into the house, not too far from my shoes, and I ran her through twice without her making a sound, then laid the body out and put silk over it. I felt that maybe some of the good had come back into my blade, but I knew also that it would take more than that to get back what had gone out of it when it got knocked loose from me.

I dragged the old man's body out of the long hall and stretched it out near the table where he and his woman had been eating. I was thinking bone, long bone; I was thinking needles. If I got up as far north as I meant to, I would have to be better than any Eskimo; whatever I could pick up in the way of know-how I had better get. I was still disgusted with myself for the time back on that yellow slope, with myself and the pelvis. This would be different, I was hoping. I peeled back the guy's sleeve, and with my small knife I cut open the inside of his forearm, running the tip of the blade down the bone from his elbow to his wrist. Then I pulled a low stout bench from the wall it had been next to, laid the arm on it and brought down the handle of the old guy's sword as hard as I could, three or four times. The bone cracked well enough, and I pried loose three long splinters and broke them off. The fire in the little cookstove on the table was still going, with some meat in the pot, and I ate it while the bone splinters dried. It was good meat. I didn't think there would be much of it in Japan, the way the war was going for them, but this guy was rich, and I guess he could have had about anything he wanted. When I finished, I took up the splinters and looked them over. They were dry now, and the points on them were sharp, as sharp as any needle you could want. I didn't want to work with them that night, but I did need to know if I could make eyes in them, so I took one of my fishhooks to see if I could penetrate the bone, and it turned out OK. I guess I could have straightened out the hooks themselves, and sewed with them, but I wanted them like they were. They had the waterfall in them, which was maybe the best place I had ever been in my life.

I was real tired, but maybe a little more excited than I should have been, so I walked around the room real slow, seeing what was there. It bothered me that there were no pictures or deco-rations, but I was not quite right about that, because off from the light, in a corner, was a table with a vase on it and one flower. Funny, the flower didn't seem to be there in any way an ordinary person would put it. It's hard to explain, but it was like it was there as part of an arrangement from which the other flowers had been taken away. It reminded me of the jackstraws my father and I used to play with up in the cabin. You let a whole bunch of sticks fall any way they want to, and so far as you know, they should've come out that way — even that they wanted to, and knew about it before they fell, and even made it happen like it did. This flower had that about it: one jackstraw, right there, and right.

Up above the flower was a picture — I could barely make it out — of a young guy in a military uniform, probably the old man's son, or grandson, maybe. I went into my first room, got my shoes from outside, and lay down on the pallet. I was not worried about anything. I thought about the needles with a lot of pleasure, because I had done something I never had before, and if I was going to live off the country when I got to where I was headed, as I planned to, this would help.

I slept pretty well, and it was first light when I woke up. Everything was very quiet, and I spent some time getting my-self reorganized. I thought that when the sun came up the men who had talked to the old guy the day before would probably come back, but that they wouldn't come into the house without being asked. Sure enough, about eight o'clock there was a light knock at the door, and I was sure it was the same people. I sat on the pallet until they went away, and then started going through the house for anything I might be able to use. I didn't believe the others would be back that day, but I didn't think, either, that it would make sense to stay there more than just that day, and planned to leave before the sun broke again.

The old man and I were about the same size, though he was a little heavier. That was good, because the bagginess of his pants made it easy for me to fill the layer between two pairs of them with feathers. I spent all day sewing, with strips of silk I cut out of some of the stuff hanging on the wall, and by the time I finished I had two pairs of pants and two coats, all layered with swan feathers. That would do for a start; that would do pretty well. I needed some socks, or at least something I could wrap around my feet, and some gloves, and I found some with three fingers, but they would be all right since I didn't have anything else.

I started the charcoal fire at the table and ate more meat, and then spent the last part of daylight going everywhere in the house I could, looking for light metals, anything thin and strong and, if possible, flexible. I wanted to streamline my bag, make it as light as I could and still have what I needed, and not any bulkier than I could help. I had some feathers left. I could have used them all, but for some reason I didn't want to: I guess I had just got used to having them with me. The clothes I had sewn were hardly heavier than the feathers themselves, and with the other feathers, a couple of long things like skewers I wrapped up in silk, gloves, an extra pair of shoes, and a heavy hat with ear flaps, I had what I wanted in the bag. That, plus the stuff I had taped on me, would be all I needed. I thought for a while that I might take the old man's sword, because I could use it for hacking brush, say, or chopping light kindling. But in the end I left it, because I couldn't see any way I would be able to do any fighting with it. I wanted to remember how the old man looked when he was coming after me, like the sword was a part of him, and the air in front of him was like a net — not on fire exactly, but electric, sparking. I put some more silk over him, dark silk, and the sword on top of that, without the scabbard. I stowed the bag next to the back door by the woman's body and lay down again, and might even have laughed a little at the idea that I would be leaving before the break of light, the only American gunner in Japan who was sighting on Polaris and carrying two feather-layered coats and two pairs of pants, shoes, a flap hat, what was left of a bag of swan feathers, and two pairs of three-fingered gloves.

❖   ❖   ❖

I woke up slow, and there was nothing around me. Then, in my mind, and more or less in the dark in front of me, too, there was that net of light again, the swarm of spark strokes that had come from the sword of the old blind fighter. This was a new place to start from, and a new way. Suddenly I could think a long distance ahead of me. I saw mountains, lakes, roads, and rivers, and on all of them it began to snow. The landscape moved upward, and was a kind of combination of what I had seen in Japan and what I remembered from Alaska, which was a lot, everything that mattered. There was a boat in it, because — and this came in last of all — I was going to have to cross water to the other island, and I already knew I would have to do it at night; that was exciting. I rolled over and sat up.

I decided to use a little of my flashlight again, to portion out the light like it was water or food, like somebody who was in a lifeboat after a shipwreck, maybe with some other people, would have to do. Before that, I needed to try to get a line on where I was as I lay there watching the storm of sparks from the sword. I had been in Japan for a week or so, and I tried to estimate how far from Tokyo I had come. On foot, not very far:

fifty miles, maybe. My main distance had been made on the log train, and I didn't have any real way to tell how many miles I had covered. I had spent a lot of the time making pictures in my mind and projecting them out on the landscape — the deer heads moving toward infinity, or somewhere — but even if I hadn't done that, I still couldn't have come up with much of an estimate. The train had been slow but steady, and I may have made a hundred miles, or even more. That sure was the best I could do in the dark. The map and the light would have to come now. Light, a little of it, a very little, a short ration. I spread the silk map on the floor and smoothed it out: silk, everything silk; I had even brought some of it myself. If I had estimated correctly, or even guessed anywhere near right, I had made two hundred miles, or maybe even as much as two hundred and twenty, and needed to go about that much more. The notion that I had come halfway from Tokyo to the northern tip of Honshu was encouraging, even though I knew that the guess was off, had to be off, and maybe by a long way. Still . . .

I looked for lakes, and there were a lot of them. They all had rivers running into them; I couldn't be sure that any of them had a waterfall just up from it. One was near where my estimate had brought me out, and if that was so, I had another checkpoint, though that could have been far out, too; far off my reality. If I was where I guessed, I was not far south of a range of mountains, and if I slanted a little to the northeast I would pass between it and a town called Morioka. If I made it through there, held course for about thirty miles, I could then take up a true-north heading and work my way onto a peninsula that would bring me as close to Hokkaido as I could get. Then would come the boat and the night water. That was a new thrill every time I thought about it. I remembered the deep, pure

interior blue of the iceberg, with Tornarssuk and I stopped
beyond words, both paddles out of the water. What a thing that
was: the only color in the world, a new color, with life in it, the
life of the heart of ice, which came clear when everything between it and us tore off, slid, and fell.

There didn't seem to be much population on the peninsula,
though there was bound to be some, because Japan depends a
lot on fishing — so said the Colonel — and right along the
coast there had to be a good many people. People and boats.
That would be for later. I saved my forward thinking about
Hokkaido for later, too; that was special in another way. I left
off all that, switched out the light, stowed it, and got up, the last
thing in my head the idea that I could scout out my position
on the peninsula by knowing — or believing, anyway — that I
would be able to see Hokkaido from the shortest distance to it
over the strait. I surely should be able to see it, since it didn't
look to be more than twenty miles, or maybe not even that.

I got my gear together, put on my shoes, and went out. I
didn't even take a last glance at anything in the house. There
was not anything to see that I hadn't already seen, and the
old man and woman would lie there until somebody found
them. I planned to be a long way from there when that happened.

I struck off to the northeast through woods and hills. I was
still in the same clothes, but the idea that I had two cold-
weather outfits in my bag gave me confidence, especially together with the fact that they had been sewn with bone needles,
that they had that kind of life. I was looking forward to getting
into one of them. That would have to be at a special time, and at
a place that had something for me.

The hills were pretty steep, and though I didn't run into

anybody, or have to make a lot of detours to keep away from people, I didn't make very good time, and got tired faster than I would have liked, with all the climbing. The hills were like foothills, and I thought that there was probably a higher range to the west, which I wanted to stay away from; it was not time for the mountains yet. In the afternoon there were some snow flurries, and I reckoned that I might have to get into one of my new outfits sooner than I'd thought. Still, I didn't yet.

Since I was getting so tired, I found that I kept pulling off my course. My feet, without my knowing until I realized it, had been trying to search out level ground, to make things easier. I crossed an east-west road, went through some trees and bushes, and then found myself moving up on a situation different, a lot different, from anything else I had ever been close to, or even thought about.

There was a light ground fog over a big field that I couldn't see the ends of, to left and right. I hadn't noticed any fog, or that the air was moist, but as soon as the field developed in front of me — or half developed is more like it — the fog was there as though the field had made it. More than that, had made it for what was happening there. Some people were moving around, and I watched them, and it wasn't long before I was studying as much as watching, they were so quiet and strange. The fog was not thick enough to do anything but blur the outlines of things, and it was not hard to see that the people — all men, I thought — were dressed the same, in long white dresses or robes, their eyes all on the ground. They seemed to be looking for something, and a few of them had baskets. They were just there in the field, in that fog, blurred, but they could not disappear.

Very slowly they crossed back and forth, and every now and

then one of them would pick something up and put it in a basket. Nobody had ever had a dream so quiet as this one which had movement in it. I remember going to sleep one summer in the Classen River valley and opening my eyes and finding a whole herd of deer, with two big bucks in it, standing not fifteen yards away, looking at me. I closed my eyes and opened them again almost right away, and they were gone. I had not heard a thing, and to this day I don't know whether they were ever really there or not. That was the quietest movement up until now. Nobody said anything, nobody did anything except sleep-walk back and forth, crisscrossing without touching, not speaking, like they were all going to do this forever, through all the seasons, through rain and snow and sun, whatever there would be. There must have been seventy-five of them at least, and with a .50 caliber — or even a hand-held .30 — I could have laid them all down in just a couple of three-second bursts. I don't think any of them would even have looked up, but just gone on crisscrossing until there was nobody left to cross. Believe me, they were not like soldiers, and I had no fear of anything to do with them. While I was standing there the fog thickened a little, and I took a couple of steps clear of the woods, and came out where they could see me, if any of them wanted to. Just as soon as I had set up in my new position, one of the men, out in the middle of the group, straightened and came toward me, not with any special hurry, but different by his motions, working through the others toward me. I let him come, not wishing for machine guns; no need.

For some reason I was thinking about the feet of the men in the field, and the way they were taking their bodies around back and forth, between, and among each other, but never with any contact. Japan must have done something to me without my knowing it, because things came into my head that had never been there before. The feet of the spider are the quietest; they must be. The quietest and the farthest off, no matter how close they are. It was those kind of feet that were coming, from the others that were like them.

He came up to me and stopped, straightening more, with an effort. He was not Japanese, and had on gold-rimmed glasses. "I guess I ought to ask you," he said in English.

I was not surprised. "Ask me what?"

"What are you doing here?"

I smiled, I really did, because I was not going to ask him the same question. I didn't want to know, particularly. If we got to talking, I was sure he would tell me anyway. "You knew I was not a Nip?"

He seemed a little puzzled, probably because he didn't understand how people in the service put things.

"Not Japanese."

"Yes, I knew it," he said.

"You mean, you know it now, when you can get a close look."

"No, I knew it when you came out of the woods and stood there. No Japanese would do that. You were too straight. You looked like you owned the place." He looked off and back. There was more fog than there had been, and the others in the field were mostly just arms and shoulders now. The ground was pretty much gone.

I glanced past him at the heads in the field crossing each other. He lifted a thumb toward them without turning around. "Don't worry about them. They don't even know you're here. They are off in a state of mind. It doesn't have anything to do with this field, or with you. Or with me either, for that matter."

I picked up my bag. "I'd better move. Can I go straight on through?"

He turned, this time toward the heads going back and forth and in and out, then he smiled carefully, like one of the company clerk-typists back in the squadron. "Well, maybe not *straight* through, but if you want to, you can make it on over to the other side. They won't bother you."

I stepped past him, and for a second didn't know what had happened to my arm, because I believed I was already on my way. He had hold of me, and not just by the sleeve, either. "Don't go," he said in a different voice. "Don't go yet." He looked at me, peering, kind of. "Stay with us. We'll take care of you. You need to hide, don't you?"

"I been hiding." I shook loose. "It would take me a while to tell you all the places. But the Nips ain't laid a hand on me up to now, and as far as I can tell they don't know where I am." I jounced the bag up and down to settle what was in there. "But some of them know where I've been. Some would, by now. I better move on."

He had me again, and for some reason I waited this time before I shook him off. There seemed to be something really important to him, and there might be some advantage in it later on, though I didn't have any idea what it might be.

"You can rest up here," he said, building up his eagerness. "Where have you been sleeping?"

"One place and another. Outside. A couple of nights under some logs. That's the closest I've been to sleeping under a roof, except a couple of nights at some guy's house. It was maybe too quiet in there."

"We've got plenty to eat, all you want. We've got some fish, rice, dried vegetables, maybe some fresh, too. I'll see. I won't say you can stay as long as you like, because I don't think you want to be a monk." He smiled again, and I wondered if he had ever typed out forms.

"You're right," I said. "Religious, I ain't."

"You're military, right?"

"Air Force. I bailed out over Tokyo the day before the big firebomb raid. I've been moving north ever since. But, like you said, not in a straight line." I might have smiled, too, but not the way he did.

"Firebomb raid?" He was puzzled again. "What does that mean?" He peered more. "Where does everything stand? Is the war almost over?"

"Maybe so. We laid down a whole lot of fire on Tokyo. And we could do it anywhere. We've got long-range aircraft, and we can go where we want. We can burn up this whole island — everything."

He turned to the field again. I had forgotten there was anybody in it. "Most of them don't even know there's a war on, and don't care. A few of them might, but they're just like the others. We never have any contact with anybody but ourselves. There's a military base just a couple of miles down the road, and we never even see any soldiers, except sometimes in trucks going by."

"Is this a north-south road?" I asked. "I mean mainly?"

"Yes. It goes up to Morioka, and then on."

So I had been more or less right about where I was, and felt good about it. I wondered now, with the kind of confidence this gave me, if it might not be a good idea to stay for a couple of days and see if I could pick up some things I could use up north. I needed heavy socks, especially. There might even be some snowshoes, and some more blades. The longer I thought about it the more I liked the idea, because if I was able to get up into the real rugged mountain country in Hokkaido, I would have to hunt and trap, and the more blades I had, and the more twine and cords, the better off I would be. I looked forward to all that like I was going on a vacation, but the right equipment would make it better, sure enough.

"Where would you put me up?"

"Our temple is across the field. You can't see it with all this mist, but it's not far. Most of the space is open, but there are a few rooms, and I can get you one, I think. Maybe you and I could stay together." His peering changed, but I couldn't read it.

"Are you sure these others won't make anything out of an American staying with them? An American soldier? That's hard to believe."

"You can believe it, though." He paused. "This mist is just right for these people. They're like ghosts, like zombies. They just float." He pulled my sleeve. "We can go up there now if you want to. I'll show you what we've got."

I shook the bag again and followed him, moving among the heads and shoulders, and I must say that I felt as secure and trouble-free as I had since I'd been in Japan: as much as at the waterfall, and, before that, watching the red box kite under water at the lake, when the sun hit clean and made it.

Past the field we began to move uphill, and I could make out a path. This went on for maybe three hundred yards, and we came out at a long low building with one of those weird curled-up Japanese roofs, like something on a postcard from a place you didn't particularly want to go to. He stopped, and I stopped.

"How long have you been here?" I asked, though I knew I might set him off to tell me all about his life, which I was sure

I would have to listen to if I stayed, but didn't want to now. There were other things to talk about.

"Six years, since '39. Time enough to get used to it."

"Seems simple enough from what I've seen. All you do is wander around in the fog — *float*, maybe. And then eat and sleep and shit, I guess."

"We do a few other things," he said, on the stairs now. "I'll tell you about them later on. Show you, too, if you like."

He slid the door and we went in. Everything slides, I thought. I hadn't seen a hinge yet, except on the water wheel that one time. I wondered why the wood didn't warp, with all the fog and wet, in a tongue-and-groove situation like that. It never seemed to happen, though. The building was cut in half, or just about, by another set of panels, but just a few feet forward, and sunk down from us was a kind of courtyard — that's the only way I can say it — made out of rocks. There were a couple of big ones, boulders, and all around them were rocks about the same size, round like they had come out of rivers and creeks. At the far end, catercornered from us, part of the yard was bare, very raw looking with the ground not covered.

"What's this all about?" I asked. I remembered hearing about this on Tinian, but here it was different. "Do they park cars in here? Trucks, maybe? Some kind of equipment?"

"No, it's a garden. You ask what it's all about. This is it. This is what the temple is all about."

"A garden?" I said, looking out over the bare rocks, all set even with each other. Not a thing was growing there, not even one of those runt trees the Nips like.

"The whole thing is ceremonial," he said, as if that explained everything, or anything.

"What do you do? Just look at it?"

"We do that, and we think. Meditate. Try to become nothing." He quit talking and then smiled. "Just lately we've been doing more than that. A few months ago we tore the whole thing up and threw the rocks out into the field where you first came up on us. That's what we were all doing out there when you came, looking for the rocks."

"Why did you tear it up to begin with?"

"So we could build it back. Over there in the corner's the only place that's left. Pretty soon the whole thing'll be just like it was, just like it's been for hundreds of years."

A notion struck me. "If the rocks are all that religious, ceremonial, like you say, wouldn't it have been better to leave them like they were to start with? I mean, isn't it important that the thing stay like it was when you got it?"

"It *is* like it was. We've been very accurate. These people believe that what their ancestors did, they can do the same. They can make the same."

"You mean to tell me that every one of those rocks is in the same place it was before?"

"I don't think we're quite *that* accurate," he said. "But there's really no difference. It works the same way."

"It couldn't be, could it," I said, and couldn't help myself, "that you just didn't have anything else to do?"

"We don't talk like that around here," he said. "Building the garden back is plenty to do. Takes a long time, a lot of hard work. They can't see it any other way. It's all natural to them."

"But *you* see it," I said. "You're an American." I knew it, though he hadn't said so.

"I've got to where I think pretty much the way they do," he said. "That's what I came over here for."

I looked around, first out into the rock yard they'd been

working on and then along the building that was put up around it. "I can stay here tonight?" I asked him.

"Sure," he said. "Nobody will bother you." Most of the other men — monks, I guess they call themselves — were still in the field down the hill picking up rocks, but a few moved along the wooden walkway that went around the yard. No one even glanced at me, and I didn't pay much attention to them. I couldn't get rid of the idea that none of them had legs, and were like the ones in the field of ground fog where I'd first seen them. It seemed righter for them just to be floating around. They were real quiet, and I thought probably nothing would have suited them better than to disappear, and not just the legs, either. It was like being in among a bunch of ghosts, or half ghosts anyway.

"Where would you like me to put my stuff?"

"I'll show you. There's no problem. If there's anything we've got, it's plenty of room."

We went to the walkway, south, and he slid open a door. There was another hall inside, and down it was another door and a big room with nothing in it but a mat and a wooden pillow in the corner.

"Who sleeps here?"

"Anybody who happens to be in this part of the building when he's sleepy. First one and then the other. I sleep here sometimes myself. Things are not territorial here. Nobody owns anything."

I put my bag down on the mat, and the other stuff I'd been lugging around.

"Would you like something to eat?"

"I could use it. What have you got?"

He looked up and smiled, meaning to be a little sly, I thought.

"What I just told you is not strictly true, you know. It might be true for the others, and probably for most of them it is. But it's not true for me. Not quite, and no harm done." He hesitated, then went on in a lower voice. "I came over here just before the war, and my mother used to send me things, mostly food that she'd put up, canned and all. She's good at that. I've got a stash. I could cook you some bean soup, and you can have all the figs and peaches and damson plums you want. I've had the stuff for a long time and don't eat much of it myself, but I keep it." And then, as though he was sure that this was something that would interest me a lot, "I always check the tops of the jars. If they bulge, what's inside is no good. But my mother's lids never bulge."

"Good. No bulges."

"Make yourself comfortable, stretch out, and I'll bring you some soup and some of those preserves."

I sat down and propped up against the corner. It was the emptiest place I had ever been in. No muskeg or mountain range could give you anything like the feeling of there being nothing to the place. The building had been made by people, but it didn't seem to have anything to do with them. It was like those gates you see in Japanese towns and in front of houses that just sit there, nothing on either side of them. They open from air into air, and there's nowhere to go.

I must have dozed off, because the American woke me by shaking my shoulder. I pushed him off and sat up. The soup was good. I just drank it out of the bowl like you would from a glass or a big cup. I hadn't realized how hungry I was, and I asked him to get me some more. When I finished I ate a whole jar of peaches, and a lot of plums and figs, and filled up real good. For some reason it didn't make me sleepy. I felt more like I had had a drink, but even more strong and alert than that would have made me.

"I might had better be moving on," I said. "I'm used to it."

"No," he said, and I couldn't tell why he should seem anxious about it. "Stay as long as you like. Or at least stay tonight."

"I guess I could do that." Then, "But no more. This place is not for me, I can tell you, figs or no figs. There's not anything in it."

"That's the idea. It's the only way the spirit can live."

"You better feed the spirit some more figs," I said, and ate two or three more.

"Are you sleepy?"

"No. I feel pretty good."

"Would you like me to put on a show for you?"

This surprised me, I don't mind admitting. "What have you got in the way of a show?" He pulled on my arm. I shook loose and stood up.

"Come outside," he said.

"You mean outside outside? Or outside inside?"

"What?"

"I mean, with the rocks on down the hill, in the fog, or the ones you got hemmed up in this empty building?"

"Inside," he said, smiling again, a little more direct this time. "Always inside."

We sat on the edge of the walkway. Snow was coming down on the rocks, and it was getting dark.

"When does the show start?"

"It's already started. It never stops."

"You just mean the snow?"

"The snow falling on rocks. Did you ever see anything more beautiful?"

"Yes, I can damn well tell you I have seen a lot of things more beautiful than that."

"What, exactly?"

"I've seen a fisher marten climb a tree and get lost in the branches of needles. That was one of the best, because I knew he was there, and because I couldn't see him. I like to see a whole herd of caribou, every one of them taking his time, all moving together through the tree line. I like to be *at* the tree line, going either way, into the trees or leaving them behind. I like slopes a lot. Any slope is better than a flat. Any natural rock is better than these you've got here. They'd look better in some creek, going along for miles."

"You must cleanse your mind," he said. "Those things you mentioned make you unhappy."

"They don't do no such of a thing," I said, bringing up the bend in the creek just below the south Brooks Range, where I had buried the college girl. That bend had power in it, a lot of real power.

"If you stayed here with us and learned to contemplate, learned to concentrate, learned to comprehend the meaning of the stones, you would never be unhappy. You would understand the secret of the void. That is the place of the spirit."

"The void? What is that?"

"Pure emptiness. Nothing. Nothingness."

"You sure got the right place for that. If you and them others want nothing — or nothingness, like you say — you got the right situation, the right place to live with it. More power to you. I'll take the pine needles around the fisher marten that don't move until he's ready to come out after something. That's some kind of strong fast little animal, I'll tell you. He's not fooling around. Him, I'll take." A quick thought hit me. "I saw some military transport back down the road, not far from here. What do those Nip soldiers think about all your rocks and what you're doing here?"

"They don't bother us. Some of them are engineers, and they work mainly on the coast. They expect an American invasion. They're building what they call pillboxes, coastal fortifications. Once they offered to grade a slope for us, but nobody followed up on it, because we didn't know what we wanted the slope to do. We might have built some stairs on it, but it wasn't that important. There could be some things later on that they might do for us, if we did something for them. I don't think it's a bad idea to keep on the good side of soldiers. But, as I say, we don't have much contact. They think we're something from another world. And that's all right with us. Maybe we are."

"*Is* it right for you? I mean *really* right? How did you get into this? Why did you come over here? Just to lose yourself?"

"I came here to lose myself, because the self I had back in St. Louis didn't suit me. It was OK with other people, but not with me."

"What did you do there?"

"I was in school, pre-med, and I had written around to get into medical school somewhere. I was accepted at Tulane, and probably would have gone there if I had stayed."

"I've heard New Orleans is not bad. One of the gunners in my outfit was from there, and went to Tulane. Played basketball."

"I couldn't get interested in a game if you paid me. I used to read all the time. I read a lot of philosophy. I read a lot of books on religion, and even about magic. Time, theories about time — I used to like those."

"Time? What kind of theory can you have about time? Time is time."

"Some say not. Some say that what most people call time is not real time."

"What is it, then?"

"What you call time is nothing but a convenience. A clock is just a machine. Real time is different from that. Real time is what you live, and not the moves of a machine. Real time is not mechanical." He turned to me — turned on me — quicker than I would have expected. "Do you dream a lot?"

"About like anybody else, I guess."

"Well, you are really two people. One of them lives the mechanical time of the clock. The other one of them watches what the first one does. He watches from the dream, when the spirit comes loose from the clock. The second self can go backward in time. He can also go forward."

I had never heard any kind of talk like this, and I tried to head it off. Not that it bothered me, but I couldn't find any way to connect with it, or get interested in it.

"Have you ever dreamed something that turned out to happen later on?" he said.

"No. I don't think so. I can't remember, anyway, if I ever did."

"When I was doing all that reading I ran across stuff like that, and it interested me a lot more than medical school did. Somehow or other I wanted to get loose from science. I wanted to get into a situation that operated according to different laws, or maybe didn't have any laws. As near as I was able to tell, the best kind of concentration of that kind of thinking, which goes beyond thinking, or before or behind thinking, was in Japan.

That's where they start with the void and try to get back to it. A total blank. That's what they want in Zen."

"In *what?*"

"Zen. Zen Buddhism. That's what it's all about."

"About nothing?"

"It's a very creative nothing. If you ever get there, you'll know what I mean. Or you won't know, and that's the best."

"Maybe for you. But I like the rocks in the creek, with water running over them, and not just put in a yard for somebody to stare at. That gets old. It's already old, as far as I'm concerned. I'm going back and sleep on your rags, where you showed me."

I got up, but he didn't.

"Remember your dreams," he said. "Later on, you might want to keep a record of them. Write them down. You might be surprised at what your Observer brings back and tells you about. He's been into the future, and you might like to know about it."

"I don't want to know about it. I'll know about it when it happens."

I told him good night and left him there, staring into the snowfall. The rocks were almost out of sight now, and the yard was smooth and bright with new moonlight. I made it back to my room and my corner. All my gear was there, and even though I had some rags and parts of blankets, I put my feet in the bag with the feathers and my arm over my eyes and went to sleep.

After a while I woke up and believed right off that somebody was standing over me. I reached out and felt around, but there was nothing there. I didn't hear anybody move. It bothered me, because I'm never that sure of something and wrong about it. I got up and walked back and forth, and then lay down again, but I couldn't go back to sleep right away. I would never get used to this country, I was sure. At least not the parts of it that had people. When I got up north it might be better. I wondered what the animals would be like.

A pain, very quick and very hard, hit me in the right side, and another one in the face, mostly in the nose and teeth. I opened my eyes and the room was full of feet and legs. Somebody was shining a light on me, and I saw the rifle butt come down again, but moved so that the plate only scraped my head just above the ear. I turned and came up on all fours and a rifle barrel moved forward down the light and ended up between my eyes. Somebody pulled me from behind, and slowly I got to my feet. There were eight or ten men in the room, all about my size or a little shorter, and all in uniform. Very dinky they looked, too, especially the caps. A kid would know better than to wear something that silly looking. A couple of them pushed me back against the wall, and another rifle came in; this one had a bayonet on it. I thought that maybe the guy was going to finish me, and if he put the bayonet in deep I was going to make somebody live hard — at least one of them. The blade only penetrated my coat and shirt, but I could feel the blood run down.

The soldier behind the light, whom I couldn't see, kept screaming something at me that could have been "American," though it could have been something else. Every time he said it I'd get another hit, either with somebody's fist or with a rifle butt. One of them smashed into my mouth and I could feel a front tooth go. I spit it out, and tried with my tongue to see how the next one to it was: loose, but still in. That Japanese excitability had hold of all of them. They screamed at each other as much as they did at me, and I figured that the only advantage I might have was that they couldn't account for me. It may have been that they thought I was a spy, because I was not in uniform and had turned up in such a strange place, but why I would be spying on a Zen monastery during wartime had them completely baffled. The trouble was that they took their frustration out on me, and I guessed I was balanced between two things: their excitability and frustration, where one of them would shoot me or stab me just because he couldn't think of what else to do. That was one possibility. With all the hits, the blades and rifle butts and fists, I was not thinking very clearly, but I did suppose that if they could control themselves they would take me to somebody else who might be able to find out who I was and what I was doing there. That was the other part of the balance.

Some way or another I was on my feet again, with the guns and blades leveled. The Nips sounded desperate, and I was afraid one of them was going to shoot. They seemed to like stabbing more, which was something I could understand. I held on, and let them chatter and poke, while I got my feet fixed on the ground solid, just so they would be that way. My face hurt a lot, but I was still fairly strong in the legs, and that was the best I had right then. Two of them went behind me, pulled my arms back, and tied my wrists. The rope was thick, which was also good; it always surprised me how much rope there is in Japan. Somebody gave me a shove. There were two of them at the sides and two in front, and all of them were trying to get me to go a certain way, which was to the outside. Before we went through the door I looked around for the American monk, the one I had talked to about the rocks and snow, but though there were three or four monks standing around, he was not one of them. It was just as well; I didn't have any hate for him. I was not mad at all. He had to be like he was — for the rest of his life, too, and that was bad enough.

We went down the hill from the building, and there was a covered truck parked by the road. Strange: as soon as we hit the open air my eyes crossed, with the pain and everything else, and even though I tried to focus on the truck, I saw it less and less like it must have been. It kept swimming and surrounding itself with yellow, which later, when I thought about it, I reckoned was probably the yellow of the valley where I had watched the convoy that was stalled, and tried to learn the gears. A few more shoves, then four of them picked me up and pitched me into the back of the truck like a sack. I lay there on my side in the corner and pulled my feet up, so that nobody would bother with them. One soldier threw a tarp over me and I stayed still, my face hurting bad, testing the rope a little, just to begin, and listening to their chatter outside, which was as excited as ever. The one guy sat down in the other corner with his gun pointed at me. The truck fired, blew, and started, and we turned around, headed back south.

The road was rough. It bashed upward and bumped around a lot, and it seemed like every lick was aimed at my face. I felt around inside my mouth with my tongue, and I was missing three teeth, with another one loose. That was not going to kill me, though like I say, I was hurting pretty good. As quiet as I could make myself, I concentrated on the rope, but I couldn't get it loose behind my back no matter what I did. But that was not the only way to go. If I could pull my legs up enough to get my feet through, I would have my hands where they belonged. That was going to be hard, but after edging around some I didn't think it would be impossible. With the road bumping like it was, it might seem to the guard that I was just joggling like everything else was, like he was himself. I could see the barrel of his rifle waving around. I was at the point of trying to put one foot through when the guard got up and lurched across to me. He braced himself against the cab, drew back, and kicked me hard. Nothing broke, or at least if it did, I didn't hear it. He kicked me again, not so solid this time, and leaned over and screamed in my face. I reckoned he was telling me not to move around. I was afraid he was going to throw back the tarp, but he didn't. He worked back across, picked up his rifle, and sat down. I lay still again, and would, for a while. My hands were where I had left them, just at the far side, the behind side, of my ankles. A little more, I thought, not much but a little more.

Still, still as a fisher marten on a branch I was, and my feet came through. I lay there with my hands; there was no hurry. I thought about how odd it was: all the riding I had done in Japan, when I had planned to do nothing but walk. I went back to the log train, and how good some of the riding had been, especially the night part when I could put out from my mind anything I wanted, overlay Japan with it, and watch the Brooks Range become everything in the world. From the train I could get the whole reason for there to be icebergs, for one thing: those big shapes made out of shadows, shadows that somehow or other had taken on a lot of weight, or that somebody or something had given the weight to, which maybe they shouldn't have. I couldn't do the same thing here, not like I had on the train. I tried hard, though: tried to see the line of deer heads in the snow, all pointed one way, the horns trued up like right dress on parade. Maybe it was because my face hurt so much, and now my ribs, that I couldn't get things to come right. The deer kept breaking formation, busting up out of the snow, when all I wanted was the heads. Maybe it was that I was hurting, and my eyes were still about half crossed, or maybe it was because the truck was headed in the wrong direction. I don't know, I really don't. But my hands were in front of me, and when the deer heads wouldn't line up I knew it was time, or almost. It was getting to be time.

I already had a one-two-three, or a sequence, like the Kansas girl would probably have said. I could take a couple more kicks if I had to. I started the number one move, which was *to* move, and move a lot. I thrashed around under the tarp, and I also started singing, as loud as I could, an old Baptist hymn, "Love Lifted Me," which had stayed with me for some reason, though I only heard it once. The guard got up again, like before. He braced on the cab. It felt like a curve we were going around now, and he had to break his grip and brace again. Then he kicked me very hard, a good one. That was the second part. He kicked again, harder this time, even. It was still the second part. I thrashed around some more, and then went quiet. I waited. He bent down almost in my face and screamed as loud as he could, as he would have to. He spit on me, and I had him.

And I had him good. There may be stronger hands somewhere in a man my size, but I haven't seen them yet. I kicked the tarp off and we rolled around, but I knew as soon as I had a hold of him that I could kill him, and probably could have done it with one hand, like with the Kansas girl. But two is better than one any time, and I got his head back in the corner where I'd been, and bore down. After not very long he shook, not fighting but like he had a chill, then stiffened out and relaxed. I held on for a minute or two more until I knew he was not dead but good and dead, and then turned loose. Using the rest of my teeth, it was easy to get the rope off, and after I did that I picked up the rifle and looked it over. It was bolt action, like an old Springfield or Enfield. There was a round in the chamber and no safety that I could find, and I knew how close it had been back at the monastery, with all those excited Nips with their fingers on the triggers — closer, even, than I thought when it was happening. I put the tarp over the guy and went over into his corner, making the plan.

There were three of them up front, and I was sure that they didn't know anything had happened, else they would have stopped and come around to have a look. That wouldn't have been good then, but it would be now; it was just what I wanted. I fired over the tailgate, worked the bolt and fired again, to see if the weapon would feed all right. Then I pulled the rifle into the dark and sighted down it, so that I could cover the whole area that showed through the space. I got set just as the brakes slammed on. I didn't think I could get all three of them, but two would be fine if the third guy ran, and one would be enough.

The first Nip showed — more from under, it seemed like, than from the side, the curb side — lifted his rifle, and screamed into the cab. Then he fired at the tarp, and another Nip showed from the driver's side. He fired at the dead man, too, because the other one was doing it, and I blew the second one's head in, because there was less of him showing, and he was closer. Before the other one could fire at my flash I hit him through the chest, and he went down and crawled. I stepped up to the tailgate and blew down on him, and was going to hit him again but the pin clicked: I was out of firepower. I could have got the two other guns, but I didn't think it was a good idea to show myself to the third man. I changed my mind around and thought with him. He'd believe that I'd have to come out the back of the truck, that it was the only way I could move. But it wasn't. Using the dead guy's bayonet, I cut open the canvas top, eased up onto the roof, and got still again. It wasn't in the Nips to run off; the last one was still in the cab, probably following orders. But with all the firing he would have to show. He didn't have any notion of what was going on, but no soldier is just going to sit when there's action that close to him, orders or no orders.

I lay with my toes against one of the struts that held up the canvas, keeping tension. I was just as glad about the guns. Let him find them, if he could get to them. And I wanted to fall on him from above. That appealed to me; I would do it before he looked up, before he could raise the rifle or even get out of the cab. He wouldn't come out the driver's side, I was more or less sure about that. Why should he? Why scramble under the steering wheel when he didn't have to? More than that, he had got in from the curb side, and that would bring him out the same way; I didn't even glance over my shoulder toward the road. I put the blade half an arm's length over my head, so I could stiffen or flex, either one. I drew back a little, to get more pressure on my feet. I could wait. I could up to a point, anyway. If any traffic showed, I would slip down at the first sign of a light and take off, but I had been making more plans while I got ready, and wanted to follow through on them. One more Nip soldier and I would have a new piece of the future, one that would work, and in a different way from anything I'd done up to now.

The door cracked. It definitely moved. It closed, then opened wider. A head came out and turned back toward the tail. I wondered if he could see the bodies, or either one of them; I hadn't had the sense to move them out of sight, or to use them as bait. He kept coming out and craning to see. When he was more out than in, when one foot was going toward the ground but hadn't reached it yet, when his balance was wrong, I pushed hard with my feet and fell, head down and blade first, sighting along the steel and ready to give it the rest of my arm just as soon as it made contact.

I hit him, but not good enough. I had cut him bad through the neck, but the blade didn't go through, and the rest of me collided with him and we fell on the ground. He had let go the rifle to grab his neck, and I went after it there on the road shoulder. I couldn't get my feet under me, but hitch-kicked toward the gun, which he had stepped on either because he wanted to or by accident. No matter about that. I couldn't get it; I tore up my fingernails trying. I got up and hit him in the side of the face with everything I had, stepping into it and turning my body to get all the weight and swing I could. He pitched forward, not falling but almost, and I uppercut him with the same hand. His foot was off the gun, but I saw it would be easier to grab the bayonet from the scabbard in his belt. I did and rammed it into him, coming up. When he was on the ground I went through him twice more. The blade was too stiff, not like my bread knife, which was why I had to use it so much. I looked around. There was no traffic, no light yet, nothing but three bodies and the power space over them, over and around. One by one I pulled the bodies off the road, down the bank, broke off weeds and twigs, and covered them up some, hurrying now, for there would likely be a light soon. Somebody would come and break my luck if I didn't get on with it.

I picked up the guns, went to the cab, and got in. All my stuff was there, the bag of feathers, everything. The bag was pushed in, like one of them had put his feet on it. What I usually carried on me had been thrown into the bag, and I fished it out by feel and put it back where it belonged. Having my long limber knife with me, having the compass and the emergency stuff — the things I had been issued and had modified, and the things I had picked up along the way — was like a transfusion. No, not like some blood had been added to mine, but like a new ration had been put in, a whole fresh supply from somebody better than I was. When I remembered the flints and the fire in them, the strength of the new blood went up even more, and up from that. Even before I took hold of the gearshift I knew I could work it, whether I had learned the right way in the yellow valley or not.

The gears were the same. When I cranked the engine and shifted down and turned around everything fell into place. I didn't look at the dials; I didn't care how much fuel I had. I would run as far as I could, and when the truck quit I would leave it, wherever it happened to be. That was not the point just yet, but it was taken care of. The main thing was that when I turned and swung north the whole situation was mine again. Too late I remembered that I hadn't checked for Polaris, just to do everything right, but I could do without it for a while; there would be plenty of other times. There was something closer: I was sure that the compass in the emergency kit came to true north not just where I carried it, over my heart, but somewhere in my body, in my mouth and nose that hurt so damned bad, maybe. The direction of the needle was just as steady. The pain was part of it, and the whole dark of the night was another piece of my equipment as I went through it on a powerful runway of road with no lights but mine.

The engine sounded all right. It wasn't missing or knocking, even though it wasn't the smoothest in the world; that didn't bother me one way or the other. What did bother me, a little, was that everything I could reach was loose: the light switch, the ignition, the gauges were bugging out of the panel like the eyes of a frog you'd stepped on, and the gas pedal, the clutch and brake pedals had at least two inches of sideways play in them. Everything in the truck was loose and rattled and didn't stop. The road was rough, not paved very well, and that made it worse, and especially bad on the teeth I had left. The pain centered around the one that had been almost knocked out, but not. It was hard to get my attention on other things.

I concentrated on driving, with the truck's particular problems, and on my lights going forward on the road. The way they were jumping around made the shadows interesting every time I passed a tree or a pole. The shadows of people, too. A few of them were walking, both ways, but they didn't pay any attention at all and didn't even look at me, although they must not have seen very many vehicles, judging from the traffic. No one passed me from behind; no one was following.

I was pretty familiar with the performance of the truck by now. Like I say, it was the worst I had ever been in. When I was at Buckingham Field, in Florida, waiting for my class in gunnery school to start, the personnel officers had to find something for us to do, and I got assigned to the motor pool. It turned out to be not a half-bad deal. My instructor was a big tough southern guy, Sergeant Hough, who had spent some time on the dirt-track circuit down there. He could drive a jeep past what it was supposed to be able to do, and was pretty near as good in any other vehicle. He taught us how to get the most out of whatever we were driving: the most mileage, the longest use, the quickest acceleration, how to use the vehicle as a fort or in an ambush. He taught us how to conceal it, how to ram with it, and how to wreck it if we had to: get down on the floor and grab one of the pedals. Muldrow, keep your head down when the vehicle rolls over, and if it doesn't have struts, the windshield and the body of the vehicle below the windows will keep you from getting killed. It was the best learning I ever did, except from my father. I got as much from Hough as I could, because I knew from the beginning that what he told us would work. With him was the one time I didn't want to do things my own way, because even then I could tell: it would be part of my own way, and we would blend it later on. Driving that road through Japan, I thought about Sergeant Hough and brought him into the situation with me as much as I could.

According to his instructions I gunned up to about sixty when the road was deserted and seemed straight for a while. I slowed down for the curves, not because I didn't think I could take them but because I didn't want to screech the tires and make things seem frantic, like somebody was after me. There was no need for that, and I didn't do it. I was making good time on the straights and didn't need to be what Hough called a cowboy. Dark and desertedness and speed were together, were one thing. I drove that way for three hours. I would think I made at least a hundred and twenty-five miles, or maybe even a hundred and fifty. Now and again I took to worrying about the gas, what I would do when it ran out, but Hough told me not to worry, just drive.

Aside from the poles, and a tree or a person now and then, walking along with his head down, I hadn't seen much of where I had been or where I was. That started to change now. There were houses, more and more of them and closer together, little houses like the one where I had set the flicker of my blade. Since

I had done that, I knew the flame was in every house in Japan. I couldn't believe, now, that I didn't know this was happening when I was doing it.

❖   ❖   ❖

For some reason, the last thing I had figured on was a town, much less a city. I drew a complete blank on the whole idea and didn't have the slightest notion about how to handle it. But I was going straight into the problem. A city: I would have to either come out of it — come out the other side of it — or stay there. It was Morioka, according to where I had been and the direction I had been going, but it very well might not have been. Suppose it was not? Was I screwed, with nothing I could do? No, I didn't think it would be that bad as long as I could adjust. North was still north, though I might have misjudged the distances and the places. But my silk map said Morioka and the road on up to the ocean. The gas was holding, and I felt I still had some miles yet.

If it was Morioka — I prayed for Morioka — it was only about seventy-five miles to the tip of the island, and a whole new game. Hokkaido was salvation: it had got that way in my mind, and stayed. The lectures on it from Tinian were the only ones I remembered, because it was all talk about cold and mountains, snow, rocks, a little game, wind, high places. Hardly any population up at the north end, my silk map said, and why would the Air Force tell me or give me anything that lied? Up there, monkeys lived in the snow, which was hard to believe and didn't seem right. But it must have been right, for up there.

But Morioka? Morioka was jammed together around me

now. On the road there hadn't been many vehicles, very few all night. But here it was like they came around me from all sides and hemmed me up. I couldn't say I was not close to panic, for the sun was coming up, more and more light. Anybody who looked right at me could tell that I was not a Jap. And where did the road go? The road I was on, where would it take me? I couldn't read the signs, and my main hope was that the town was built around the highway — like most American cities, or a lot of them — and that if I kept straight on I would come out the far side, headed right. I thought of that, and the ocean, and the bergs.

But things got worse, a lot worse. With the light, people poured into the streets, and there were vehicles — some of them military — all around me, and carts, bicycles, wheelbarrows, wagons of every kind you could think of, including kids' wagons. And right in the middle of things I was nearly stalled. There was no way I could move. Panic: I was nearly there. My head was working, but it didn't give me anything. The nearest I had ever come to something like this was in Tokyo, in the fire, when people were jammed up in the streets and I was hunkered down in the door with the .45, waiting for what I wanted. The panic, that huge panic of all those people, the fire and the smoke and the heat, were a kind of safety for me; I could pick and choose. This was different. The only panic was mine, and I didn't have any camouflage: no hillside, no pine straw, no rocks, no bushes, no snow. It is terrible to be exposed like that, I can tell you. I pulled down my hat as low as I could and slumped, to wait it out. There was no telling what the holdup was.

Something banged on the door, not the driver's door. It was not a gun butt or anything hard, but it still put a shock wave through me. The bang came again, but not any harder. There was not any urgency in it, or any authority. I leaned over and got a glance. Two kids, about eight or ten, were going along the stalled traffic, hitting everything they came to with sticks. That was all, that was all.

What should I do? I had the two guns with full clips, and I could have made a fight if I had to. I could have got out and run, and tried to lose myself, but that wouldn't have worked for long. Again I drew a blank. The Brooks Range left me, the fisher marten left me.

Nobody seemed interested in me except the kids and their sticks, and they came and went. I stayed low, leaned up, and looked around at the city, at the people. Life was going on: men, but more especially women, were carrying things, crossing the street with short steps. There was a lot of wood, bundles of it that the women and girls were toting, and every now and then a log that it took two or three or even four of them to handle. I wondered if it might be possible for me to go to sleep, but that would have been taking things too far, giving away too much. A cart was in front of me, and a boy on a three-wheeled bicycle was behind. This was the hand that I had been dealt for right now, and there was no way I could have changed it. I sat for what must have been at least an hour, all sorts of things running through my head, and none of them any good. But somebody blew a whistle, and the cart pulled off to one side. I could move forward about half a block, and I did. A truck like mine pulled in ahead of me. Behind me from the same street another vehicle, another military vehicle, closed up, near enough but keeping distance, more or less like Sergeant Hough had taught us to do back in Florida. We crawled through the streets with the kids rattling sticks along us like they would have along a fence. Then we stalled again. The truck in front of me stopped and the driver got out. He grabbed hold of a woman with what looked like a bundle of laundry on her back and hit her across the face very hard. She stumbled over to the side of the road, and we went on. This was the way people treated each other over here; I was getting used to it. But she was out of the way, and we could move.

It was a much bigger town than I had any notion it would be when I started through it. At first, as far as I was concerned, I was just in between the truck in front of me and what looked to be about like a six-by-six or a weapons carrier from back at Buckingham. I wondered where we were going, going like we were going. But in the end, the direction was all that mattered, and I drove along out of town, keeping distance, not getting any closer to either the truck or the weapons carrier.

The town dropped off us little by little, and we were in the scrubby country, clocking along at about thirty-five or forty. It was not bad at all; I could have been driving in a convoy anywhere. A convoy? I thought. Could that be what it was? I craned, half stood up from the seat, and tried to see over the truck in front of me. Sure enough, there was another truck in front of it, and I reckoned there were probably others in front of that one, too. Here I was, damned if I wasn't, doing what I was doing: driving a truck in an enemy convoy. Who would have thought anything like it? Believe me, I wouldn't have. It was not anything I could ever have imagined.

I couldn't tell what, right off, but something was getting to me, and I didn't like it at first. I didn't like it, and then I did like it. I realized that I had hardly seen any of the land we had been going through because this feeling — this other feeling — was getting at me from the inside and I didn't know what to do with it. Usually I would have made myself happy by the idea that I was controlling things; that I was actually driving one of the enemy's trucks, just as the Japanese military personnel in the other vehicles were doing; that I had taken them in, and they were taking me in the direction I wanted to go. I did feel that, and I tried to encourage the feeling as much as I could. But it was being crowded out by another one that had a real disturbing side to it. Disturbing is the word; I can't think of a better one. What was it, though? I couldn't fence it off, I couldn't pin it down. It just came over me. First, the feeling of being trapped, of being locked into a convoy, started to leave me little by little. Maybe it was the constant speed that we were all moving forward with. It may have been that I was right out there in full view, not in a Japanese uniform, not disguised as anything, and still free. Maybe it was because I didn't look at anything but the vehicle in front of me and the other one behind, in the rear-view mirror. Whatever, I was comfortable, more comfortable than I had been since I bailed out, except possibly that time next to the waterfall.

But this was not like the waterfall, really. Other things were part of it, which were caused in some way by my being in a line of trucks. Even the fact that they belonged to the enemy was not as bothersome as certain parts of the military life began to be. I could not get past the idea that I was under orders, was following them the same as the soldiers in the other trucks and vehicles were doing. It was hard to believe — it was hard for *me* to believe — that this notion was more reassuring than anything else: there was a sort of plan that I didn't have to make myself just now. That was good, and I rode with it for a long time, most of the morning. In with the idea of following orders, though, came two people: my father and Major Sorbo, my commanding officer and the pilot of the 29 I'd bailed out of.

My father had been the loner of all loners. He made himself that way, and it was right for him. Because of something that had happened to him back in Virginia — he never told me, but I always thought this — he had taken it on himself to get as far away from other people as he possibly could. To him that meant Alaska, and it made the life I lived while I was growing up. He wanted me to be like him, and believe me, I *wanted* to be like him. He was not a natural outdoorsman or any kind of pioneer type, but all the time I was living with him up there, I could tell that he took right to it. A lot of times he told me he wished he had been raised like he was raising me. In a way we grew up together, learning the same things, the same ways to connect with the land, the mountains, the animals and fish and birds, and with the seasons, and most especially with the cold.

I was more sure than ever, now, that I had to get to Hokkaido, and if I could, up into the mountains on the northern part, by the ocean. If I could do that, I could do anything. It would be like opening the door of the cabin on the Brooks and having that red wall my father'd painted hit you like a blast, an explosion, more than just a color, after being so long in the no-color of the snow, under the emptiness of the sky, blue or overcast, either one. That red wall was my father's only strangeness, though other people might have told you different. If they did, none of them ever told me. It wouldn't have mattered anyway; I knew what I knew. If I could make it to northern Hokkaido, it would be like throwing the door open and having that red wall come at me, and I would live, or at least die, where I wanted to be.

Well, I thought, God help us. The spirit of the team. I never had it in my life, but I had it now, damned if I didn't, driving in the enemy's convoy. Any of the others in it would have killed me, cut my balls off, or my head, or both, gouged my eyes out, spilled my guts all over the road, wound them around barbed wire, strung me up, used me for bayonet practice. But in a way I wanted to go where they went. We were all under orders.

I never took my eyes off the truck in front of me, whose driver I never saw. In the rear-view mirror, I did get some notion of the guy behind me. He was just a kid. He smiled a lot, as though pretty much to himself, and it seemed right for him to be doing that, in the sunlight we were in, going along. I wondered, from that, if the Nip in front of me was catching a glimpse of me every now and then, like I was doing into the truck behind. What would he see? Off one of the Nips I had shot I had taken the hat and put it on. Even if I had had his whole uniform, though, I wouldn't have passed for a Japanese soldier in a million years, but in a rear-view mirror, with just the hat on, I might do all right. I didn't think anyone would notice all that much; we were going along.

The road was rough but pretty good, and we began to make a lot of turns. I wondered if it might be possible to get out my map, to see if the country around the ocean was hilly or mountainous, but the map was not very good on terrain, and I doubted if it would have helped much. I was not real anxious about getting to the ocean, but, like I always do, I started to make plans, plans with a big forward sweep to them, all the way to the mountains at the tip of Hokkaido, on past the monkeys in the snow. In any place in the world there is game. If there was snow or tundra or even rocks, the game I understood would be there, and I knew how to get it. I could outthink any animal or bird that lived in the cold, by thinking more like he did than he could do. All I had to do was get there.

We rode. There was nothing else to do, and by now I had got used to it. I could not bring up in my mind any notion of how the line of trucks was going to end up or where it was going, but I was sure of one thing: I was not going to turn off the road I was on, no matter what the rest of them did. It bothered me that all this would stop, later on, and everybody would get out. That would be hard to handle, but I didn't think it was likely. If the convoy was going to some army base, or to a depot or a fortification of some kind, it would not be on the main road; there would have to be a turnoff. If there was, and I didn't turn, they might take out after me, and I would have to gun up and run for it. But I didn't think that would happen, either. If they turned and I didn't, a few of them might think it was strange, maybe, for a minute or two, and then forget about it and get on with what they were doing. Besides that, we were curving around so much that only two of them at the same time could see me; the others wouldn't even notice, no matter what happened. So that part of it should be all right. Maybe.

None of this happened, though. On into the afternoon, when we had come down into a valley and were on a straight stretch for a little while, the trucks started to turn, one by one. Three ahead of me, one of them went off to the right. After a few more miles, the one in front of me turned off to the right, too. I looked in the mirror, and the weapons carrier just behind me turned — it was to the left for him — and I saw the kid's smile for the last time: it wiped across and was gone. I waved, but only inside the cab.

The rest had turned off, and I was by myself again. I won't say something went out of me when the convoy broke up, but I did have more fear after it left than I had when I was in it.

There didn't seem to be any death in the line of trucks, and I had lost the orders that somebody or something had given me. I came back into my status, as they say in the Army, but I was not in an army anymore, and never was again.

❖   ❖   ❖

I came to be pretty sure, by now, that I might not be on the main north-south road, because there was not enough traffic. Vehicles I saw were all military, but there were not many of them. I tried to keep up an even speed, but once something like a jeep passed me and sounded its horn, and the driver leaned out and made some kind of signal. I held on, since there wasn't anything else I could do. He put his head out and looked back, and I got ready to fight one more time. He pulled away, though, and pretty soon I had the road to myself again.

By this time I had a notion of how the gas gauge was set up, and if I was right I didn't have much left. There was not any way to get more, because I didn't know where there was any, and even if I did, I would have had to steal it, which would have brought in more risk than I wanted: there are always a lot of people around a depot, or anywhere there's fuel. Besides, I was tired of driving. Even the fact that I had made a lot of distance didn't get rid of the idea that there was something not fair about my doing things this way. I wanted to pick up my bag of feathers and my other things and go on the way I had been doing before I ran into the monks in the monastery fog, before the American monk and I had sat looking at the rocks in the courtyard. I thought of something I should have said to him when he was coming at me with all that religious stuff he had learned how to say. This would have been good, I thought: when he said something like, God is everywhere there is, God is in this snow, I should have come back at him and said, No, the snow is in the snow. That would have settled his hash, and it made me feel better when I realized I could have said it.

Driving along on the dregs of my gas, I tried my best to get back into my feelings and thoughts on the log train, where everything seemed so easy. Then, I could project forward and back, and get involved in the landscape of my own head. The whole world of cold and snow and wind and winter was all mine then; it just seemed to come to me. The caribou at the tree line, going from range to range, were more beautiful in my mind than they were where they were alive, and I remembered my father, now, as part of all that in a way he never really was. It was that red side of the cabin that hit me, the one whole wall of blood red, but brighter than blood: brighter and brighter. When my father painted the inside of the cabin, and made the wall that way, he said it was because you got starved for color up there in all that snow, and craved it like elk and caribou crave salt. I believed him then, believed that was the reason for the paint, but now I had come to think, without any notion why, that there was another reason. The red was more than the color you were starved for. It was something else. Something real definite happened when you opened the door and came in out of the snow and faced into that red wall. Whatever it was hit you like a hammer right over the heart — not in the head or the guts but the heart. You could feel yourself stagger and come back.

Now, in Japan, after all those years, I thought I had it. I had what the wall really did. It was nothing but this: you had to stand out against it. In the snow, on the muskeg, the animals and birds blended with what was there, with what they were in.

The tern did, the ptarmigan and the winter weasel and the lynx did, and I did my best to do the same thing. But when I came in from the white and up against that wild red, I couldn't do it anymore. I was trapped, you could see me, and there was death in that. There's no other way to put it: there was no place to go. The background, the world, was against me. That's why the change came when I moved from white to red, moved against the red and stopped. Or maybe you could say I *was* stopped. There was always the need to look around, to look this way and that way, trying to find some other place. It was panic, sure enough, and I won't deny it. But there was also, along with the panic, a terrific joy, in that I knew I would never be up against anything worse, any place where everything was against me, where there was no way to turn, and when you reach that kind of limit you can't keep the happiness down. I was at home in the snow; I was all right. I knew, in the white outfit I used to wear, that if I closed my eyes I would be as out of the world as the snowshoe hare — the snowshoe hare on one side or the lynx on the other. I could hide or attack, wait for danger to pass or kill something before it even knew I was there. All the time I was growing up I must have known, in my way, that the red wall where I couldn't hide was part of the other; it made invisibility possible. If the wall was a place where I couldn't hide, it would make hiding better when the conditions were right. I don't know why I believed this, but I did, and it seemed to work. I went along forward in my mind. Sooner or later I was going to have to get on water, and it would be like the wall: no camouflage, no cover. And it would have to be at night. That was one thing. A few others shaped up, too, as the gas in the truck went down. I needed to find where Honshu came closest to Hokkaido, and I needed a boat with no engine, one that ran on nothing but silence. But first I had to get to the ocean, and then we would see.

Meantime my face was hurting pretty bad, especially my nose and mouth. My nose didn't crunch when I pinched it, so I thought that it probably wasn't broken and would heal up in a few days or maybe a week. I had lost three teeth, and another one that would probably come out, though I kept trying to stuff it back in with my fingers, but couldn't tell yet if it was taking hold. Whenever I left off from planning and let my mind wander, my head would start to hurt, and I wouldn't feel as good about what I was doing, or what I had been planning. And so I knocked it off and began to wonder what I was going to do with the truck.

I could just have left it at the side of the road and gone on. I might even have turned it around and left it headed south. I doubted whether that would fool anybody. Not for long it wouldn't. If the Japanese had any sense at all they would know they were missing a truck and some men, and would look, and when they found it would want to know why it was here, this far north, no matter which way it was headed when they found it. A good idea seemed to be to run it off into the water, but I didn't pass any rivers or lakes. The map showed two lakes off to the west, but I didn't want to go hunting for them. They were too far off the track I wanted to take. Some dirt roads went into hills on the right, and one of them was the best I could do. I couldn't think of any way to get the truck clean out of sight, so I turned off, went over one rise and then another, didn't see anybody, stopped the truck, and got out. I went all over the cab and the rest of the truck, looking for whatever would help, but there was not anything. I went through the engine, too, and pulled out some wires that I might be able to strip down and use for snares up north. I could have struck my flints and set fire to the thing, but there didn't seem to be any real good to that, though I would have done it if I thought it would confuse them a little and buy me some more time. As it was, I just walked away, topped out the two rises, stayed on the east side of the hills, but high enough so that I could check the road now and then, and went on, carrying my bag of feathers and fish heads and other stuff, foraging around for a place to sleep. If my silk map and I had any sort of good relation, I was not far from the ocean, and might even come out somewhere near the strait. I formed a picture of it in my mind, which would not be anything like it would turn out, but it would do for now, sure enough.

No trees, but bushes. Not plenty of them, or thick together, but some. If nobody came along, I thought I would rest up a bit as soon as I had put some distance between the truck and me. It would not be bad if I ate something, the way I felt, slept until I woke up, and then went on up north for the rest of the night. I might even be able to use the road part of the way.

❖   ❖   ❖

I slept in a bush between two other bushes, covered with leaves and my bag covered with leaves, my feet pulled up and in the bag. I was real tired, and dropped right off. I believe I might have tried to catch the reflection of lights from the road, but there were not any, or if there were they went right on.

I was rested when I woke up, but I could have used more, and tried to go back to sleep. It was cold, not the real stuff I could get with and into, and would be ready for, and prepared for, but cold enough to make it hard to sleep. I didn't want to wear myself out — believe me, not right now — and wished I could have had as good a night's sleep as I did back in the house where I fought with the old guy and his sword. Though the soldiers had beat me up pretty bad, none of them scared me as much as that old guy did, because he was on to something I didn't know anything about and didn't have any way to deal with. If I could have got him out in the snow it would have been different. He would have never known what hit him, or where it came from, or even if it was there, before it was too late. I felt like I had lost a round back there. But the sleeping sure was good, and I wished I had it back.

I saw there wasn't any use in staying where I was, and got up and moved on. There wasn't much light, but I could see well enough, and there was at least a chance that I could make a few miles before the sun came up. But the ocean — when would it be there? A whole new turnaround of my situation, maybe even a whole new life, would start just as soon as I saw it. A day? Two days? Two days and two nights? When? I was ready to kill somebody if he had a boat. That would be my decision; I would pick him. I was looking forward to more time that I would control. Let whoever it would be come into my time.

I kept walking, along the low side of a hill. One hill connected to another, and I really didn't know whether this was good or bad. I was real tired, and I was not walking anymore, much less stalking, but I guess what you could call trudging, and this could have been bad, because my alertness was low. I remember the Air Force people talking about alertness — alertness in the air, alertness at the base, alertness in your personal life — but I didn't have any of that now. I was only fucking tired, and I was trudging. The best things I had were leaving me, and I went on and on. I really didn't care.

But there was a convoy. It seemed to me that I had a special connection with convoys, that there were guys amongst those trucks who could understand me. They pulled up. This was good. My interest took on, tired as I was.

They all stopped. This was something. I watched them, all those trucks, over the crest of the hill. There was a whole long line of them. Even at night you could see the dust; you could see the dust around them in their own lights. It was a scene that I would not have wanted to be in, and yet I was in it, under orders. Why not?

I heaved up some, where I could get a look. Everything had stopped, and I watched the lights. They were doing something to the lights. At first the low dusty hills were caught in the glow, and it made the shadows strong. Then everything began to tone down. The lights started to go, but not disappear. The shadows rounded off, and I inched up. From what I could tell, the drivers and the other people in the trucks were working with the headlights, putting something over them. They were making slits, taking most of the light out of the light, probably with tape of some kind. The light kept dimming, and still stayed. Still stayed; then they all started up. The hills shook. The shadows traveled and moved very easily as the trucks went on, on out of sight.

What about all this? I thought. Were they heading for some secret installation, or what? I couldn't tell, but I had another notion, another interpretation, and if I was right things would break in my favor. In the dimming of the lights I saw the ocean: a port, some kind of anchorage, something they didn't want to show from far off, over an open space. I shook and gripped myself. Maybe I had made it through the fire, through the fields and the terraces, through the fights, through my own blood and gone teeth, through the lakes and the creeks, through the stars, through the good times and the bad. If the ocean opened up in front of me, I didn't think there was anything I couldn't do. And if I could find a way to get to the other island, and into the cold country, the real country, the mountains and the isolation, and find just a little game, I believed there was not a person in Japan, or any bunch of them, who could stay in it with me. I had plenty of confidence, if the guys in the trucks had been dimming down for the reasons I was hoping for. I thought I would stretch out, and move and take a look when the dawn gave me a shot at it.

I waited, lying between some scrub bushes, but I couldn't get to sleep to save my soul. I was too excited thinking the ocean, even the north island, might be in sight just over the next rise. There was nothing to keep me from trying to look, even just as things were, and I decided to change, go forward a little. I picked up my stuff and went on through the bushes.

When I got to the crest of the hill I couldn't make out anything. I couldn't see any better than I had before. But the night felt more open; the way you breathe is different when there's lots of space in front of you. There were some clouds and not much moon, but I stayed and waited, listened and tried to see. If the ocean was really down there in front of me, something would flash sooner or later.

It happened, very faint and far off, but a dim flicker with a levelness to it that I didn't think anything on land could have caused. What there was of a moon came out and it happened again, and then again, and then all at once, all over. I was still not absolutely sure that I was looking at what I wanted to see, but I was on the knife edge of believing that I might be dead sure, if I stood there long enough. I would have to wait for daylight, though, to be as sure as I wanted. I lay down again, just under the south side of the hill, made myself as small as I could, and slept.

❖   ❖   ❖

Light came. The sky had cleared. There were plenty of stars everywhere, and I lay for a while looking at them through the bushes; I had got used to looking at stars through bushes. Then, keeping low, almost crawling, I went up to the crest of the hill and turned all my eyesight on what would be there, on what was there.

It was the greatest sight I have ever seen, I tell you. About a quarter of a mile away was a brown village of wood huts, and beyond that was the ocean, blue-gray and restless and going out of sight. I scanned for the other island, but it was not anywhere I could see it. There must have been a dock or wharf in the town, because there was a big black ship next to it, and soldiers were taking stuff out of the backs of the trucks and carrying it toward the ship. Some kind of loading operation was going on. The ship was probably a supply ship, and if that was true it would probably take a good long time to load.

None of that would do me any good, though. I didn't want to steal a skiff or a rowboat — even if I could have with all those soldiers around — and just get out on the water and hope for the best. I needed to know exactly where I was going, because I would have to get across the strait in a night, and there couldn't be any fumbling around about it, or the waste of any time. I knelt down and got out the map. As far as I was able to figure, there were not but a couple of towns big enough to service any

kind of heavy shipping, and they were both west of where
Honshu and Hokkaido came closest together. It would be east,
then. I needed to get away from the soldiers as fast and as far as
I could: try to make a forced march for a couple of hours, then
hole up in the bushes, get some rest, and work east at night for
as long as I could stand up to it. And I needed something to eat.
I was tired of dried fish heads mixed with feathers and uncooked
rice, but I was not desperate yet. The main thing was to move
out, make a line where I could check the ocean whenever it
was light enough, and make time to the east whichever way I
could.

I was in the bushes for two days and two nights. I've never
been so bored with bushes or so tired in my life. I've crossed
forty miles of muskeg, between the Tlicit River and Rabbit
Creek, a hundred miles south of where I lived, when the spring
thaw was on. The land was more than half water, and you had to
pull your foot out of the shit after every step you took, sometimes with your hands, but that was not nearly as bad as this,
because in the flats up there you've got something to look at:
coming on a nest in the hummocks, or feathers where some
predator got a bird, and the live birds keep rising up out of the
water or planing down onto it. Here, where I was now, in these
uninteresting dead hills, there was not one sign of life, nothing
but scruffy bushes with tough twigs. I thought once about striking the flints and trying to boil some rice when the dark came,
but I didn't have any water, and I decided that the twigs were
probably too worthless to burn, growing in that black soil that
was too sorry to grow anything else in. That was most likely the
reason they hadn't terraced these hills, though there might have
been some other reason they didn't do it. Both days, at early
morning and twilight, I'd scan the horizon for the other island,

but it didn't show. If it was not east of where I had started out, I had plumbered myself sure enough, because I didn't have the energy to go back the other way. Everything was riding on my being able to see the island, and it may have been farther off than I had thought, too far to see from anywhere on Honshu. If that was so, it was too bad for me — too bad, tough shit, and so long.

With all the thousands of twigs pulling at me for two days, I didn't make a lot of distance, but I made some. All the time, nobody came up to where I was. It may have been that all the interest was in fishing. Back on Tinian they told us how dependent the Japs were on fishing, and looking down on the water and the beaches I could believe it. There were lots of boats of all sizes on the beaches and on the water, everywhere you looked. I watched a little during the day, and a lot at night. When it got dark all the boats that were out, or going out, put on a light of some sort, probably an oil lantern. Exactly why the drivers in the convoy had taped all the truck lights was something I couldn't understand. I reckoned to myself that that was just like the Japanese, and let it go at that; it's an answer you can't argue with.

I was discouraged, I don't mind telling you. If the other island didn't show pretty soon, I would be too weak and played out to get to it. Three things were in my favor, though, and they buoyed me up, because there was nothing else but them to do it. First, the weather was good, and real clear; if anybody could see Hokkaido from Honshu, I would be able to, if I found the strait. It had turned off warm and there was a fresh breeze, even blowing over the hill. Being as tired as I was from the twigs, I could sleep good, and I did. The third thing was that there were all those boats, and if I played my cards right I could have just about any of them I wanted. When people were not actually in them, they just walked away, like it was never their idea to have anything to do with them. Half the time they didn't even bother to tie them up, but just anchored them to the beach with a rope and a heavy rock, or something that looked like a building block.

Nobody took the trouble to guard anything, and it came to me that I could change my plan now, and that I ought to. Before, I thought I would probably have to kill somebody, maybe even two people, to get a boat, and if that was so, I could see how they might come out into the water after me, though I hadn't made out any patrol boats or military craft at all. Right then I added one item to the list of what I wanted to get, besides two oars I could lash together to make a two-bladed paddle like a kayak's. It was whatever made the light — a lantern, whatever. If I could get out from the beach on the night part of the fishing shift, I could just be one of the boys, out there working for a living. There would be that about the light: it would kind of make me official. That much was settled. I moved east over a couple of hills, and the ocean moved off to the north. Taking my time, I followed it. In broad daylight I stood up and looked.

What happened then was more like a film on my eyes than anything real. It was a far-off film, but it did seem to me that the ocean in one place was not like it was everywhere else. I could not be sure, but it may have been that there was a difference in one place. I blinked and tried again, and the same thing happened. There was not a definite shape, but there was — there might have been — a difference that I could feel more than I could see. I got down, tried to clear my eyes with my fingers, got up, and tried again. I told myself not to fake it, not to make things up. I wanted so much for the land to be there that it was almost like I was trying to think it into the real world, whether it wanted to come or not: land, a whole island where the real snow was, the real space, a place where I could live the way I knew how. I gave it another try. The same.

I had time. I worked to the east over three hills, stood up, and scanned again. This time the ocean was dead even, all the way left and right. I came back to the place where I had been, over a rickety little fishing village, and it was the same as it had been before. It was not so much that I knew something was there, at the absolute limit of what I could see, but there might have been, and right then I knew I had to go with it, and I *would* go with it. I didn't think of it as my only chance, because I kept that notion down, but all the time I knew it was, and my blood began to pump. I sat down just under the brow of the hill and got out my emergency kit for the compass, the asshole compass. No matter what we called it, the needle was true, as true as it was on any other compass; I had checked it out. I raised up and sighted on true north, and took a bearing on the part of the ocean that might have been not quite the same as the rest. I made it out to be nine degrees east of where I was, and that was good enough. I put the compass back in the kit and checked my gear, everything in it, and waited for the first of the dark and for the first of the boats to go out.

Before it got dark I took a last look at the land below me. Past the shacks of the little village was a long point of land, and I figured to go around the village and out to the point and try to find a boat there, where there didn't seem to be anything but beach. But by the way the fishermen treated their boats, leaving them just wherever they happened to come to, I was pretty sure there would be some on the point, and unless a bunch of people went out to them together, I felt like I could handle just one or even two of them, and I might not even have to do that. My plans began to heat up.

I needed the whole night, so the sooner I got started, the better. On the other hand, it would not be a good idea for me to try to go out with the first group of them. There would be too many at the same time. It would be better for me to be a straggler, but not too much of one.

I hung back a while, watching how they put out. I concentrated on one, just a young guy by himself. He put a few things in — I couldn't tell what they were — cast the rope off the paving block, got in, and went on out. And that was that. There was no hurry about it. It was very simple, something that nobody would pay any attention to. But that might be the hardest thing of all for me: to keep it simple and slow and just do like everybody else. Any sort of fast motion or violence would not be good. I gave up the idea of killing anybody. I had to find myself an empty boat and get out on the water. That was all, and it was everything.

I started walking out toward the spit. I passed seven or eight people getting ready to go, and nobody even looked at me. I went on beyond what little light there was, out onto the spit. I would have been surprised if somebody didn't keep his boat out there. Maybe there would be more than one.

But there were no boats there, and I wondered what to do next. If I went back through town and into the hills again, what would that get me? I wouldn't do that no matter what. I was bound for the other island, any way I could get there. I decided to try another fifty yards on the spit, where it got darker and darker.

And then I saw two boats right together. The smaller one would do, and there was nobody around. I went to it and used my flashlight, which still had some juice. The boat was about ten feet long, had oars and the lamp. It also had some thin ropes in it. There was no reason to wait, and I got in and shoved off. The water felt like a million dollars, especially after all the walking I had been doing on land through the twigs and thorns. I rocked a little, just for the feeling. It was great in that big quiet. There was not much moon, but using my flashlight again I started to do a couple of things. I took the oars and the rope and lashed the oars together so they would make a two-bladed paddle, like I was used to. That meant I could move the boat like a kayak, facing forward; it was better for me to see where I was going. The oars were light, and would work well that way. Then I got out the compass, set my heading, and looked for a star to line up the heading with. I couldn't make out Polaris, but there was a big star, maybe even a planet, that was not more than a few points off the compass heading. That would be good enough.

There were only a couple of boats between me and the open dark water, and I worked out past them. I didn't think anybody would notice how I sat in the boat, but somebody in one of the other ones said something, probably to me, then said it again. At first I thought I'd paddle hard, make a run for it, but I kept down the panic and tried something else. I knelt down on the floorboards, got out the flints, and lit the lamp. That seemed to do it, because nobody said anything else. Like I say, maybe the lamp was it, or maybe they just lost interest. Anyway, I was out in the big dark of water now, by myself.

The only sound was mine, and it was a nice rhythm, one side and then the other, holding to the course, putting the prow right under the star, and moving toward it. The water rocked me; I rocked the water. It was almost-black dark, but not quite.

I got where I could see a little, but not much. Nothing happened for four hours. I was into my rhythm, and deeper and deeper into it. I didn't have any notion as to how much distance I had made except by the time it took me to make it. My main worry was that I wouldn't be able to get all the way across in the dark. In daylight I would be a sitting duck for sure, with no cover and camouflage, and no scheme I could come up with would be good enough. But that was not the point. The point was that I was moving on the water, and that I was moving the water. But the thought kept coming back to me: what was I *doing* here, halfway between the enemy's two countries, something nobody could even have dreamed up? The water hit the sides of the boat as I kept up my rhythm. Who had a better right to it? But again, what was I doing here? The water was right, felt right, I could have been here on vacation and nobody would have said anything about it. But I was not fooling myself. I was where I was. But after a minute I didn't let myself think like that. Only for a second did I think like that, but it was wrong. Only for a second: a flash, a night flash. Then, no more.

But when the oars had come into my hands double-bladed, a kayak paddle now, something happened to the strait between Honshu and Hokkaido, something the place could never have imagined, that would never be there again. The snow came back, and the real cold, the gut-blue water and the long stretches and, above all, the ice. There was the glacier. The glacier was coming to me with every dig of the paddle, every stroke, every slant of the body to go with the paddle, left and right. I had seen it, and would see it again, the real pure thing, the pure color. Believe me when I tell you that when the glacier calves off there is something that you don't get with every day.

You would have to be out there in a kayak, where it is quiet, no engines; where you lift your paddle out of the water because there's not anything else you can do. The ice slides, you with your mouth open, slides down and falls: falls groaning like a woman, somebody said, but it doesn't sound like that to me. If there was ever a woman in the world who sounded like that, I wouldn't want to be around. No, it was something else, something that the world said itself, that nobody could know except what said it. But there it was, right ahead of me, the shucked-out middle of the glacier, the same color as the star where I set the prow, and was going right-left for it, through the channel. Well, where I was heading I couldn't get enough of remembering it, the pure blue: the pure more-than-blue. It was the most intense and most pure, a clean shot to the inside. And so *bright*, so deep bright, not like anything else, nothing like it. When you were out in the kayak you started with some notion of walrus, of seal, of whatever you might find on the floe, even a polar bear. But when the glacier starts to calve, all animals go somewhere else; there is nothing but what is. When I told you before that you wouldn't see this every day, I was right. It was the most intense, and the most pure, it was — well, you could say — secret, the best of it, the heart of ice, the heart you never had any idea was there, and when you saw it, knew had to be there.

That was what I thought about in my rhythm. And when I wanted to stop and look, I stopped and looked, back and forward, but mostly back.

Here I was, here I was. The log train had been snow, the fields where I was going, where I hoped to get to. It was the long line of deer, buried to the briskets in snow, all facing one way. You bet: the line of deer heads, all bucks, bound for infinity.

But now it was the ice, the water and the ice, the white sea; what I said.

I must have made ten miles by now. I was not sure, but I thought I had; I had to think it. There were no other boats around. I rested a minute and started out again. But something had happened that I couldn't explain. I didn't have the star anymore. I looked up. The sky was clear enough, and had plenty of stars in it, but not that one. I knew that the star would not stay in exactly the same place, but it wouldn't matter all that much; it would be close enough. Hokkaido was a big island, but now I didn't know where it was except generally, and if I didn't make it across at the narrowest point, I wouldn't make it by daylight, and I would be gone — no hope, no chance, no north. I looked for the star again.

Between me and the land was as dark as anything you could imagine. It was that dark before, and it was that dark now. No, it was darker. Darker, more solid, and it might have been moving. I strained my eyes out over the water. I tried to contrast. And it came, and it was big. An enormous ship — it couldn't have been anything but a battleship — was right in front of me. And now I could hear it, hear it cutting the water. My boat began to rock, a little at first and then more. I held still where I was, backwatering with the paddle. I could handle it all right, and now I could make out more than I had been able to before. The shape in front of me was so damn big, it was like a mountain or a city, going from left to right. I thought I even made out a couple of towers on it. I had the impression that the whole thing was stiff, like it was cut out of wood or cardboard, that it didn't really have any weight, that it was flat and didn't have any insides, only an outline. And so *quiet*. The faint sound it did make was a kind of run-together bubbling, and it was strange to me, and funny more than not, that a battleship, as far as I was concerned, was a huge flat cardboard cutout that bubbled.

I waited for it to pass, and the star to come back. Just to have something to do, I turned around and looked back, and what I saw shook me up a little. Another big ship was going by in the opposite direction. This one I could make out better, and it was big, maybe even bigger than the other one. I was right between them, and the water around my boat and the boat itself began to boil. No bull elk at rutting time ever bucked more. The whole strait was swirling around me from both directions; it was like being sawed in two by water. I dropped the paddle on the floor and held on, doing everything I could to keep from turning over. It would be bad news sure enough if I got thrown out and lost the boat, or it sank. Goodbye, goodbye, I said; this may just be it.

But it wasn't. Both ships went by, bubbling front and back, the water came quiet around me, and the star was where it had been, or almost. I picked up the paddle, made a couple of adjustments, put the prow under the star, grabbed hold of the water on one side, shifted the blade to the other, and plowed on forward, glad to be going.

Three more hours, four, eight hours now. I was getting very tired, my arms and my hands mainly, but also my back, from sitting so long in the same position. I judged that it was about two or two and a half hours until first light. Two and a half, no more. Where was Hokkaido? Had I played everything wrong? No way back, no way out. I kept going forward.

Another hour, and nothing. My arms were about to fall out of their sockets, my hands were raw. I would not have been surprised if I'd got seasick from the constant right-left, left-right movement that it took to move the boat. I thought that maybe my eyes had learned something about the situation from straining to look at the battleships, and it might have been that they had. I did my best to concentrate the land into being where I wanted it to be, but I didn't make a very good job of it, because to add to my other troubles I was getting sleepy. I could hardly keep my lids up. They were not so much heavy to fall, just determined to come down. Don't do it, I said; don't let it happen.

But it did. I woke up and shook it off. I looked for light: light would get me castrated, light would kill me. Still dark, still the star, still headed right. My lantern had gone out. There was the same kind of dark that the first ship had made, the darker than the other dark, the solid, the dark inside the dark. I checked again, I strained my guts, I put everything I had into it. If it was not land, I couldn't find it, and I couldn't make it, no matter how hard I tried.

I was almost sure it was, though, and as I came closer I was more sure. I passed a boat a couple of hundred yards off, and it sure hadn't come from the side I'd started from. I must be getting close. Closer and closer, and the best sign of all was that the star was right on it, though a lot higher. I kept moving, I picked up. I kept up.

It was land, dark and solid. I didn't see a thing about it, except that there were not any lights. Patrols, I thought; are there any patrols? Some guy walking the beach who would shoot at anything? Anything that moved? Or a couple of guys, talking that excited talk before they opened up, opened fire. There was nothing but silence, a great good quiet, as I drifted in.

I grounded, and it was a feeling, up through the backbone, that you wouldn't forget. Land. All right. Land. Now what?

Could I risk the flashlight? There didn't seem to be any reason why not. But I hung back, my thumb on the slide. If I struck that light, a whole barrage, an enfilade, might hit me, just because of a spark.

But they were not expecting that spark. They would not be that ready.

I was already thinking ahead, right away. First secure the beach, then move inland, northwest at first. So said my silk map, which had come to be so much a part of what I was doing that I would not have taken on a big topo map, to swap for it. I began to understand what they had told us on Tinian about survival: cherish your equipment. But I knew more. A lot more. I could tell them about it, whoever would want to listen.

Ground, solid. I turned to the boat that had got me across. What to say? What to do? There was no other way we would ever meet again, and we both knew it. I kissed the palm of my hand and put it on the gunwale: that was all I had, but it was what I meant.

Then I turned to the new thing, the new island. Now. Now. What to do? There were no patrols, no coast guard, no nothing. What were things like here? It was dark and that was good, but it had its problems. The map — the silk, the body silk — said go northwest first. Then, after you pass a certain point, swing due north. That would be the point, right. But first northwest, and get away from the coast and the boat. There was no place to hide the boat, and it wouldn't have done any good if I had tried to drag it around and conceal it; somebody would have found it. So I left it where it was, wondering what the Japanese would think of their own oars made into a kayak paddle. Let them wonder while I moved.

Moved, moved inland, northwest. I needed a mile at least, and I could lie down, let go, let everything go. There was not anything I wanted so much except just to let go. And yet the strait, the battleships, the whipsawing of the water, were right there, and the hills, if I could find them, would feed in, would, like you could say, be fed by all that water, by those ships, and the rest of it, to the northwest on the new island.

I got the impression that there might be a town or even a city over the hills to my left, and that I might be fairly close to it, but I didn't do anything about it. Before I left I sat down on the beach around a turn from the boat and picked up stuff from underneath me: sand, shells. None of it would do, and I moved inland thirty or forty yards, with all the water I could carry in my hands, to where there was real dirt. I plastered it all over me. Whatever was there: whatever, I would look like it. Then I picked up my bag and started walking, one more time.

One mile, I thought. I was sure ready to sleep. Trees, if I could find them. Bushes. A tree. A rock. Not a road. Not a field. I didn't see a soul, and could have gone on and made a little distance, but I was too tired, and the light was coming up. I could see now, and I put in under some bushes and lay down. They were not much for concealment, but they were all that was there, and I could hardly stand up. I was on the north island, and that was enough for now. I felt very beat up and out of things, but I kept telling myself that I had made it to the north island, and if I could just keep going I would be in the deserted part of things, and I could stalk, could find a way to trap. I would be where I could control and live. I didn't ask anything else.

❖   ❖   ❖

I must have slept all day, because the stars were coming out when I woke up. I got on my feet, picked up my bag, and went on in much better shape. At first, when I had carried the bag around with me everywhere, I thought that surely somebody would ask me about it, what was in it, where I had got it, or make some kind of trouble about it. Nobody ever did, though, and gradually, from looking around a lot, I came to understand that everybody in Japan is carrying something. They can't walk without carrying something. The men can't, and the women sure-God can't. So it was all right if I went along toting a bag of swan feathers and fish heads. Nobody knew, and nobody cared. It made me feel a lot safer.

When it got full into night I started traveling again, using my flashlight whenever I needed to. The ground was rocky and rough, and it would take me maybe a couple of days to cover enough ground to turn due north again. I found a road and moved along parallel to it, keeping it in sight but never on it. In three days I only saw three vehicles, and I began to think that Hokkaido was completely deserted. But I was not taking any chances, and was just as cautious as I had been before.

When I made the change from northwest to full north I felt like a millionaire: better. Polaris swung around and trued up, and the land started to rise. Underfoot was good; all I needed was snow, and game. The animal never lived that I couldn't stalk.

I went on, and on, and up, traveling some in the daytime now, because I saw I could. With all that time alone, I took to checking myself, to see how I was doing. Three of my teeth were gone, but the gums were healing up all right and didn't hurt so much anymore, and the tooth that had been loose had stayed in and got solid again, and I took that to be a good sign. I could chew on one side as well as I ever could, if I had something decent to chew. For the rest, I felt OK. There was nothing

wrong with my hands, and my feet and legs were better than
they'd been since I left Alaska. My nose would probably be
crooked for the rest of my life, but that didn't bother me at all.
Why should it? The main thing was that the land was rising,
and I was going up with it. I looked forward to plateauing out,
and living high and cold.

It kept happening. As I got higher the trees got better and
started to look like trees ought to look. I didn't know what they
were, but they were not far from being oaks, with thick bark and
a lot of branches. I happened to glance up into one of them just
as a light snow — the kind the Eskimos call eyelash snow —
was beginning to come down, and I'll be damned if there were
not five or six monkeys sitting in it. I had never seen any
monkeys except in the Denver zoo, and these were not like any
of them. I gave the tree a kick, just to see if I could stir them up,
but it didn't bother them. I didn't want to bother them; just
playing a little.

The snow was good, because when there was more of it I
could get a fix on what game might be around. I would be able
to track. I had problems, though, like always. With the snow my
heart came up, and I also knew I had to do something about my
hands and feet. The gloves I had got from the old warrior were
not thick enough for really cold weather, and my feet were
numb enough to be dangerous. What to do? I didn't have the
answer, but figured, like all the other times, that I'd find some
way to deal with it.

I sat down with my back to a tree, waiting for the snow to
settle in and the animals to run around, to run from or hide or
stalk, to leave me the signs that they had to leave. The ground
with a nice roll to it, the trees in a kind of open woods: there
would have to be things that lived here. I got up and looked for

a straight branch, and finally found one about fifteen feet from the ground. I hitched up the tree, cut it off, and came back down. I trimmed the branch and lashed on my short GI knife to make it a spear. That and my long bread knife were the only weapons I had, and unless I could find a way to trap something, I would have to use one or the other if I found game. I didn't have any notion I could kill an animal with my bare hands, or maybe my bare hands and teeth, but if I had to, I would try. Men have a real disadvantage, with such short teeth; almost any animal is better off, even rats. I got up and tried out the spear, gave it a couple of short casts. My throwing arm is not one of my strong points, so it struck me that it would be best if I didn't try to throw, but worked in close enough to stab. The best of all would be to make whatever animal there was come to me, come by me, or maybe I could hit him while he was grazing, nuzzling stuff through the snow. When animals have their heads down they can't see you. That's why they always look up before they go back down.

The spear was good enough, and I left the bag under the tree and went looking. When I was a few hundreds yards into the woods things began to happen underfoot. There were rabbits here, and I picked up the pugmarks of some kind of cat. And there were hoofprints, too — the best sign of all. All of these had just come out in the last hour or so, which was also good. It meant there was plenty of life. The hoofprints had me stumped, though. I didn't believe they were from deer; they were too small. What on earth, then? Some kind of goat was as close as I could come. What kind of goat lived in the mountains on the north island of Japan? We had had some survival courses on Tinian, and I tried to think back. But the truth was that I never paid much attention to them, figuring that I knew more about it than the instructors did, who got everything out of a book.

I went on in, in the general direction of the hoofprints, checking my compass now and again. I didn't want to lose track of my bag; it was like home. It was the closest I could get, and the closest I wanted.

I followed one set of hoofprints, which was getting harder to do because more snow was coming down, more flakes and bigger, but still not real heavy. The sky was overcast everywhere you looked, and I expected that the snow would go on for a long time. And then I saw — whatever it was, whatever they were. No more than twenty-five yards off was a herd of about fifteen, grayish, not too much darker than the snow, in a clump of trees upwind from me. They were about the size of goats, from what I could make out, with the visibility like it was. They surely had to be goats of some kind: short goats and heavy, that's the best I can say it. They were meat, though, and maybe hides, too, and I got over behind a tree to plan my stalk. I really wanted to fall on them — or one of them — from above, like I had the Jap soldier in the truck. That was the most satisfying thing that ever happened to me in my life, because if I hadn't been as close to being a fisher marten as a human being can get, there was nobody else who could: the fisher, which is the best animal ever made.

I was about to step and move forward one tree when something spooked the herd, and they came right toward me. I got ready, and had a big one picked out. But I didn't make any move, because I was too surprised. The one I was getting ready to hit had an arrow in him. And behind the foreleg joint, too, right in the boiler room, the heart-lung section. He was already staggering, and didn't have too far to go before he would fall and kick.

I took a stab at another one, but all I did was turn the herd, and they went back the way they had come from. They stopped then, all together with their heads down and making a lot of commotion. I heard a voice scream out, and it was not any goat voice, nothing that came from those ghost-goats, and I realized they were ganging up on the other hunter, probably goring him, and might kill him, sure enough. I took a few steps and was there, and stuck one of them deep, then pulled out and stuck him again. He moved away, but two of the others came off the guy on the ground and hit me in the legs before I could even think. One of them didn't get in a good lick, and didn't do much more than just graze me, but the other one did, and hit me in the big-meat part of the leg with both horns. They went in deep, especially one of them did, went in like needles. They were as sharp and thin and pointed as a mountain goat's horns. This goat, or whatever he was, was not fooling around: he even shook his horn inside of me, to tear things up a little more. I stayed on my feet; if I had hit the ground it would have been all over. I jerked the horns out of me and kicked the shit out of him with the other foot, and he and the rest of the herd took off, except the one I had stuck and the other one with the arrow in him.

I looked around. I looked at my leg. It hurt bad but it wasn't bleeding much yet; with puncture wounds the blood just kind of wells up. As deep as the place was, I knew there would be plenty of blood and it would be hard to get it stopped. I put a handful of snow on it and went over to look at the other guy. He was still on the ground, rolling back and forth, and I knelt down by him, mainly to see what he was like. He had a beard, a long

one, about half white. A beard was something I hadn't seen
in Japan, not even a mustache. He was not a soldier, and he
didn't even look like a decent civilian. He was a scrawny guy,
smaller than I am, and was dressed mostly in furs. He must
belong to some kind of tribe around here, was the best I could
figure. He was not civilized, I can tell you. That I would have
vouched for.

I went over to him, as best I could. His outfit was torn in a
couple of places, but I didn't see any blood, and I was pretty sure
he was not hurt nearly as bad as I was. We both got on our feet,
and he stared into my face for a long time. With him, I didn't
feel that I ought to pretend I was Japanese or try to keep him
from looking straight at me, and that was a relief. He picked up
his bow, turned his back, and left.

I was down to myself again, with nothing but two dead goats.
The blood was welling up in my leg pretty good, but in a way I
had done what I came to do, with some help from another guy. I
fell down beside the goat with the arrow and started cutting
him, stripping away the pelt, trying to keep it as whole as I
could. I meant to try to make an outfit out of it. But when I got
that meat bared off, I forgot about the hide. I started to eat, first
off the hip and then up around the spine, bringing the blood in
too, as much as I could get. Don't let anybody ever tell you
blood is not good to drink. If you make gravy out of it there's
really not much difference between it and raw blood. Every
now and then I'd look at my leg, where my own blood kept
coming, and I couldn't get away from the idea that the more
blood I lost, the more I was replacing from the goat. It was a
strange thing, losing and getting back at the same time.

I ate and ate, cramming the hole in my leg with snow whenever I thought about it. The meat was like a transfusion. I hadn't

tasted meat in such a long time that it was like something from a place I had never been. My body just went all around it, and I was sure that I would live. They say about the wolverine that it will never be driven off a kill, that it will stay with a down caribou or elk until the last piece of marrow is cracked out of the bones, that it'll die before it will leave what it's eating. I could believe it; I out-ate any wolverine. When I'd had enough, I packed my leg with snow again and finished stripping the hide off the goat, then went to the other one, the one I had stuck, and skinned him, too. I didn't eat much off the second one, but drank some blood. When I got through I was real bloated and hurting bad. I wondered whether that goat's horn had hit the bone of my leg. There was a deep electric feeling in the puncture that I couldn't account for in any other way. I looked at the place and wondered if I ought not to try and sew it up with some of my fishing line, but I really didn't think that would do any good, and came to the conclusion that it would probably be better to let it bleed and clean out. I've always healed up fairly fast, faster than most, and even though it was a puncture wound, I believed I could trust my luck, and my body. Just get the bleeding stopped: freeze it, lots of snow.

But I may have been fooling myself. Since my leg hadn't started to heal yet, and so didn't have the stiffness that you get with clotting, I could still move around, though I had to take it slow. I got together some brush and made a kind of lean-to, more like a blind for still-hunting than anything else, and got into it, pulling the bloody hides over me. After that, I don't know. I either fainted or went to sleep. Maybe both, but I don't think I was even worried about what was going to happen to me, I was so full of meat and hurt. The night was coming on, and it was still snowing, very peaceful and quiet. I was out real quick.

When I woke up I didn't remember where I was or what had happened. The snow had stopped, and it was colder than before. My leg was stiff when I looked at it; blood was all the way down to the ankle. Sitting up to look cost me a lot, and I lay back down. It was day, one day or the other, and the blind had chinks in it. Through one of them a man was looking at me, and then I knew there was another. Probably more than two. I raised up and put some of the branches out of the way. There was not anything I could do, so I just lay there and looked back at them. Then I got up on the good knee. They were all armed — all ten or twelve — with spears and bows and arrows, but they didn't make any move to use them.

They seemed curious and even friendly, though maybe puzzled. The fact that I was an enemy of theirs and would kill them if I needed to did not seem to be a part of their thinking. From the way they looked and their expressions I would not have been surprised to find out they did not even know there was a war going on. As far as they were concerned I might have dropped out of the clouds, which I guess is true, in a way. I tried my best to stand up, and mostly made it. I pointed at my leg, and the closest one to me bent down to look at it. When he straightened I could not believe he was not really sympathetic toward my situation. They had a horse with them, a short shaggy one, and they pushed me — not hard — toward it. I had never ridden a horse in my life, but it looked like they wanted to give me some help, and I could sure use it. It cost me every bit of pain I could stand, but I got on, and they were in favor of it, I could tell. I happened to glance down, and one of them had my bag, from a couple of miles off. I was surprised at first, and then not. They were woods people, and knew what was on their turf.

We went along through the trees, every step that the horse took going through my leg like the horn of the goat that made it. Some goat, I thought, or whatever it was. A lot more goat than any other goat, even a mountain goat. I had never seen anything on hooves fight like that, or a bunch of them gang up on anything. I tell you, I admired that animal, and I was glad the woods people brought along the two hides I had skinned off them. I didn't want to leave them behind in the blind I had thrown together.

I don't know how long it took to get where we were going. I was close to passing out some of the time, but I didn't seem to be bleeding as much as I was before. I could have been wrong about that, though. I spent the time thinking about the damn goats. I was glad I had eaten so much of their meat. Maybe something would come over, maybe their blood would give me back some of mine; with a little difference, it could be. They could sure fight — I couldn't get over it. They were quick and mean, and they went after it; they came after you.

We went on, into a village. My head was down and I couldn't see very much. But what I did see set me up straight. Two guys on those little horses were dragging a bear, a dead bear, into a clear space in the middle of the huts. I didn't even give myself a chance to see what the huts were like, or what the village was like, because they were dragging a bear into town, and that has to matter. It was a fair-sized black, not too much different from the ones at home. They pulled him on his back through the snow, his paws up, and near to being stiff. Most of the people there came around him, very still, the guys with long beards, little bent-over women and kids. Nobody touched the bear, whose mouth was open, with the big teeth and the tongue hanging out on one side with blood dripping off it. I was beginning to haze out again, and concentrated on the bear to keep me going. But he couldn't do it for me and I couldn't do it for myself, and the next thing I remember I was lying with my bad leg up, probably on some furs in one of the huts. I was not hungry, but I was real sleepy, and I went back under.

I woke up once, when it was dead night. Whatever my situation was, it was not as bad, and I eased my leg and fell, fell one more time, and deep; it was best to do it. Sleeping and waking up went on for a while, and the people kept coming in and out. They fed me real well: meat, probably bear meat as long as it lasted, but chicken, too, which would have amazed anybody. They had bread right in there with everything else, made into little cakes, and their gravy was the best yet, thick and salty. They seemed to be anxious to do anything they could for me, get me anything I signaled to them I wanted, and a lot that I never asked for: heavy fur pants made out of the same kind of goat that had gored me, and a long bearskin shirt like a robe, fur gloves, mukluks, the works. I wondered if they treated all strangers like this, or if they ever saw any, and put down their attitude toward me to the other guy, the other hunter who had been down under the goats. The fact that I had run them off him and had got gored doing it might have been the reason, or else they might have cut me up like the bear I had seen them dragging in. Everywhere you looked there were parts and pieces of bears: bear hides, bear paws, bear teeth on necklaces, bear paws nailed up to the walls. In my hut there was a big bear head right over where I was lying, and I looked at it for a long time every day. As I said, I hadn't known there were any bears around, for I hadn't seen any sign. But these little men with the whiskers sure must have known how to find them.

Finally I got to where I could sit up and stay awake for a while and begin to have an interest in things. The women, I think it was, had left the hides I had taken off the goats in the hut with me, and I thought I might have a try at curing them, softening them, and making clothes out of them in case I had to use them later. I had seen Eskimo women chew on seal hides, and knew more or less how they did it, but I didn't have the knack and gave up before I let myself get discouraged and frustrated. I signed to the women who fed me that they could have the hides, to take them away, even though I really didn't want to let them go. I had got where I liked them, in the same way I admired the animals they came from.

My wound was filling in and didn't hurt nearly so much anymore, even though that leg was stiff. When I had been there about ten days, I'd judge, I tried to stand up on it, but it began to pain me so much that I was glad to give it more time. Five days more I stayed there, doing the same things and limping to another hut that had this big pit for a toilet. The village was the cleanest place I had ever seen men live in. It was very neat indeed; it was a pleasure to be there.

I could walk around some now, and when I could do it without favoring my leg so much, it seemed like it made the whole village happy. I had never in my life seen such friendly people; even Eskimos couldn't compare with them. The men came back to see me, including the fellow the goats had been after. He wanted to see my wounded place, and I showed it to him. He smiled a little and looked me in the eyes, and we went outside together, and damned if they hadn't just brought in another bear, bigger than the first one, as far as I could tell. This time I watched what they did with him. A bunch of them picked him up — he must have weighed about three hundred pounds — and carried him to a hut that had part of the wall knocked out. Some of the men ran inside, and the ones with the bear handed him through the window to the others. The fellow who shot the goat touched me on the arm and pointed, and started toward the house.

I followed and went inside with the rest of them. It was as dark as my hut, and there was a low fire on rocks in the middle of the room. I noticed, then, that there was a strange sound coming from outside. A good many women came in, carrying it with them, singing together and doing small-footed dance steps, or I guess that's what they thought they were. The bear was lying on the ground in front of the fire, and one of the guys, in a kind of a bear helmet, in bear fur and with a lot of bear teeth around his neck, started talking to him. The women and girls were singing and dancing, and it was warm in there, and I went to sleep. I kept hazing in and out all night, and the guy kept talking to the bear, and the women kept up that high song, and moving around, moving around me and the one guy and the bear. I held out till it got light, because there was not any other special place to go, and I didn't want to hurt their feelings by walking out. This was important to them, though I couldn't tell you why.

All the time I was growing up, I had never seen more than six or seven bears: two blacks like these, two grizzlies, one big brown, and one polar. I had always stayed away from them, because they, especially the grizzlies, will make a point to come after you, and nobody would want that. They can take your head off with one lick. More: they can take a horse's head off, or an elk's.

But this was different. My feeling passed over to the other side. They showed me two cubs in a wood cage, and I thought at first that they were being kept for pets, a couple of live ones in amongst all the pieces of dead ones; it was good to see a bear move around. But they were putting up little sticks around the cage, painted sticks with the top ends shaved down with the wood curling, and there was a lot of carrying on, with the women singing and dancing and now the men coming into it, too, and I knew they were going to kill one of the cubs, or maybe both, probably with a lot of noise and singing and speeches. I was never one for any of that. Whatever animal they decided on, they could have done this with. They could have done it with the lynx — if there had been any of them — with the arctic fox or the wolverine. I had been wrong, I had been dead wrong about them. No matter how friendly they were, these were men like all the others, and they did the same things as the others. They wanted bear meat and furs, and their guilt about it set up all that singing, to agree on it, to put it right; set up all that singing and dancing, and playing those twanging instruments that all sounded out of tune. I say screw that. The animals are a lot better than any such. Better, a lot better, than the people. My heart turned around and locked.

It locked more when they cut off the big bear's head and put it on a little bench in front of the fire, and laid some of his own meat, with cakes and wine, in front of it, the same stuff that I was getting ready to eat with the rest of them. We all waited while the singing went on, high and lost, and I would just as soon have lost it.

They finished chopping up the bear and passed out the meat. And there was the head, sitting in front of the fire, taking everything in.

All the time I was thinking about the cubs. But I didn't believe the men would do anything to them that morning, because they had the big bear to eat, and his head was looking on. As soon as things quieted down a little I took off and went back to my hut, glad to be out of the noise. I slept good, all day, and as the sun was going down the women brought me some more to eat, more meat, some cakes and some saki, and I went to sleep one more time, hoping the tundra would come to me, not with grazing animals but with predators. I was reaching it one more time, and went deep, and stayed till I was ready to come back.

I lay about half asleep, looking at the bear head on my wall, as I had been doing for hours every day for the last two weeks. But I could get up and get around now, and I started collecting things in my head. Four women came in with some goatskins. I thought they were just being generous, but there seemed to be something special about the skins, which had been made into a thick shaggy shirt and pants. They wanted me to notice something about them, and I got it. These were the hides I had skinned off the goats in the woods, and I can tell you I was plenty grateful, because I wanted to have that kind of vitality and fight and fire pass into me. I had already eaten a lot of the goats, and now to wear them, too, would be luck beyond the best of luck: the best I'd had in Japan, the best anywhere. I lay back and grabbed them up around me. This was the good wilderness smell, and I didn't want anything else. I went down for another night, and I knew that the next day would be stronger for me.

It was, sure enough. I was ready for anything, and when the men came for me, acting as much as they could like new brothers, I went with them, out of my hut, out into the open space,

into the other house with the knocked-out window where the
bear and the bear's head had been. It was all cleared away now,
and I sat down with the others in amongst the shaved colored
sticks. The women were singing, and moved in and around us.
We were all there with the two cubs. They were nervous, as any
animal is liable to be when there is all that human carrying-on
going around them. This was not something that ought to be
done, and there's not any doubt about it. The people put poles
down with the skulls of animals on them. I could tell, without
too much trouble, bear, deer, fox, squirrels, some birds, could
have been pheasants. But nothing like a fisher and sure-God
not like a wolverine. A wolverine would have eaten up that
whole dinky little village in half an hour and not thought anything about it.

We sat there, and the women carried on, singing and dancing
to the point that you'd wish singing and dancing had never been
invented. Everybody drank a lot, and so did I, for there was not
any other way to stand it. I kept looking at the bears, which
were going back and forth at a great rate, banging up against the
bars of the cage. They were not happy with all this, and neither
was I. But that didn't seem to matter to the people around me
and around the bears. The men took bows and arrows, and
shook them in front of the bears, and one of the guys took a
long necklace of bear teeth, reached into the cage, and hung
them around the neck of one of the cubs. He looked good there
for a second, but then, with the handclapping and carrying-on,
the bear started to howl and bawl, and banged on the bars. All
this was enough for me. I don't believe in cruelty, in tormenting
animals, no matter how much you dance and sing. But that
doesn't have anything to do with it. The thing that bothered me
most was that the people seemed to have come on the idea that

they were doing something special for me, that I was being let in on something. Believe me, I had news for them.

Three men went over to the cage and started talking to the bears, the women dancing and handclapping behind them. There were big rocks holding down the logs on top of the cage, and two young guys got up and took them off. The cage opened up, and some of the older fellows threw lassos around one of the bears and pulled him out. Everybody — men and women, and especially the kids — screamed and clapped when the bear was dragged down, and some other ropes went around him. The younger fellows and some of the children had got hold of bows and arrows, and they shot at him, but I don't think any of the arrows were hunting arrows or were strong enough or sharp enough to do any real damage; they were just to make him mad. Why they wanted to make him mad I was never able to tell, but that's what they wanted to do, and they did it. He lurched around from one side to the other, half trying to get away and half trying to get at the men who were holding him, but he couldn't do either one. The guys on the ropes were used to this, I could tell. They pulled him around in a circle in front of all the screaming women and the others.

The guy who had hunted the goats was standing next to me. He looked at me and smiled, like he was sure I was enjoying this as much as he was, and that pissed me off worse than what they were doing to the bear. Finally they dragged him to a pole with a lot of colored ribbons on it. One of the older men, wrapped around with bear hides, with two or three necklaces of teeth and claws, kept talking to the bear like he was reasoning with him. It didn't do anybody any good, though, especially not the bear. Six of the young guys held him by the legs, the head, and the tail, and four others brought out some heavy poles, almost like logs.

253

Now what? I thought. What the hell now? They put the logs on both sides of the bear's head and stood him on his hind legs. A middle-aged man with a bow moved up about ten feet from him, where it would be hard to miss, and shot him, a good shot, a center shot at any range, heart and probably one lung. The bear jerked and struggled a little, then everybody turned loose everything and he fell and didn't move. I have seen bad things happen in my life, but never anything that made me as sick or as mean as that. I didn't care what I did to any of them.

They cut off the bear's head and skinned him, and carried him into the nearest hut. But I had had enough, and went back to my own hut. I wanted to get things together, to move out. I felt like I couldn't wait. But I waited. I would wait.

In the weeks I had been there I had accumulated a good deal of stuff, and I wanted to make some sort of selection of what to take with me, and come out with a weight that would have everything I needed and not be too heavy for long distances. My clothes, all bearskins and goatskins, were all right. I had mukluks and gloves. I still had most of my original stuff from Tinian, and the bag of feathers, and odds and ends. I had the wires I had taken out of the soldiers' truck I had driven, and I hoped to make some snares on up the road. The women had made me a rack out of bones — bear bones, there was not much doubt — for a backpack. It was very stout and light, and the shoulder straps were real strong. I had the skin I had been sleeping on, which I could use for a ground sheet, and one of their spears was leaning in the corner; I could take that. The head was stone — stone-sharp, and that's sharp, for sure. That, plus my old homemade spear from the goat hunt, would do me for weapons. I had tried out one of their bows, but couldn't do much with it. I didn't want the trouble of carrying one of those around with me, anyway. The whole idea of a bow was nothing but frustration; the spears would do fine. I'm mainly a stalker, and not somebody who operates from long range. I leaned my snowshoes against the pack and lay down on the ground and went to sleep, figuring to wake up around three, when most of the people in the village had gone to sleep, or at least I hoped they would have.

I didn't have any plans about where I wanted to go except to keep pushing north, checking out the game signs as I went. For these people in the village to live as well as they did, with all the food they had, and the different kinds, there had to be plenty of game, and I looked forward to getting off by myself, in any place I wanted to, any place I liked where there were no people, and set things up to live, live there, maybe build a shack out of branches or rocks, or whatever was around, and just see what happened. All the time I had been in Japan I judged how the next day would go by how well I slept, and that depended on how I felt when I closed my eyes. I nudged the pack and the snowshoes with my foot, and knew that this would be a good night. I wanted to sleep deep in it, but not all the way through it.

I woke up on time, and nobody bothered me. There it was. Everything was around me. I stayed a minute. My bearskin ground sheet was lashed into the pack, but I remembered the other nights I had been there, when I lay on the bearskin as I might have done on the bear, if he had loved me. I got up. I touched the snowshoes and the pack and the old GI knife on the stick and the spear with the stone head. I put my brain all through the pack, to see if everything was there. I looked for the things I might have forgotten, and they were not there; they were all in the pack. To say it another way: they were there. I left the hut and walked to the other one. A light snow was coming down on me, light and steady, on everything. I went to the hut where the other bear was, the last one they had.

Inside, the light was real low. The fellow from the goat hunt was there, like he was on guard duty. He looked at me like he always did. He pointed to the bear in the cage, lying down. He pointed, and one more time he smiled at me, real brotherly, I'm sure he thought it was. He touched my arm, and that was it for him. He was dead before he even thought about it. My bread knife was through him and out the other side, a lick that nobody can live with. I waited a second with him still standing, and then pulled out and let him go down. That was not one of the worst times, I tell you. I hit him one more time, in the throat, and went to the cage. I had a problem, for a minute or two, getting all those wood catches unfastened in the dark, but I did it, and opened the cage. The bear didn't seem to want to come out, but I grabbed him by the neck fur with both hands and pulled him clear. I dragged the guy over and put him in the cage, and then tried to get the bear out of the hut. Finally he got the idea. I gave him a boot in the ass, and he took off through the village, heading for the woods if he had any sense. One is enough, I said, and went back, all set. There was nobody around, but I was ready to fight, with men, women, or all of them.

But I walked right out, the snow falling, real even it was, and probably it would come down for a long time. That would take care of the tracks. If it had been clear, I would not have been hard to follow, but like this there was no way for them to tell which way I was headed. They might have figured I was going north, but even then, I don't think they would have followed me. If this was so, it might have been that they were afraid of me, but probably that was not it. I don't think they were interested in me, except as something strange that had been there for a while for no reason, and then gone off for no reason. They were hunters, though, and good ones, and I watched my back trail pretty close. But they didn't come, and I went on all night feeling like I owned things, and there was not a sign of them. They just wanted the bears, I reckon, and that was all right with me.

❖   ❖   ❖

I slept in a grove, good and warm, with the bearskin sheet over me and the sky clear and cold and full of stars again. I could not really believe I was where I was, that all this territory was mine, that I could go where I wanted to, find what I would find. For the first time — even with my busted-up face and my gored leg that still hurt some and everything that had happened — I felt young, young and on top of the whole situation, to go on up north, to go *into* it.

When I woke up it was like the beginning of everything. There was nothing like this cold: clear and right at zero. There's nothing like it, nothing. It threads down through your nose like steel that gives you life, gives you some reason to get out here and live in it, do things, find out what's around, what's in the world where you are. When I ate the goat meat was the closest thing to it, but I had been hurt then, and bad hurt, and it was not like that now. My leg pained me a little, but I could use it almost as good as the other one, and the notion of ranging all over this new country in this cold gave more energy to me than any beer or whiskey on this earth. Beer and whiskey and wine are all right for bars, but that cold wire down your nose, the wire from the woods and the tundra, the real wild country, is something else. And that was where I was now, what I had. I went on. I wanted to go on anywhere it was like this. I had waited a long time, and it was as good as home, as the north face of the Brooks, or even better, because now I didn't have any father, much as I loved him, as much as he taught me. It was just me now, and what I could do, and how I could make out. It was all mine.

I kept traveling: three days, four. There were bigger trees than I had seen anywhere in Japan, and then there would be long open stretches. Open. Empty. I like empty. I also liked what I had come through to get where I was; I liked my knocked-out teeth and my thigh gored to the bloody bone. I had gone through it, and I carried the marks of it here. I had got here any way it took, and there was no human thing or animal thing that could stand against me. In the middle of one of the biggest bare places, one I could hardly see across, I stopped and put both feet together in the best of breathing in the sky, and the good, the great steel went down both nostrils and all over me, and if heaven has got anything better I don't want to know it. I can't know it, because heaven has not got it. Not yet. The clear cold was so wonderful that I damned near cried. I could stand in it, I could sleep in it, I could jump up and down in it. What I did was dance, danced on the snowshoes, as much as I felt like, which was plenty. Then I went on, still dancing a little.

The land dropped some. It fell off in tremendous plateaus that I footed across hour after hour, looking at the tracks of whatever was there. Rabbits were around, a lot of them, and I came on some hoofprints that might have been made by the same kind of goats that gored me. I didn't see any bear sign, though, and reckoned most of them were back of me, back up higher where there were more trees, and probably rocks with caves where they could hole up. In a way I was disappointed that I couldn't find anything that had to do with bears, because I had a connection with them, one I never had in Alaska. A connection for sure, like with the goats. Goatskin and bearskin I had on, had all around me, and on my hands and feet, helping me to live, to get along. And I had the round purple scar on my leg, which had quit hurting and was feeling great, even though the hole of it would not ever leave me. That was all right: I've got that goat right down to the bone, in my left leg, and he won't leave.

Bears, though: it might not be a situation I'd want, to run up on one of them in the open. I didn't have any reason to tangle with them, but I wanted to know where they were. I just did, that's all.

On the fifth day from the village, I had just finished eating some of the dried salty meat I had brought from there, and was starting across another field. I cold-trailed a rabbit just to have something to do, and went with it for about half a mile, out into the middle of a field. The rabbit wasn't doing anything but traveling — not too fast, from the print make. He was going north, generally, zigzagging but vectoring out north, and I appreciated that: I was not in any hurry. I was getting to like him for leading me on, for not going too fast, for not being in sight, both of us going where we wanted to go. But then the tracks stopped, just gave out, never went anywhere else for as long as there was. His prints stopped in the middle of the open, the middle of the flat-field snow. It was not something I had never seen before, because I had, but it really startled me to find it here. Something had come down out of the air and got it. A hawk, an eagle, an owl — there was no way to know. It was like the rabbit had taken off into the air, as it had, in a way it wouldn't have liked. There was some blood on the snow, but not much. Some blood and no fur. That was it.

I spent an afternoon in the trees without seeing any game, or much sign. About two o'clock I came out on another plain. I was getting used to plains and the time it would take to cross them, and knuckled down to slog on through this one for the hours until it got dark. But in the middle of the field, this time, there was something, a kind of clot. It was not like the other flats, not pure. A clot, sure; it didn't belong there. Or maybe it belonged there more than I did. Maybe, maybe not, maybe both. I went closer. A wing lifted out of it. Lifted, went back. It was a hawk on a down rabbit. A down hawk on a down rabbit — that, I could understand. I went on in. I didn't want the rabbit; I wanted to see things go on. I wanted to see what happened, and how it was happening now.

It was a real big bird, bigger than any hawk I had ever seen, but not as big as an eagle or an osprey. He stood back off the rabbit, clappering his bill, as I came in. Then he took off. It all came back to me from the time I was little. I really do like to watch things fly. But this was not any wild hawk. He circled and I caught a faint sound — a bell — that went around the circle with him, around me and the rabbit. I just barely heard it once, but it was there. He gained altitude. I picked up his angle with the compass, because it might be worth something; the hawk and I and the rabbit were all going the same way. I put the rabbit into my bear pants. He was not too clawed up, none of the fur was split, no meat was showing, and there was not much blood.

I slept that night in the wide open, in another field like all the others I had been going across. I was tired, but the spread of stars was so enormous and the clearness going up to them and all around them was so great that it was hard for me to go to sleep for just watching. It was all about too much for me, especially since the land had dropped off more and I thought it might be possible that I was getting near the ocean, where everything would end and I would begin — begin to live for the rest of my life, the way I wanted to, in a place that was made for me.

I got up early and the ground fell, fell more. I topped out over a ridge, and the day was dead still; the sun was dead still. There was what looked like a shack way off in front, and a rise behind it, and I would have bet my life that the ocean was on the other side of the rise.

There couldn't be anything in the shack to hurt me, and no way for whoever was in it to tell anybody that I had showed up. It took me most of the morning to get to it, and when I was about seventy-five yards away a big bird took off from it, maybe from inside it, and went back out the way I had come, over the ridges, over the field where I had picked up the rabbit.

There was no concealment, no notion of hiding, no stalking, no camouflage. All I wanted to know was who was around. I didn't think it would be anything like the little bearded people, the bear people, because they needed their village; you couldn't imagine them without it. But somebody lived here. Smoke was coming out of the place and standing in the air without blowing. It was real still. I thought it would be funny, in the wrong way, for me to knock on what passed for a door, so I just pulled to one side the slabs of wood and branches and went in.

There was nothing much in there, but a pot of something was cooking in a hole in the floor, and behind that, in the dark of the back wall, was a bunch of rags and skins with a man in it. I went around the pot and over to him. He raised his head. The light through the cracks caught him, and he was about a thousand years old, or sure did seem like it, with the kind of oldness that only Oriental people have: the wrinkles are so damned deep, an eighth of an inch at least, you'd think, and cut out, or cut in, like with a razor blade that didn't bring any blood. I stood there while he got himself together and got up, even shorter than I was, hardly over five feet. He said something. I said nothing, but handed him the rabbit. He looked at me like he couldn't believe it, then took the rabbit and put it on the floor beside the pot. I got ready to go, because he didn't have anything I wanted, but he took me by the sleeve and wouldn't turn loose.

I couldn't for the life of me tell what he wanted, but then he pointed at the pot and maybe at the rabbit, and all I could come up with was that he wanted me to eat with him. I was not all that hungry, but I didn't see anything wrong with it, so I sat down on the floor to see how he would go about things. He didn't make any move to do anything with the rabbit, so I took the GI knife off my branch spear and started in to gut it and clean it. I'm pretty good at this, and I could tell that he thought so, too, and when I finished he chopped the meat up and put it in the pot, along with whatever else was in there. We ate it all, and it was very good. Living with the bear people, I had got used to cooked meat, but I didn't want to lose the liking for meat when it was raw, because if you have to cook it before you can eat it, you can't live the way I wanted to, and was probably going to have to. Anyway, I finished my part, had all I wanted, and got ready to go again. He stood up on the other side of the pot and made a motion with his hand. He pulled at my sleeve again and pointed to the door. He went out and I followed him around to the side of the shack. There, on a low perch tied together with strips of what looked like hide, were two big birds with cloth around their heads. I could see their beaks, though, that beautiful hook they both had, and nobody had to tell me they were predators. One of them was probably the hawk I had seen in the field, the one that had brought down the rabbit. I went closer, and the biggest one shifted on his perch. My God, they were big! I had seen eagles, from a distance; these were not quite as big as that. I had seen plenty of hawks, too, but never this size. I didn't have any idea what you'd name them, but like all meat eaters they had the look, even with their heads in rags: if you turned them loose, they'd get after something. The old guy put a piece of leather around his forearm, tapped on the perch with his other hand, and pulled the bird off the wood, guiding it over to his arm. This seemed all right, and we stepped clear of the shack and out into the snow. He took the rags off, and it sat looking around with quick jerks. Finally it got to me, and I knew a thing I had never known before. Predatory birds, most of them, have something like the eyesight a telescope gives you, or field glasses, and right then I was sure that it could not only bring things close up, but see through them, too. I had that seen-through feeling, like I had been shot by something that wouldn't kill me but would change me. The old man lifted his arm and the bird flew, first dipping down almost to the ground, then going up, working hard at first and then, getting into it, working easy. This is something, I thought; this is really something. I say I'd changed, and the longer time went on the more I knew it: I had sold birds short. I would let that idea stay with me and see what came of it.

The old man pointed back to the hut. I shook my head and tightened up my shoulder straps. He grabbed me by the sleeve again, and there was not any doubt that he didn't have the slightest notion I was any danger to him, an enemy, some part of a war with his country. The snow was his country, the snow and the hawks, the hawks and the rabbits, and getting on every day; there was nothing else to it. If I stayed, say, for a night, he couldn't tell anybody I was there. Who would he tell? It would not be like the American monk at the monastery, who lived not far from a military base he wanted to get in good with. There wouldn't be any harm in staying for the night. Besides, I wanted to see the bird come back. I had got real interested, like I say.

Maybe it was the rabbit that did it. The old guy was mighty old, and I couldn't see how he had the strength to go out and find whatever game the birds brought down. He might have starved to death even if his hawks killed ten rabbits a day, because he couldn't go out and find them and bring them back. That was his problem, though, and not mine. I didn't think anywhere beyond the one night.

In a couple of hours the bird came back. I was outside the shack taking a piss when I saw it. It was making a long circle, and the old man was out to meet it. When I saw those feathers and that beak and those eyes again, I knew that the bird was never going to be an "it" again, but "he"; that would be best. The old man got him back on his perch and put the rags over his head. He looked close at the claws, and pulled me down to do the same thing. There was no blood on them.

And so I stayed. With that night I started living there. I figured I would for a while, anyway. I didn't have anywhere special to go anymore. And I had been right on one thing: the old man was so weak that he could hardly get up to feed the birds and take care of them. More and more of that I learned how to do. They got to where they would come to my forearm just as well as they would to the old man's, and it was good to feel the grip in those feet, which would hold with just enough pressure to keep the balance. But behind that was a tremendous force, a power that I couldn't even guess at, heartless and right there when the bird needed it. With the bird sitting on it, if my arm moved he would tighten, and if I moved more than just a little it could have been bad. But I never did, and we got along. I would feed them — usually rabbit meat, but sometimes birds they'd knocked down — with the old man, but when he saw that I could do it all right he just stayed down and more or less let me take care of things. I was glad to do it, for the birds were the best predators I had ever seen, and I had seen a lot of them.

I began to transfer my feelings — or soul, or spirit, or whatever you want to call it — to them, because they did more than any other creatures for the wish I had that was most like me: not only the need to attack but to fall on something from above. Up until now it had been the fisher marten, which is the fastest thing in trees, and also one of the best hunters on the ground: they can tear up a porcupine before you can even think; they have good camouflage and good moves; and I had enormous respect and love for them. But the birds were different. There was another side to them, another dimension, you might say. I never put names to them. Names are chickenshit; they didn't need any names. There's this about them, and when I realized it I was nearer being what I wanted to be, and needed to be. I would tell anybody who hears me saying this, look around you and be honest with yourself. For most of you, flight is not in you, and never will be in you. Even when you're in aircraft it's not. The great thing about the birds, especially if they're predators, is that anybody who loves them and understands how they operate gets to be like them; his mind, his imagination, can fly with them, and the birds know it. The hawks were flying day and night, whether they were in the air or on the perch. They're always out there over the snow, over the woods and trees, over the rocks, with that superhuman eyesight, with power over everything they can see, or ever will see. I don't think God himself could ever want anything more.

In the morning, if it was not snowing too hard, I would go out and take their eyes out of the rags and then turn them loose, one at a time. The old man just liked to hunt one bird a day, for some reason, but I hunted both of them, because it made more sense. Besides that, I had the pleasure of watching two takeoffs instead of one, and two flights. When a bird left my arm he seemed to fall, just enough to open his wings and get them going, and then beat hard and go up. The feathers made a sound, a whisper sound, when he was really working, but then didn't make any at all. And when they came back in, whenever they got ready to, it was in a soft swoop, and they'd fasten on my arm, first hard and then easy. Every day I was glad that I had got out of the trees, as much as I liked being there. I was glad that I had gone from the trees up, from the fisher marten to the hawk, over the snow, high, and seeing everything.

The day always started good, because the birds were in it, and I was with them, and in a way going with them. I'd give them a little time — an hour or an hour and a half — and then put on my snowshoes and head for the big fields, because that was where I could usually — but not always — find them. I covered a lot of territory, with some woods and frozen creeks in it, and I couldn't always connect with them. But most of the time I could; they would head for the open places to come down in, and I would take whatever they had brought down and head back for the shed and the cook pot. It was a situation I could not ever have had any other way, or at any other time. There was not anything like it. After the birds left in the morning, I went out with my snowshoes and the bear spear I had picked up from the bearded people. I was in another mind, which I liked better than the other one I had. The birds were in it; and what they would do, I would try to follow and pick up, and go on.

Could the snow, could the snow and the cold and the birds, have knocked me out, made it where I was crazy? If this was crazy, I was for more of it. I couldn't tell about any of it, but it was all great; it was greater than great. I went out with my spear and with what I knew about the real cold — the snow and the wind, and what you have to do with them, and can do with them, and how, if you know what you're doing, it all works together — and went with the birds over the open fields. I went out into a snow situation where I didn't know who did what, or where anything was, or would be. That was part of the good. You couldn't want any more freedom, and I didn't want any more than I was having; there was not any more. Every time I left the shack I was already over the fields with the hawks, looking down like they looked with those wild accurate eyes, with a heart way up in the air, where it belonged all the time, ready to come down, ready to fall from all that height on what was put there for them to eat, for me to eat, for me and the old man.

Almost every day I went out with the bear spear. I had really come to love that thing, especially the head of it, and never got enough of it. The stone of the head was saw-toothed, which means that somebody had chipped it, chip for chip. That shows you something about the human mind, because when a cutting edge is made that way it doesn't cut, it rips. Lots of injury, lots of blood. I appreciated that, but mainly I just liked to look at it and feel of it, because it was beautiful and delicate and must have cost a lot of time. To learn how to make it would be something it'd be worth your while to do.

Like: I used to go out, and maybe there was wind and a light snow, or maybe it was clear. I was all of everything, the bear-skins I had on, the snowshoes and the spear, and the birds overhead. I went out every day into what would be, what-ever was there. Really, I was just supposed to bring back the game the birds had downed, but it was more than that, a lot more.

There was a lot of time. When I got into the first big field and didn't see anything, I was ready to foot it across into the next one. But there had to be something to do, instead of just snow-shoeing and nothing else, so I took to chucking the spear. I used to scale it out as far as I could into the flat snow. The spear had great balance, and if you threw it right, would ride up and then nose over and come down just exactly as you'd think a spear ought to do. That was a beautiful thing, and I couldn't get enough of it. I threw the spear hundreds of times, and after a while I really didn't care whether I ever drew down on either an animal or a man with it: that was not why I did it, not anymore. The thing was the arch of it, the flight that was not too much different from the way the birds did now and again.

As far as game was concerned, I got to be sort of halfhearted. I took a couple of shots at rabbits, one of them not bad, if I do say, but never hit anything. I was more interested in spearing the snowbanks, which I got to where I could do pretty well. My arm was better than I had given it credit for, and all those days out in the snow fields, with nothing to do but throw, it got better, until I was real proud of it. I didn't even know how far the spear would go. I just scaled it out, then went and picked it up and scaled it again. This was something, and I'll pass it on to anybody who's listening to me. Just get yourself a spear and start throwing it. If you could have the situation I had, you would be throwing out over level snow, snow that went on and on. In the best field, the one where the hawks came down more times than they did anywhere else, you could just barely see the trees on the other side, and I would believe, every time I pulled my arm back to throw, that I was going to put it all the way out into the trees, trees that were a good mile and a half off. No possibility. No matter. When I cranked back my arm with the spear in it, the feeling, what you might call the wonder of it, and I'm not afraid to use that word now and then, when no other one will do. Lord, I thought every time I pulled back my arm, what if it never comes down? And if I was right on the edge of everything, with nothing but the big nothing out in front of me, and turned loose the bear spear, where would it go? The birds didn't know anything about all of this, but I can tell them now that it was part of it, part of them, part of what went with me when I went out to find where they were, where they had come down, what they had killed.

Again, one more time. When I would throw into a snowbank, when I laid the spear in there with everything I had, I imagined what I might be hitting. It could have been anything, animal or human or something on the other side of it, all of it — beyond, way beyond. Beyond. Beyond was what I said when I leveled the spear, beyond what I thought when I threw it, when I put everything I had into it. Beyond when it was in the air, a real balance, a true balance, and when it hit the snowbank. It was snow that had taken it, had taken everything I had to give, had taken my body and gored my leg and my new arm. A lot of the time I forgot what I was out there to do. But then, with all the rambling and throwing, I would most likely come on one of the birds. There was some strange game around there. There were plenty of rabbits, some of them with ears long enough so you could call them hares, like snowshoe hares, and two or three times there was a real odd animal, somewhere between a raccoon and a dog, which the old man called a moyuk. I would have thought that they were too big for the birds to fool with, but they killed them just the same, and we ate them. The hides were not bad, and when we had some sun I cured them out, though I never did find anything to do with them.

Snow, and the push, the thrust of the new arm, which had got much better than the one I'd been born with. The spear and the arm, the snowbank with the hawks over it, sweeping, penetrating with their superhuman sight, maybe even piercing into the snowbanks, seeing what I might be hitting. I gave it my whole thrust, my whole body, and the hawks circled and saw. That was it, and who could want anything else?

When I got back to the shack — or the shed is what it really was — I used to look at the spearhead real close, because I was always afraid that there might be a rock in the snowbank that would chip the point, or even break it. I had really come to love that head, and the whole spear, and more than one time I was sorry I had killed the little bearded man who had hunted the goats at the same time as I did. I wish I hadn't done it, because in a way he had been a good friend, and he was a hunter, too. Too bad, but there was not anything I could do about it now.

I wondered where the bear people had got that kind of stone. I remembered a guy, a kind of nut or fanatic at Point Barrow, who used to go out and hunt with a bow and arrows, and always used stone points that he chipped himself; it was some kind of black rock that he got from New Mexico. He would take a lot of time with those rocks. I never went with him out on the hunt, but I really liked what he did: all that chipping hour after hour, day after day. He swore by those stone points, and I could see why. They were beautiful, and they worked. He killed a sea leopard with them, and you don't see that every day. My spear with the chipped head and the hawks. The hawk's view, which was beyond any man's. It was being able to see what you don't. It was being able to see into the snowbank, into the stone. To see beyond what any human, any man who has ever been born, could see. Like I tell you, out of the snowdrift, into the snowdrift, into the stone.

❖   ❖   ❖

But now. Now. I was asleep, and the birds were not restless. I thought that maybe the old man might need something, some water I could get out of the snow, something. I went over to him and did what I could to shake him, but there was no shake in him. No shake, no breath. I put my head down on him, and there was not anything. I mean, nothing at all. Could it be he was dead? He was dead. He was dead and he was mighty dead, and that was all. No rabbit meat would bring him back, no moyuk, no nothing. I put all the furs over him and went back down, myself. Sleep was enough for me. The next day I would bury him and then take over. I had more or less inherited from him, and nobody could say it was any other way. I don't have any doubt that it would have been all right with him. We had eaten a lot of rabbits together, cooked and fed the birds, and he'd nodded his head when I chucked the spear at my best, really got it out there. That was enough.

      ❖   ❖   ❖

But now. But now. This was the thing you call sleep. In it was the Canadian lynx. I have always loved the fisher marten, and now the hawk, but in a way maybe the lynx is better than the marten, because his camouflage is better. Unless. Unless. Unless the animal is so close to the space he is in that there is not any difference. All the time I'd been in Japan, all the time I'd been living, this seemed to me to be the truth of the thing: you can get to the perfect blend if you know exactly how to do it, and if the time is right. The same thing is true of the predator and the thing he is after: both. Both. True of the lynx and the snowshoe hare. I just felt, in the middle of the night, that it was my time now, and I believed I could do it. I believed that everything led up to where I was. The notion rose up in my throat, and there was not any doubt about it anymore. There were people outside the hut, and maybe a lot more than had ever been there. I was ready to deal: I had my terms.

The old man was dead, that was sure. I was not, and that was sure, too. I could look, I could see, I could feel. Where to turn, where to put the eyes? Outside. There was something out there. I went to the reeds and branches, which were all I had as a door. It was snowing, not bad but steady, and I looked out. At first I couldn't see anything but little flakes. I kept watching, because I could tell it was not like the other nights. I didn't have the conviction that I could go out with the spear and the birds into the open fields the next day. No, that was over. I had had everything I would ever get from the situation. This was something else.

There was air, not steady but in quick pulses. The wind, blowing like it was doing, would have to gust, to set the snow aside, sooner or later. Enough for a look. Enough, just enough. It was enough. I saw one black shape, and right away I could see that there was not just one. There was another one beside it, and on the other side, too. The whole ridge was full of men, and I would have bet that there were others behind them. Everything told me it was right; that they should be there. It was not the bear people. This was a whole lot of other men, most likely civilians, and maybe some soldiers, too, don't ask me. I don't know. But I was ready for them. It was time.

I tell you, it was right for them to be there. I knew I was close, and that this was the time. It was, it was. The birds had helped me — I had come down with them on game from hundreds of feet, because I understood what was going on and so did the hawks. That was the best feeling of all: to come down, to have all that air behind you, that would always be there, any time you were in it. The birds had helped me, but had never been able to get me all the way there. They were open, and coming down, and it was a part of what I wanted, what was right, but not all. The real deep part was what I had always been sure of: to blend with the place you're in, but with a mind to do something. To do something, then to leave, so that nothing around you could do anything about it until it was too late.

Right now, it was time. Again. Now. I stripped off. I kicked open my old bag of swan feathers and slung the feathers out on the floor. I was saying — I was saying — that many a Canadian lynx, many a fisher, because his camouflage was too perfect, disappeared into where he was, and was not ever heard from again. On the other side, I most believe that same thing could happen with the snowshoe hare, had happened a whole lot of times. There must be plenty of rabbits on the other side, a whole heaven of them, ready to be the stillest that it is possible to be. A whole heaven of them, and I like to think about that.

It was my time now. The feathers were all over the floor. The old man was dead, and the guys with the guns — one of them fired and blew in part of the door — should be out there, trying to gun me down, to blow away anything that moved. I had news for them. I opened up my right arm, the one that scaled the spear out toward the woods. Blood poured out, and I smeared it, put it all over me. I cut the old man's throat for whatever blood there might be, and got it on me everywhere I could reach to. I hit my knees to the floor and rolled in the feathers, like I was rolling in the snow. I was close. I was very close.

I walked out and I knew I had found it, what I had been looking for all my life, in all the blood and the fucking and the right arm and the fast move, in everything I had done and everybody I had had to deal with. I knew I had found it, but up till now I had never had the full thing. In the wind the swan feathers fluttered on me, and I could have flown. I could have flown with the hawks and the swans if I had wanted to. But I didn't want to. I wanted to stand there.

I laid my bread knife in the snow and stood up straight again. They fired, a lot of them fired, the whole ridge sparked and crackled. Splinters flew off the shack behind me. A bullet went through me but didn't touch me. It was happening. More splinters flew off behind.

When I tell you this, just say that it came from a voice in the wind: a voice without a voice, which doesn't make a sound. You can pick it up any time it snows, where you are, or even just when the wind is from the north, from anywhere north of east or west. I was in the place I tried to get to. I had made it in exactly the shape I wanted to be in, though maybe just a little beat up. But the main thing was that I had got to the landscape and the weather, and you can remember me standing there with the bullets going through, and me not feeling a thing. There it was. A red wall blazed. For a second there was a terrific heat, like somebody had opened a furnace door, the most terrible heat, something that could have burned up the world, and I was sure I was gone. But the cold and the snow came back. The wind mixed the flakes, and I knew I had it. I was in it, and part of it. I matched it all. And I will be everywhere in it from now on. You will be able to hear me, just like you're hearing me now. Everywhere in it, for the first time and the last, as soon as I close my eyes.